BACKSLIDE

KEITH THOMAS WALKER

KEITHWALKERBOOKS, INC

KEITHWALKERBOOKS

Publishing Company
KeithWalkerBooks, Inc.
P.O. Box 690
Allen, TX 75013

For information write
KeithWalkerBooks, Inc.
P.O. Box 690
Allen, TX 75013

All characters in this book have no existence outside the imagination of the author and have no relation whatsoever to anyone bearing the same name or names. They are not even distantly inspired by any individual known or unknown to the author and all incidents are pure invention.

ISBN-13 DIGIT: 978-0-9967505-6-1
ISBN-10 DIGIT: 0996750568
Library of Congress Control Number: 2017907361

Visit us at www.keiththomaswalker.com

CONTENTS

MORE BOOKS BY KEITH THOMAS WALKER

Blurred Lines: The Monster
Blurred Lines: Cop Killer
Blurred Lines: Copycat Killer
Blurred Lines: Mister Me Too

Asha and Boom Part 1
Asha and Boom Part 2
Asha and Boom Part 3

Backslide
Backslide 2

The Realest Ever
The Realest Christmas Ever

Prom Night at Finley High
Fast Girls at Finley High
Bullies at Finley High

Jackson Memorial
Jackson Memorial 2

Brick House
Brick House 2
Brick House 3

Threesome
Threesome 2

Take One of Mine

Take one of Mine Part 2

Fixin' Tyrone
How to Kill Your Husband
A Good Dude
Riding the Corporate Ladder
The Finley Sisters' Oath of Romance
Blow by Blow
Jewell and the Dapper Dan
Harlot
Plan C (And More KWB Shorts)
Dripping Chocolate
Sleeping With the Strangler
Life After
Blood for Isaiah
One on One
Election Day
Evan's Heart
Poor Righteous Poet
Might be Bi Part One
Harder
Primal Part One
Hotline Fling

Visit www.keiththomaswalker.com for information about these
and upcoming titles from KeithWalkerBooks

PROLOGUE
SPEED BUMP

CHAPTER
1

DANA MOORE HAD not reached the halfway point of her shift at Jackson Memorial when she received the call every mother dreads. Her son had been blowing up her cell for the past five minutes. Tariq knew better than to call so many times over something frivolous, so she stepped out of the exam room and told another radiology tech, "I got a patient on their way down. I'll be back in a second."

Julie told her, "Okay," without looking up from her magazine.

In the hallway, Dana returned her son's call. He answered with a breathless, "*Mama.*"

"What's going on?" she asked him. "This better be imp–"

"Mama, I'm at the police station," Tariq informed her.

The fear and anxiety in his voice made Dana's whole body grow numb. She backed into the wall behind her and leaned on it for support. A sudden chill made goose bumps sprout all over her body. Her voice wavered when she responded.

"Wha, what?"

"*We had an accident,*" Tariq cried. "I hit somebody, Mama. *They said I killed him.* People was – *they was shooting at us!* Brendon got shot. He at the hospital."

Tariq was crying, near panic. Dana's eyes glossed over. The hospital corridor began to tilt to and fro as her mind swam. She felt like she was tumbling down a rabbit hole. Everything her son told her made sense, but at the same time it didn't – maybe for someone else's child, but not Tariq. He was–

"They said you don't have to be here for them to talk to me," he said, his breath coming in shudders. "They said since I'm seventeen, I can talk to them without you here. *But, I'm scared, Mama.* I don't know what to do. I don't know what to say. You gotta come down here. *They said that man's dead."*

He sniffled. Dana's heart shattered in a million pieces as her muddled mind tried to comprehend everything he was telling her. The word **DEAD** assailed her like a punch to the throat. It was hard to take in another breath, hard to tell if her heart was still beating. None of this was right for her baby. *Not Tariq.* Even though he was delivering the dreadful news firsthand, he had to be talking about someone else's child!

"Baby, calm down," she said, though she needed to take that advice herself. Tears spilled from both of her eyes. She squeezed them shut and saw her only child behind her closed lids. Tariq only had one year left in high school. He was gonna be somebody. Realizing she was thinking of his future in the past tense broke her heart all over again.

"Are you in jail?" she cried.

"No, Mama. I'm at the police station – on Lancaster. They wanna question me. *Mama, I didn't mean to hit nobody.* He ran out in the middle of the street. *You can ask anybody!"*

"Who was shooting?"

"I don't know. The man, the guy I hit, his friends was."

"Are you okay?"

"Yes. Brendon got shot."

"What's the address where you're at?" Dana asked. She rubbed the tears from her eyes and opened them. Looking around, she realized she wasn't the only person in the hallway. A coworker from Ultrasound watched her with wide-eyed worry.

"I – I don't know," Tariq said. "Hold on, Mama."

Dana turned and reentered her department. Julie looked up at her, and the magazine slipped from her hands.

"Oh my God, Dana. What's wrong?"

Dana headed for her workstation without responding. Her hand was shaking so badly, it would've been a miracle if she managed to write the address legibly. Rather than her son, a woman's voice came to the line.

"Hi. This is Officer Ruby Hutt. Do you need the address to the station?"

"Yes. *Please tell me what's going on.* Is my son under arrest?" Saying those words aloud made the contents of her stomach shift uncomfortably. She reached for the wastebasket under her desk, thinking she might vomit.

"No, ma'am. He was involved in a fatality accident, and they would like to question him. He's being detained, but he's not in handcuffs."

"Some, somebody died?" Dana didn't think the world moved at all while she waited for the woman to respond.

"Yes, ma'am. I'm sorry."

A fresh trail of tears leaked from Dana's eyes. Her department never looked so dark and wretched.

Tariq had really killed someone.

She brought a fist to her mouth and squeezed her throat closed on a wail that tried to force itself up. Her whole body trembled.

"Ma'am, are you ready for the address?"

Dana's mouth fell open, but she couldn't respond. She turned and saw her coworker standing in the doorway. Julie had no idea what was going on, but her eyes filled with tears as well.

Dana held out her phone. Julie stood frozen for a moment before she took it. Dana tried to hand her a pen and notepad, but both items fell to the floor. Julie quickly stooped to pick them up before she brought the phone to her ear.

"Hello?" After a pause, Julie said, "Um, okay." She approached Dana's desk and used it to jot down the information she received from the officer. When she disconnected, her heart kicked as she asked her friend, "What's going on? Does this have something to do with Tariq?"

Dana nodded. It was impossible to get her thoughts together. "*I gotta go*," she managed. She lifted the notepad and took her phone from her friend. "Where's, do you know where Steve is?"

Julie had never seen her friend so upset. "He's in a meeting," she said. "It's okay. *Go.* I'll let him know you had to leave."

Dana knew she should speak with her supervisor directly, but every second she waited left Tariq vulnerable to the criminal justice system. Every black woman in America knows how quickly that scenario could go from bad to worse.

"Okay," she said. "*Thank you.*"

Her tears were still flowing like rain when she reached the parking garage.

CHAPTER 2

ONE HOUR EARLIER

Tariq looked over at his friend with a disappointed expression as he turned into the Stone Crest Apartment complex on the far east side of town. His SUV was built for all terrains, but Tariq still took care to avoid a humongous pothole directly in their path.

"Really, nigga?" he said to his friend Brendon, who sat grinning in the passenger seat.

Brendon's eyes were glued to his cellphone. Nearly all of his teeth were showing. "What? What's wrong?"

Brendon had dark skin, whereas Tariq's was fair. Both teens kept their hair trimmed short, but Tariq frequented a barber more often than his classmate. His crew cut was clean. Brendon's was borderline nappy.

The boys were around the same height and build. They both considered themselves the more handsome of the duo, but most girls gave the edge to Tariq. Tariq was also smarter, when it came to books, and his family had a better financial standing. His mother worked as a radiology tech at Jackson Memorial. Brendon's mom hadn't held a steady job in over a decade. He couldn't even say for sure where she was at the moment.

The summer temperature was stifling. Thankfully the AC in Tariq's 2005 Explorer worked well. The afternoon outing was Brendon's idea. Two weeks into summer vacation, cruising the streets and pulling down (or lifting up) skirts was all the boys cared about. Having a car at seventeen was a blessing few of their peers enjoyed. Tariq's license was considered *provisional* until his 18th birthday, but his mother trusted him enough to drive on the freeway and stay out past dark, as long as he made it home by midnight.

From the looks of the Stone Crest Apartments, Tariq doubted if he'd be interested in the freaks Brendon was texting. Even with a pocket full of condoms, the risk of contracting an STD were high. He didn't think it was possible for anyone who cared about their personal hygiene to live in a place so rundown.

"Really nigga?" he said again as they neared the apartment's leasing office. Both of the largest windows were boarded up, but a big sign on the door proclaimed "*Yes, We're Open!*"

Brendon looked at the office and laughed. "We in the hood now, boy. Don't start acting all scary when we get to they apartment."

"Man, I don't even know if I wanna get out the car," Tariq said honestly. "Somebody might steal it while we're gone."

"Yeah, right. Don't nobody want this piece of shit."

"It's always a nigga with *no* car that got something to say about *my* car," Tariq noticed. "You know I ain't worried about no hood. I just went to *another hood* when I picked you up."

"This one's worse," Brendon said.

He was right about that. These apartments made his crappy neighborhood look upscale.

"This the one I'm finna smash," Brendon told him.

Tariq violated a cardinal sin by looking over at his friend's electronic device while driving. If his mother saw him do that, she'd take away his keys for at least a couple of days. The girl in the picture Brendon showed him looked like a stripper in training. Tariq frowned.

"Man, how old is she?"

"Sixteen."

"You can't be with no sixteen-year-old no more," Tariq advised him, not for the first time.

"I just turned eighteen last month," Brendon complained.

"It don't matter. As far as the law is concerned, she a minor, and you're an adult."

"You listen to everything yo mama tell you?"

Tariq shook his head, rather than keep it real with him. What was so bad about kids listening to their mother – especially when it came to something like avoiding jail? Tariq had never been arrested, and he planned to keep it that way.

They rounded a few more corners and spotted three girls standing outside of one of the buildings. Before they were close enough to see their faces, Tariq told his friend, "*Man, hell naw!* Them some little girls."

"They in high school," Brendon assured him. "They go to Western Hills."

"What, they *freshmen*?"

"I don't know."

Tariq smacked his lips. "I can't believe you got me out here for this mess…"

"We can still smash, since we all in high school."

"Where the hell you get that from?"

"Whatever," Brendon said. "I know *I'm* finna hit. You wanna stay out here with the other two while I'm upstairs?"

"No, I don't," Tariq said honestly. "But if you want it that bad, I will."

"That's what I'm talking about. Bruh, you won't believe some of the shit she said she'll do to me." He scrolled through his text messages, getting more excited by the second.

"Long as she do it in less than ten minutes, I don't even care."

"*Ten*? Nigga, I'll be back in *five!*"

They both laughed. Brendon was a nut job. The boys had been best friends since middle school. Tariq was used to his outlandish behavior. Most of the time he found it amusing.

The girls introduced themselves as *Toneisha*, *Keisha* and *LaTisha*. Tariq didn't have anything against girls whose names ended with "*sha*," but three in a row. *Damn*. It didn't take long to determine the girls' level of sophistication was on par with their crummy apartments. And one of them was still in middle school!

The one Brendon tried to hook Tariq up with, Toneisha, was okay-looking. But her tank top had spaghetti straps, and Tariq saw that her bra straps were dirty. Nope. Any girl who didn't think it was important to wear clean underwear had to be harboring cooties.

"You with them Bideker Boys?" LaTisha asked Brendon when he got out of the truck.

Tariq sighed inwardly. Brendon had been wearing a bead necklace for the past few weeks. The beads were black and yellow. In a normal world, there was nothing wrong with that. But in the ghettos of Overbrook Meadows, black and yellow was the color of a street gang. Brendon was not officially part of the gang, but he was working on it. At the moment, he was more of a tagalong or *wannabe*.

Tariq didn't know if Brendon wasn't ready to endure the beat-down required to become an official member of the set or if the gang had rejected him. But he did know (and had told Brendon multiple times) that they couldn't be friends anymore if he joined the Bideker Boys. Tariq's mother was from Chicago. She'd seen a lot of bad things. She'd do anything in her power to keep her son away from hoodlums.

"What about it?" Brendon asked his new friend. "You got a problem with Bideker niggas?"

"No," the girl said, grinning broadly. "I was just asking." She continued to stare at his beads, much like a groupie would admire a rapper's gold medallions.

"So we going upstairs or what?" Brendon asked her.

"Yeah," she said. "Come on." She turned, revealing a bubble butt even Tariq found enticing. Brendon followed her like a dog in heat.

LaTisha looked back and asked, "What about your friend?"

"He ain't trying to do nothing," Brendon informed her. "But your friends can hang out here and kick it with him."

The two rejected girls didn't appear to like that idea, but Tariq was definitely uninterested.

"Alright, we'll be back," LaTisha told her friends, and the matter was settled.

CHAPTER 3

SEVENTEEN MINUTES LATER, Brendon and his friend emerged from the apartment. Tariq was so grateful to see him, he closed his eyes and gave thanks to God. The rejected girls had been waiting in his car, listening to the radio, and one of them had a serious case of B.O. Tariq didn't know if the odor came from her underarms or her panties, but even with all four windows down, his whole car smelled funky. He couldn't hide his excitement when Brendon bid his friend adieu, and the other girls hopped out of his ride.

Brendon smiled brightly as they drove away. "Say, man, you should'a came up there. That ho a freak."

"Yeah, I could tell," Tariq replied.

"Naw, she a *freak* freak," Brendon insisted. "We wouldn't have had to take turns. You know what I'm saying?"

"Yeah, I do. So is she your woman now?" he joked.

"*Hell naw!*" Brendon said with a sneer.

"You know she gon' be blowing your phone up."

"Yeah, that's a problem when you put it down like I do," Brendon boasted. "If she start getting on my nerves, she getting straight *blocked*. Her cellphone don't got no service anyway. She be calling me on Facebook."

"I'm surprised she got WiFi."

"She don't. She logged into her neighbor's router!"

They both laughed.

When they exited the apartments, Tariq made a right on Lancaster, headed west. The three-lane thoroughfare was always busy, especially at that time of day; with commuters headed home from work. The posted speed limit was 45 miles per hour. Tariq was more comfortable with residential streets, but he didn't have a problem catching up with the flow of traffic.

He checked the speedometer and saw the needle on 44 mph when he passed through a green light at Oakland Blvd. He didn't know it at the time, but this information would be crucial. He was still laughing with his friend six blocks down the road when he noticed a crowd hanging out in front of a Beefer's restaurant.

Brendon asked him, "Nigga, did you know they still got Beefer's over here?"

Tariq didn't believe he took his eyes off the road, but he would later acknowledge that for a moment he did look up at the restaurant's marquee, which advertised a triple-beef heart attack in a paper bag.

Tariq told his friend, "Man, if you eat that, it'll be your *last* burger."

Brendon shouted, "***Say, look out!***"

And Tariq realized one of the men loitering outside of the restaurant had broken away from the group. The man wore a white tee shirt with black pants. He was moving quickly. Tariq believed he was trying to cross the street, but that didn't make sense. They weren't at a light, and he'd have to make it past three lanes of heavy traffic before he got to the median.

More importantly, the man didn't wait for a lull in traffic. His chance of making it across safely was exactly *zero percent*, which would explain the shout Tariq heard from a member of his group. He thought one of the men reached to stop the jaywalker.

But it all happened so fast. Tariq had less than a second to react.

He saw the crowd.

He saw the marquee with the triple beef burger.

He heard Brendon shout.

He saw a man break away from the group.

His brain calculated all of this at the speed of light and immediately transmitted instructions to his right foot.

BRAKE! BRAKE NOW!

Tariq's foot was obedient to these instructions, but he couldn't say for sure if he managed to stomp the brakes before the crazed man was directly in front of his bumper. His eyes were wide, his heart a frozen knot in his chest. He heard a loud **BOOMP!**, which was somehow more horrifying than then feel of his half-ton SUV impacting soft flesh and bones.

And then the man was gone.

Tariq prayed he'd imagined all of it, but half a second later there was a **BOOMP-BOMP!** as his rear wheels scaled a speed bump that shouldn't have been in the middle of the road.

Tariq's truck finally came to a complete stop. He looked over at Brendon, his wide eyes tinged with dread. Brendon had the same look on his face. Tariq checked the rearview mirror and saw that all of the traffic behind him had come to a screeching halt.

"*Oh shit*," Tariq muttered as the acrid smell of brake pads and tire smoke filled his nostrils. "*Oh shit*," he moaned. His horrified expression made him appear a few years younger than seventeen. "Did I hit him? *Did I hit somebody*?"

"That nigga just ran in the middle of the street," Brendon said. He was freaked out too, but Tariq appreciated that he was already on the defensive.

"*No, man. Shit. No...*" Tariq brought a hand to his mouth. He shook his head as he checked the rear view mirror again. His eyes glossed over when he saw that the speed bump wasn't a speed bump. It was exactly what he thought it was. One of the drivers behind them exited his vehicle and cautiously approached the body. The crowd from Beefer's began to spill into the street.

"*Damn, what do I do?*" Tariq's voice quavered. He felt like his heart was trying to jump up his throat. He felt sick all over. His intestines looped and tied themselves in knots when he looked over at his friend. "*Shit, man. What do I do?*"

"*Run,*" Brendon breathed.

But even in the midst of the most frightening encounter he'd ever experienced, Tariq knew he couldn't do that. He didn't think he could step out of the car and face what he'd done either, but his hand moved to the door handle, and he pushed it open.

He looked through the opening before stepping out into the bright sunlight. The body behind him was twisted and crumpled, his arms bent at unnatural angles. Tariq didn't see any blood, but the man's tee shirt was now soiled with bold, dark blotches. Tariq knew those were tire marks. *His* tire marks. His legs felt like rubber bands, but somehow they supported him.

People were yelling. Horns blaring. Lost in a whirlwind of emotions, Tariq half-believed this was only a dream. His eyes were glued to the body in the street. Skid marks from his tires led directly to it. As he drew nearer, Tariq saw that there *was* blood. There was plenty of it.

He inched closer, trying to get a look at the man's face. He wasn't sure why that was important. The victim's bloody visage would surely mar his dreams for decades if he laid eyes on it, but he had to see. Was the man conscious? Bleeding from the mouth or nose? Gasping for air like a fish out of water?

Or were his eyes already wide and transfixed; staring past the world of the living?

Was he dead?

Jesus, that would be – *no*. There was no way he actually *killed a man*. But he was going so fast. And the body was twisted so badly. Despite the extreme gravity of the situation, Tariq couldn't help but consider his mother's reaction to this. She would take his keys for sure. He'd be grounded for months, maybe for the rest of his life.

He never saw the victim's face, because the crowd had grown dense in a matter of seconds. All of the men from Beefer's converged on the scene. Some tried to help the injured man up. Tariq wanted to tell them that was the absolute *last* thing they should do to an accident victim, but by then he noticed the man's friends were what his mother would call *hood niggas*. They were loud and rowdy, yelling and pleading. A few turned and fixed angry eyes on the only person they could lay blame on. Tariq stopped in his tracks when they began to advance on him.

"*Man, what the fuck you do*?!"

"*You saw that nigga!*"

"*I di – I didn't, wha, I did–*" Tariq wanted to tell them he didn't do anything wrong, and any attempt to blame him for the accident reeked of immature-quick-to-judge ignorance. But his fight or flight instincts had his heart revving. He couldn't get his tongue to articulate a proper defense.

He backpedaled as they marched forward. Visions of Reginald Denny filled his mind. Was this for real? Could people really be this outrageous? Tariq had experienced countless *Nigga Moments* during his short time on earth, but never had he seen such dark, angry eyes fixed solely on him. The body lying on the pavement became an afterthought as self-preservation became his primary concern.

Tariq was completely dumbfounded when he heard someone shout, "*Hey, them niggas from Bideker!*"

Bideker? What the hell?

That comment made no sense at all. Tariq had forgotten about their marginal connection to the south side gang until he followed the voice and saw that one of the aggressors had approached the passenger side of his truck. This one was a teen, around the same age as Tariq. As he watched, the boy reached through the open window and began to struggle with Brendon. Tariq's eyes widened when the tussling progressed to punching.

From his vantage point, Tariq couldn't see Brendon's reaction, but the boy on the outside of the truck was animated. He tried to jerk the passenger door open and then kicked it when it wouldn't come free. The whole time he struggled with Brendon, he continued to rally the troops.

"These Bideker niggas! They killed Shank!"

Tariq didn't bother trying to explain that he and his friend were not in a gang, and they didn't kill anyone. The victim just needed to wait on an ambulance, and everything would be alright.

Instead he backed quickly towards his SUV, which was the only clear route to safety. If the mob caught him out in the open, he was finished. They wouldn't stop dragging him through the streets until the police arrived.

Tariq's only saving grace was most of the men converged on the passenger side of his truck, hoping to snatch Brendon from the vehicle. Tariq hopped in on the driver's side before they realized he was attempting to escape.

"Get 'em!"

"Get them niggas! They trying to take off!"

Beyond the screams of the angry crowd, Tariq heard his friend now. Brendon was pleading, begging them to, *"Get off me! I didn't do nothing!"*

His words didn't stop a barrage of arms and fists raining through the open window. Tariq was so shocked, he wasted several precious seconds, staring in awe, until he felt a hand on his throat.

"Aagh!"

He pushed it away, and the dark hand gripped his shirt instead. Tariq turned and locked eyes with Satan himself. The man was twice his age and size. His fair skin revealed bold tattoos on his neck and even a few on his face. His forearm was the size of Tariq's thigh, his fist the size of a football.

"Get out the car, nigga!"

The man's eyebrows bunched together when Tariq screamed again and reached for the steering wheel with one hand and the gear shift with the other.

"Get out the car!"

"*Gooo!*" Brendon shouted. "*Goooo!*"

A glimpse to the right revealed nothing but black faces and black arms. Some reached for the inner door handle. Some held Brendon in a death grip. Others continued striking. Brendon pulled away from them, catching most of the blows in the back of the neck and head. Tears streamed down his face and mixed with the blood leaking from his mouth and nose.

"*Man, goooo!*" he yelled. He met Tariq's eyes and begged for his life. "*Drive off, man! Goooo!*"

Tariq threw his car in DRIVE and stomped the gas pedal. The engine screamed as the truck lurched forward. For a moment, it didn't seem like they were moving. The mob had them almost completely surrounded. The arms poking through the windows didn't go away, and neither did the devilish mug on the driver's side. Tariq couldn't tell if the man was running alongside the truck or somehow *flying*.

Gradually, as he increased speed, the faces on Brendon's side of the vehicle fell away one by one. But Tariq's demon held on. When his speedometer inched past fifteen miles per hour, Tariq's whole body jerked off the seat. His attacker had stopped running, but he refused to let go. Tariq's screams stopped abruptly when his tee shirt cut off his air supply and began to strangle him. He pressed the gas pedal harder, thinking there was no way –

POP!
POP!
POP!POP!POP!

Despite everything that had transpired in the past thirty seconds, the sound of gunfire was surreal. Tariq was an A/B student, for Christ's sake. A good boy, by any one's account. His pastimes included video games, comic books, and helping his mother with her garden. This type of stuff wasn't supposed to happen to him!

Yet there he was; caught up in the ultimate Nigga Moment; a life or death struggle in a bad neighborhood he never should've visited.

He didn't notice that the hand gripping his shirt had disappeared, but Tariq did see the bright, red lights ahead. He didn't slow or even consider stopping. More horns blared as he roared through the intersection, but no one hit them, so it didn't matter. The more distance he put between himself and the body in the road, the safer he felt.

A minute down the road, Tariq was ready to proclaim his getaway a success when his friend delivered grim news.

"Say, I'm hit, man." Brendon's voice was low and raspy.

Tariq didn't take his eyes off the road – dared not. But his face registered confusion. Of course Brendon was hit. He saw him get punched multiple times. Why would his friend feel the need to make a formal announcement?

"I'm *shot*," Brendon clarified. He lifted his sleeve to reveal blood seeping from his shoulder. *"You gotta take me to the hospital."*

Tariq looked to the right – just for a second – to assess his injuries. When his eyes returned to the road, they were once again filled with horror.

PART ONE
BEADS

CHAPTER 4

And when I drive by where he died
Where sirens screamed and mourners cried
I hear moans come from everywhere
I dodge a body no longer there
I see dark blood dried on the street
Where his body used to be
Sometimes I cry into my hands
I now know fear
I killed a man

AT THE POLICE station, Dana listened quietly as her son told his story. Tariq didn't tell her *every little detail*. His mom didn't need to know about the thots they were visiting. She didn't need to know that Brendon bedded one of them, and he didn't think he should tell her about Brendon's bead necklace. If Dana found out about that, it would be the end of their friendship. Plus it wouldn't change the fact that the mob's reaction was completely unjustified, since Brendon was not really in a gang.

"We drove for about five miles, until we saw this police station," Tariq continued.

He and Dana sat in an interrogation room that was probably wired for audio and video. But since she hadn't agreed to let Tariq give an official statement, she didn't think any information they obtained from the cameras could be used against him in court. In any event, by this point in the story, Dana was fairly sure her son hadn't done anything illegal.

The man he hit was jaywalking, and Tariq swore he wasn't speeding at the time. It was tragic that the victim had died, but Tariq couldn't be held responsible for an idiot running into the street. The only thing the police might say he did wrong was flee the scene of the accident, but the mitigating circumstances should take care of that. No judge in the country would expect a motorist to render aid while they were getting shot at.

"The police came out, and they called an ambulance for Brendon," Tariq told her. "They brought me in here and said they wanted to question me, and that's when I called you."

There was a small table in the interrogation room. Dana sat on the same side as her son. The room was a little chilly. Tariq had both arms tucked inside his tattered tee shirt. He wasn't as distraught as he was when his mother first arrived, and Dana had gotten her tears under control. Seeing that he was okay and embracing him had relieved her tension substantially.

She reached and touched the red welts on his neck. Tariq had said the scrapes came from his tee shirt being yanked by one of the assailants. His shirt was ripped badly, nearly in tatters. The neck portion was stretched so violently, he could fit it around his torso.

Dana's heart beat sweetly for him. Hearing what he and Brendon had been through sent shockwaves all the way to her soul.

"Are you okay?" she asked, for what had to be the tenth time.

He nodded. "I am, Mama. They got Brendon way worse."

"Have you heard anything about him? Is he okay?"

Tariq shrugged. "He was bleeding bad, but he only got hit in the arm. They haven't told me anything." His eyes watered. He lowered his head, and his face reddened. "Mama, I killed that man."

Dana pulled him closer. She held his head against her chest. She wanted to tell him it would be okay, but she knew it wouldn't be. Accident or not, Tariq would have to live with the memories of his fatal accident for the rest of his life. The feel of his SUV rolling over the victim would haunt his dreams for years. Rather than speak, she held him while he cried, as she had done countless times throughout his life.

After awhile someone knocked on the door of the small room and then opened it. A plainclothes detective stepped in and asked, "Is he ready to give a statement?"

Tariq sat up and looked his mother in the eyes. He nodded.

Dana looked to the officer and said, "Yeah. We're ready."

CHAPTER 5

THE INTERVIEW WAS a lot less taxing than Dana expected. The detective treated Tariq like he was a victim, which may have been because his mother was present. He was calm and patient, even when pressing for details about how fast Tariq was going, when he noticed the crowd at Beefer's and when he realized someone had ran into the street.

The only time Tariq didn't provide quick, factual information was when the policeman asked why the crowd turned on him and Brendon. Initially Tariq didn't want his mother to know about his friend's necklace. Now he felt like he'd be snitching if he told the police about the beads.

"I don't know." He shook his head. "They were mad because their friend got hit. They said my friend was in a gang, but he's not. I don't know why they thought that."

Sweat blossomed on Tariq's forehead. Lying to an authority figure was not something he was accustomed to. He hoped they'd attribute his discomfort to the overall stress of the ordeal.

"Brendon's never been in a gang," he told the cop.

Dana frowned at that but didn't say anything. Tariq didn't include this information in the story he told her.

"Did they say what gang they thought your friend was in?" the detective asked. He was a black man with a moustache/goatee combo that would've looked better if it was trimmed lower.

Tariq's heart kicked even harder. "Bid – *Bideker*... something..." He hoped that appearing ignorant about the gang would help his defense.

"*Bideker Boys*?" the cop asked.

Tariq's eyes lit up. He nodded. "Yeah. That's what they said."

The detective added this information to a notepad he'd been writing in. "How do you know Brendon isn't a member of that gang?"

Dana wanted to interrupt the interview at that moment, but she held back. She didn't want to seem defensive.

"He's my best friend," Tariq said. "I know he's not in a gang."

"The crowd that attacked you and your friend, were they gang members?" the policeman asked.

Tariq shrugged. "I don't know. They looked like, um, *thugs*. But they didn't have bandanas on or nothing like that. I mean, I don't think they did. It all happened so fast."

"Were they wearing any particular colors?"

Tariq thought about that. "Um, black," he said. "I think most of them were wearing black and white."

The cop scribbled more in his notebook before asking Tariq, "Are we gonna find any drugs or weapons in your vehicle?"

Dana's eyes narrowed as she stared at her son, waiting for him to answer.

Tariq quickly shook his head. "No. No, sir."

"At any point did Brendon encourage you to hit the man who walked into the street?"

This time Dana fixed a look on the detective.

"No," Tariq said, still shaking his head. "As soon as we saw him, he yelled, '*Watch out*.' That was the only thing he had time to say."

31

Again Dana wanted to intervene, to make sure they weren't trying to railroad her son. But the detective closed his notebook at that moment and nodded.

"Okay, thank you," he said to Tariq. "That's all the questions I have for now."

Neither Dana nor her son moved. She knew they didn't have cause to detain Tariq, but this was the south, and stranger things had happened.

"We can leave?" she asked the detective.

He nodded. "Yes. We don't believe the accident was your son's fault. What happened is extremely tragic. But so far it appears Tariq has been truthful and forthcoming with the information we need. It doesn't look like he could've prevented this accident. Investigators are still collecting evidence from the scene, but I don't think they'll find anything to change our decision. There are a lot of businesses in that area. Footage from their surveillance cameras should corroborate your son's story."

Dana sighed inwardly, trying not to let on how relieved she was. She switched gears and asked, "What about those people who attacked Tariq and Brendon? Have y'all arrested any of them?"

The detective couldn't hide his disappointment when he shook his head. "No, ma'am. I'm sorry, we haven't. The crowd had mostly dispersed by the time the first unit arrived on the scene. We've taken witness statements that confirm everything Tariq told us. The witnesses said the man with the gun took off immediately after the shooting. A few more people who were involved in the altercation also fled on foot.

"The ones who remained with the victim, the officers couldn't say for sure if they were involved in the assault or shooting. We may be able to identify a suspect when we review the surveillance footage. We'll give you a call when the investigators are done with your truck," he told Tariq before rising to his feet.

The thought of getting his murder vehicle back wasn't appealing to Tariq or his mother. Neither of them responded.

CHAPTER 6

BY THE TIME they exited the police station, the sun had completely set. The night was warm. Lancaster Avenue was as hectic as ever. The sight of the busy street sent a chill through Tariq's body, despite the 80-degree temperature. As they approached Dana's car, he looked down the road, in the direction of the accident. The street was nearly flat enough to see for miles, but he couldn't spot Beefer's marquee from their vantage point.

The time was 8:30 p.m. This was two hours earlier than Dana would've gotten off work if she had completed her shift at the hospital, but she felt completely drained. Her eyes were red and puffy from crying. The mental fatigue had culminated in a headache. She wanted nothing more than to transport her baby to the safety of their home, but she wasn't upset when they got in the car and Tariq asked her, "Can we stop by the hospital to see Brendon?"

Dana realized that was the right thing to do, and she was selfish for not considering it beforehand.

"Yeah," she said as she started her car. "But you're gonna need another shirt." She pushed the trunk release and told him, "Check the trunk. I think I have some tee shirts back there."

Tariq exited the vehicle and found an acceptable tee. He closed the trunk and changed shirts before he got back inside the car. Dana watched him in the rearview mirror. She didn't think he'd always appeared so small and skinny.

She noticed him looking to the right as she exited the parking lot. She planned to make a left, but she asked, "Do you want to show me where the accident happened?"

Tariq shook his head right away. He'd seen episodes of *The First 48* where the detectives left a murder victim in the street for hours after their death. This probably wasn't the same type of investigation, but there was no point in risking it.

Dana made a left on Lancaster, heading towards the hospital district.

CHAPTER
7

SHE HOPED THEY'D taken Brendon to Jackson
Memorial. Dana planned to visit her unit and let her coworkers
know what was going on while Tariq was visiting his friend. But
he called Brendon and learned he was at John Peter Paul; one of
the neighboring hospitals.

Despite being admitted over two hours ago, Brendon was
still in the ER when they arrived. Fortunately he'd already been
treated and was awaiting his discharge orders. He sat up on a
stretcher with his legs dangling over the side. Dana gasped and
fought to minimize her reaction when she first laid eyes on him.

Tariq had told her that members of the crowd attacked
them, targeting Brendon almost exclusively. But after seeing her
son's minimal wounds, she didn't expect Brendon's injuries to be
so severe. The boy looked like he'd gone a full round with a
heavyweight. His right eye was swollen, almost fully closed. His
bottom lip was twice it's normal size, with a cut down the middle.
He had a few contusions on his cheeks and forehead.

But he smiled at his visitors. Dana managed to stop her
jaw from dropping, but she couldn't force her lips to smile back.

"Jesus, Brendon. Are you alright?"

"Yeah, I'm good," he said. "I don't look that bad, do I?"

Dana sighed rather than respond.

Tariq approached the stretcher and was honest enough to tell him, "Man, you look *messed up*! You good, though?"

"Yeah, I'm good."

The boys grasped hands and came together for a bro hug. Tariq continued to stare at his injuries when he backed away. He shook his head, his expression solemn.

"Dang. I didn't know they hit you that many times."

"I told you to drive off," Brendon reminded him. "Half these licks I took are your fault," he joked.

Tariq didn't find the humor in it. "I'm sorry," he said. "I was scared. If I would've known–"

"Quit tripping," Brendon said, still grinning with his misshapen mouth. "Considering it was six against one, I think I came out alright."

Tariq wished he could be as upbeat as his running buddy.

"I can still get more girls than you," Brendon said, "even with my eye all swole up."

Tariq cracked a smile then. "Yeah, and they'll still be uglier than my girlfriends. But at least now you got an excuse: You can say you couldn't see what they looked like."

The friends chuckled.

Dana said, "Hey, Victoria," to one of the other visitors in the room. She walked to the woman and gave her a hug.

Brendon's aunt looked as exhausted as Dana felt. She said, "Hey, Dana."

"Y'all been here long?" Dana asked, looking down at Victoria's daughter Kim. The five-year-old was fiddling with extra linens on a rack in the exam room.

"I just got here an hour ago," Victoria said. She was a short woman with big lips and gaunt features. "I was at work when he called. They was gonna let me go, but Brendon said he only got grazed, so I went ahead and finished my shift."

Dana thought it was sad that Brendon's aunt didn't head to the hospital immediately upon hearing he got shot. But Tariq had told her Victoria was a reluctant *guardian*. She didn't make much money working as a cashier at Krogers, and she had three children of her own to take care of. It wasn't Victoria's fault that her sister would rather run the streets, going back and forth between jail and rehab, than care for Brendon. Victoria provided her nephew a roof over his head and at least one hot meal a day. Other parental duties, like trips to the school and hospital, was pushing it.

"You only got grazed?" Tariq asked his friend. Next to the police deciding not to prosecute him for the accident, that was the best news he'd heard in the past few hours.

"*Yeeh*," Brendon said. He lifted the sleeve of his hospital gown to show off the gauze taped on his shoulder. "Ain't nothing. Only needed six stitches."

"Mama, I'm hungry," the smallest person in the room announced.

"I told you we'll get something to eat when we leave," Victoria snapped. "These people need to hurry up," she said, frowning. "They said they was gon' let us go thirty minutes ago."

The little girl lowered her gaze and returned her attention to the boring hospital sheets and blankets.

Feeling sorry for her, Dana said, "I think I saw some vending machines in the waiting room. I can take her to get a bag of chips or something, if that's okay..."

Kim's eyes lit up. "Do they have cookies?"

Dana smiled down at her. "I think they do."

Victoria pushed off the wall and said, "Hell, I might as well go with you. I'm hungry too. Do you think you can get me a Snickers or something?" she asked Dana. "I'll pay you back next week."

Victoria didn't know how much Dana got paid at the hospital, but she knew she took X-rays, and she assumed it was a lot.

"Uh, yeah," Dana said. "I can get you something. You don't have to pay me back. We'll be back in a second," she told her son as the three ladies left the room.

Brendon rolled his good eye at his begging-ass aunt. He knew she had no shame, but it never failed to surprise him when he witnessed it firsthand. When it was just him and Tariq in the room, he lowered his voice and asked his friend, "Say, what did you tell the police?"

Tariq was confused by his conspiratorial tone. "I told them what happened," he said, frowning. "What you mean?"

"What about my beads?" Brendon clarified. "Did they ask about them?"

Tariq shook his head. "They asked why them fools thought we was down with Bideker Street. I told them I didn't know."

Tariq checked his friend's neck, noticing for the first time that his necklace was missing. "What happened to them?"

"I chunked them," Brendon revealed.

"*Chunked them*? Where?"

"Out the window – after we got away from them."

Tariq didn't remember his friend disposing of evidence during their getaway, but then again, he had other things to worry about at the time, like getting away.

"I told you you was stupid for wearing those fucking beads," he growled. "You almost got us killed."

"They was mad 'cause they think you hit ol' boy on purpose."

"*They thought that because of your fucking beads.*"

"Well it's over now," Brendon said. "The police can't prove I had 'em. Even if they could, it didn't have nothing to do with that accident. Them niggas was just tripping. That fool deserved to get hit; running out in the street like that."

Tariq continued to frown at him. He had lied to the police to protect his friend. Brendon took it a step further by disposing of evidence. If some of the thugs who attacked them decided to come forward and offer their version of events, the missing beads could come back and bite them in the ass.

"Did that nigga make it?" Brendon asked.

"Who?"

"The one you ran over."

Tariq had left his gloom cloud at the police station, but it was back in an instant. The lights in the exam room suddenly felt dimmer. He shook his head. "The police didn't tell you?"

Brendon shook his head. "I didn't ask about him. I was trying to hurry and get them out of here, before they found something to arrest me for."

"He dead," Tariq revealed.

Due to Brendon's facial injuries, it was hard to judge his reaction. "Oh. Word?"

Tariq nodded. He backed towards one of the chairs in the room and took a seat, feeling nauseous all of a sudden.

"The police turned you loose, though," Brendon said. "That mean it wasn't your fault."

Tariq nodded vacantly.

"I know it's messed up what happened," Brendon went on. "But look what they did to us. Plus it wasn't even your fault. I ain't got no sympathy for that nigga."

Tariq thought his friend was being unnecessarily callous. But Brendon had been beat up and shot by the thugs. Maybe it was okay for him to harden his heart.

Tariq lowered his head and sighed. "I'm just glad it's over with."

But deep down, he knew he was probably wrong about that.

CHAPTER 8

And when the night finds me alone
His ghastly presence prowls my home
My mirrors are now home to his face
He's in the darkness when I awake
The memories won't let me go
My existence is an anchor for his soul

DANA AND TARIQ lived in a quiet neighborhood on the southwest part of town. They finally pulled into their driveway, with hopes of putting an end to their tragic day, at a quarter till ten.

"You hungry?" Dana asked as she entered their home, turning on lights in the living room and kitchen.

"No, I'm good," her son said. He went to his room and closed the door.

Dana wanted to talk more, but she allowed him time to himself. In her bedroom, she undressed and showered. She didn't know anything about the person who died, but she could imagine what her son must be going through. She thought about everything Tariq had told her and replayed the accident in her mind as she bathed. Her vision was so surreal, she could hear the screeching of tires, the shouting from the thugs in the crowd. Her heart hammered when she looked down and saw blood mixed with the water swirling down the shower drain.

But when she blinked and rubbed her eyes, it went away.

Tariq was still holed up in his room when she put on her night clothes and left her bedroom. He had said he wasn't hungry, but Dana went to the kitchen and made spaghetti anyway. Her son didn't make an appearance when the savory smell of garlic and pasta filled the house. But he was agreeable to supper when Dana knocked on his door. She had hoped he'd showered and changed by then, but Tariq still wore the same outfit. The bruises on his neck looked more swollen, more pronounced.

He followed her to the kitchen, and they ate quietly. Afterwards Dana washed the few dishes, while he remained at the table. Tariq didn't have his cellphone with him, which was a rarity. He just stared at the bare table top, with his hands clasped together in his lap.

"Do you wanna talk about it?" Dana asked when she put the last dish away and dried her hands.

He shook his head.

She stepped closer and stood over him until he looked up at her. Tariq was six months away from his eighteenth birthday. Lately he'd been doing little, annoying things to assert his position as a man. But tonight he looked every bit like a teenage boy. She reached for his hand.

"Come here."

He accepted the gesture and rose to his feet. She led him to the living room and took a seat on the couch. The lights were off, but there was enough illumination from the kitchen to make out his sullen features. Tariq took a seat next to her. He slowly leaned her way, resting his head on her bosom, and started to cry. Dana held him, and her tears fell silently.

Tariq hadn't been this accepting of her affection in years. Dana wasn't sure how long they remained in that position before she heard him snoring lightly. By then he had both arms wrapped around her. Dana didn't want to break the embrace, so she closed her eyes and gradually drifted off to sleep herself.

CHAPTER 9

THEY WERE STILL locked together in grief when the morning sun brightened the front room with warm sunrays. Dana awakened first. Tariq stirred moments later when she reached overhead to stretch her arms. He looked around, momentarily confused about how they ended up on the couch overnight.

He scooted over and asked, "Why you didn't take me to bed?"

She grinned. "You mean pick you up and carry you, like when you were five? I think you might be a little too big for that."

He smiled too. It did Dana's heart good to see that.

"I don't mean carry me," he said. "You could've woke me up and told me to go to bed."

"What's wrong? You don't like cuddling with your mama?"

"I guess," he mumbled.

"Hey, I got the worst end of it," she informed him. "When was the last time you bathed?"

Tariq raised his arm and tried to sniff his armpit. "I stink?"

She gave him a comforting look. "Not *horribly*..."

"Well, I'm not doing nothing today, so I don't have to bathe," Tariq joked.

Dana almost asked why he wasn't going anywhere, but then she remembered where his truck was and why the police had it. Apparently Tariq was flooded with the same memories at that moment, because his smile slipped away.

"Do you work today?" he asked.

Dana was on the schedule, but she told him, "I don't have to. I can stay here with you."

He smacked his lips. "Why would you do that?"

"I didn't think you'd want to be here by yourself."

"Why? Just because *you* don't get a summer break doesn't mean you can slack off with me."

Dana was relieved to hear that he still had his sense of humor. "So you're okay here by yourself?"

"I'm here by myself all the time. What you think I'm gonna do, throw a party?"

Dana didn't think that. She worked two to ten-thirty. None of Tariq's friends would be interested in a party that had to end that early. Plus he'd never been the type to try something like that.

What Dana worried about was him being home alone and depressed, with memories of a dead man running through his mind all day.

"What are you gonna do, just play games?" she asked. She didn't like him vegetating with his PlayStation during the school year. But she was more lenient during the summer.

"Mama, don't worry about me. I'm alright. Seriously."

She sighed softly. "Alright. Do you want me to make dinner before I go, or are you okay cooking for yourself?"

"I could just go–" Tariq caught himself. No, he couldn't go buy fast food without a car. "What do we have to eat?" he asked.

"I don't know." She stood and headed for the kitchen. "I'll check."

CHAPTER 10

FIVE HOURS LATER, Dana got dressed and headed to work as planned. She had misgivings about leaving her son alone, but since they'd been awake, he made it clear that her pampering and hovering was not appreciated. By noon, he didn't seem like the same boy who fell asleep in her arms last night. He was back to asserting his independence, and Dana had no choice but to let him.

When she got to work, her coworker Julie was the first to express concern about what happened yesterday. Julie had to take the phone and jot down the address for the police station, when Dana was too distraught to do so herself. She felt bad for not calling back to give her an update.

Their supervisor Steve was in the office that afternoon. He and Julie listened with wide-eyes as Dana recounted Tariq's harrowing Friday night. When she was done, Julie was the first to respond.

"Oh my God, Dana. That's horrible!"

"Yeah, that's..." Steve shook his head. "I can't imagine anything like that happening to one of my children. I don't know what I would do."

Steve and Julie were both white, but when it came to parenting, the concern they felt was universal.

"They were *shooting*?" Steve couldn't believe it. "Why would – how could they think Tariq hit someone on *purpose*?"

"Stupid mob mentality," Dana said, shaking her head.

Julie continued to frown. "What does that mean?"

"Something like this happened, um, in Detroit, I think," Dana said. "It was a couple of years ago. A man was driving through a residential area, and he hit a little kid that ran in the road. He got out to help, and a bunch of people attacked him. They beat him so bad, he was in a coma. Skull fractures. He almost died."

"I remember that," Steve said. "But that was racial, wasn't it?"

"He was white," Dana recalled. "The people who attacked him were black. But I don't think it was racial. They just reacted to that little boy lying in the street."

Steve looked like he disagreed with her assessment, but he didn't mention it.

Dana said, "I think the guys who attacked Tariq and his friend were in a gang. They accused Brendon of being in a gang. That's why they think Tariq did it on purpose."

"That's stupid," Steve said. "I never heard of a gangbanger mowing down an enemy with his car."

"Stranger things have happened," Dana said thoughtfully. "I've seen some really ugly things. That's why I left Chicago. The gangbanging has gotten way worse since then. Moving south was the best thing I ever did." She considered the irony of fleeing a gang-ridden city only to encounter more gang trouble in Overbrook Meadows. She shook her head. "At least I thought it was."

"No, it is better here," Steve said. "This is, I'm sure this is an isolated event; just some idiots overreacting to something that could've been handled with *words*. Tariq will probably never run into those people again, if he stays out of the hood."

Dana appreciated her supervisor's encouragement, but he seemed a little naïve to some racial issues. Just because Dana managed to find a home in a nice neighborhood didn't mean Tariq's friends were so fortunate. Brendon lived in an area that could be considered *impoverished*. The same could be said about a lot of their friends from school. To completely avoid the hoods in Overbrook Meadows, Tariq would have to avoid a whole lot of black people. Maybe that's what Steve had in mind.

"How's Tariq doing?" Julie asked. "If that happened to me, I don't know if I'd ever want to drive again."

"He seems okay," Dana said. "The police have his car. I don't know how he'll feel about driving when he gets it back."

"You should get him into counseling," Steve suggested.

"You should," Julie agreed. "He might say he's alright, but how could he be? Someone *died*. And he got shot at. Boys – they never want to admit when they're traumatized, but you know he is."

Again Dana felt guilty for leaving Tariq home alone that day. He could be curled up in his room crying right now, for all she knew.

"You're right," she told her coworkers. "I'm gonna call someone."

CHAPTER
11

THANKS TO THE insurance plan at the hospital, Dana had no trouble making an appointment for Tariq to see a grief counselor. She called him after lunch to see how he was holding up.

"Hello?"

"Hey. How's it going?"

"I'm fine," he told her.

Dana could hear battlefield noises in the background, so she knew he was on his game. "You feeling alright?" she pressed.

"Mama, I'm fine. For real," Tariq said. "You don't have to worry about me."

"Since when? I been worrying about you for the past seventeen years. What makes you think it's gonna stop today?"

"I'm just saying. I'm not over here crying or nothing."

"Okay," Dana said. "That's good. Look, I made an appointment for you to see a counselor, but he can't take you until next week..."

After a pause, Tariq said, "A counselor for what?"

"It's a crisis counselor."

Another pause.

"You mean, for like, kids who lose their parents?"

"Um, yeah. But that's not all they do. They try to help anyone with a stressful situation, like what happened last night."

"I don't need a counselor, Mama. I'm telling you I'm fine."

"Maybe you are, Tariq. But a man died yesterday. That has to have some kind of effect on you."

"Why do you keep talking about it? You act like you want me to have a breakdown."

"I don't want that. But it's not healthy for you to act like you can forget about it and keep it moving. You will end up having a breakdown, if you do that."

"Alright. Whatever. I guess you're gonna make me go, even if I say no."

His insolence was starting to irritate her. Dana had to remind herself that her baby was hurting, even if he didn't realize it.

She told him, "Yes, you're going, even if you don't want to."

He sighed loudly into the phone. "Is that it?"

Dana's nostrils flared as she sucked in a deep breath. If the boy wasn't grief-stricken, she would've given him a piece of her mind.

"Yes, Tariq. That's it. I'll talk to you when I get home."

CHAPTER
12

HE CALLED BACK near the end of her shift, but Dana was busy with a patient. She returned his call twenty minutes later.

"Hey, what's up?"

"Mama, there's, um..."

His voice was laced with dread. The hairs stood on the back of Dana's neck while she waited for him to finish his statement.

"Some guy came by the house," he informed her.

Dana's eyebrows bunched together. That didn't sound like something he should be apprehensive about.

"At first I thought it was a burglar," Tariq went on. "'Cause I don't know him, and he... I don't know. He just looked like he was up to no good. I didn't want to open the door, so I yelled through it, asking him what he wanted."

That was the advice Dana had given him in regards to a visit from a stranger. So far so good...

"He asked if somebody who drove a blue Explorer stayed here," Tariq said.

Dana's heart froze. Her eyes narrowed even more as she approached her desk and took a seat. "Wait. He asked about your car?"

"Yeah," Tariq said. He sounded slightly winded.

"And you never seen him before?"

"No, Mama. It was – he's not from around here."

"What'd you, what'd you tell him?"

"I told him no," Tariq recounted. "And then he walked off. I watched him through the window. He went and got in a car with some other dudes, and they drove off."

Dana's mind raced. A stranger at her door asking about Tariq's car? She couldn't imagine what that was about. But her son had another piece of the puzzle.

"Mama, it look like some of them dudes from yesterday."

Dana's eyes widened. Every ounce of blood in her body chilled. For the second time in as many days, a deep sense of foreboding darkened her department.

"I been looking out the window," Tariq said. "They drove by again, a couple of times. They keep looking at the house, but they didn't stop. You, what do you think I should do? Should I call the police?"

Dana's heart started beating again; thunderously hard. What was happening to their cozy, little life? Raising a son as a single mother was hard enough. She'd managed to make it seventeen years without Tariq getting caught up in any serious trouble. A freak accident had changed everything. If it was the same hoodlums from yesterday, how the hell did they find out where Tariq lived? More importantly, what were their intentions? Yesterday they fired shots at him and Brendon, thinking they hit their friend on purpose. If they took the time to–

"Mama."

Dana's eyes glossed over. *God, please don't let anything happen to my baby.* She swallowed hard. "I'm, I'm here," she breathed.

"Do you want me to–"

"When was the last time they drove by?" Dana realized she was starting to hyperventilate. She closed her eyes and tried to steady her breaths.

"About ten minutes ago. Should I call the police?" he asked again.

"Yeah," Dana said, nodding. She yanked one of her desk drawers open and grabbed her purse.

"You want me to call them, or you're gonna do it?"

"I'll call them," Dana said. She knew her son was capable, but Tariq might not be able to convey the urgency she felt. Would the police stop by, just because a stranger knocked on the door? Dana wouldn't get off the phone with them until they promised a unit was on the way.

"Okay. What do you want me to—"

"I'm on my way," she told her son. "Don't go outside, and don't answer the door. If they come back, call 911!"

"Alright, Mama. Do you think—"

"Baby, I gotta go." Dana left her desk and saw that Julie was busy with a patient. She hated to leave her department shorthanded again, but there was no other option. "I gotta find my supervisor, and I gotta call the police," she told Tariq. "I'll call you when I'm on my way."

PART TWO
SHANK

CHAPTER 13

This simple scene of serenity
Awaits the arrival of anticipated action
Beneath my bold bravado
Is a frantic, fragmented fear
Crazy cowards come creeping
Cruising in a crowded Crown Vic
Reeking of ripe revenge
Firing for a fallen friend

DANA'S RIDE HOME was frantic. The speed limit on the interstate got bumped up to 70 miles per hour a few years ago, but that wasn't fast enough for her to get to her only child. Her heart drummed, like the pistons under the hood of her Kia. She barely maintained enough composure to plead with the police; begging them to go to her home and protect her son. They agreed to stop by, but it was clearly not a priority. Thankfully when she finally made it to her neighborhood, Dana saw a black and white parked in her driveway. The squad car didn't have its sirens on, and there was no ambulance idling on the curb, so she was finally able to breathe a sigh of relief.

As she slowed to a stop, Dana noticed a few of her neighbors had come outside to gawk at the police activity. Among them was a tall, brooding brother who lived across the street, three houses down. The man wore jeans with a dark blue tee that was probably an extra-large – but the shirt wasn't big enough to conceal his above average physique. He stood stoically with his hands by his sides. The muscles in his arms looked toned and powerful. His skin was nearly as dark as his eyes, which appeared concerned when he momentarily locked eyes with Dana.

The sight of him added to the discomfort she already felt. But the tug at her heart wasn't as bad as it used to be. There was a time, not too long ago, when her neighbor's intense gaze was enough to bring her to tears. Nowadays he was only a minor annoyance, which was easily pushed out of her thoughts completely when Dana looked away and turned into her driveway. She rushed from her car as if it was on fire and met up with the police officers Tariq had invited inside their home.

CHAPTER
14

"SO, THAT'S IT?"

Ten minutes later Dana's tension had not dissipated. Rather than ease her stress, the police only added to it with their inactivity and nonchalance.

"Ma'am, I don't know what you want us to do," the first cop said. He was Hispanic with dark skin and a full beard.

"I want you to do some type of *investigation*," Dana told him. She stood in the foyer with her hands on her hips.

Tariq sat on the couch behind her with his hands in his lap, his expression as strained as his mother's. The two policemen were trying their best to vacate the premises, but a concerned citizen was holding them up; telling them how to do their job.

"What exactly do you want us to investigate?" the second cop asked. He was black and very unattractive, in Dana's opinion.

"Tariq says it looked like some of the guys he got into it with yesterday," Dana said. "This could be the same people who shot at him and his friend. Isn't that something you should investigate?"

"We're gonna write a report," the first cop said.

"A *report*? What the hell—"

"That's actually more than we *should* do," the second cop said, cutting her off.

"And why is that?" she spat.

"Because there's no law against someone knocking on your door," the policeman said. "Your son got a good look at him, and he can't say for sure if this person was involved with the incident from yesterday."

"We *know* it was the same guys," Dana said defiantly. "What do you think, thugs just randomly roll through this neighborhood, knocking on doors? No one like that has ever come by here before. This isn't a coincidence!"

"You might be right about that," the first cop said. "But without proof, all you're doing is speculating. There's no law against someone knocking on your door," he reiterated. "Your son says the man was not threatening. He only asked a question, and then he left."

"What?" Dana let go of her anger and pleaded with the men. "He wanted to know who drove my son's car. That means they're looking for the person who killed their friend." Her eyes were wide and glistening. "What do you think they're gonna do when they find out it's Tariq? You gotta wait until something bad happens before you try to help us?"

"Ma'am, *no crime has been committed*," the first policeman repeated. Frustration had hardened his features and his heart.

"We understand what you're going through," the other cop said, his tone more sympathetic. "But you need to understand our limitations. We can't go around arresting people for nothing. Just like citizens have to obey the law, we do too. If the man that came to your home threatened your son, that would be different."

"We don't want to wait until they threaten us," Dana insisted. "Please, can't you at least..."

The officers waited, but Dana had no idea what course of action they should take.

"The detectives from yesterday," she said. "Can you pass this along to them? They're still investigating the shooting. If this has something to do with it, maybe they can follow up on it..."

"Okay," the black cop said. "We'll make sure to pass this along to the detectives who are investigating your incident from yesterday."

He waited a few beats. When Dana couldn't think of anything else to tell them, the cops turned and eagerly left her home. She followed them out.

"If anyone comes back and harasses you, don't hesitate to call 9-1-1," the first cop said as they returned to their patrol car.

Dana stood on her porch with her arms folded over her stomach. She shook her head slightly, still not convinced the policemen were doing all they could. She didn't think they'd actually go out and arrest someone after she called. But questioning a few gangbangers seemed reasonable.

As the police backed out of her driveway, she surveyed her quiet street and saw that all of her neighbors had gone back inside – except one. The brother down the road stood in the same position; with his arms at his sides, his eyes fixed squarely on her. Dana knew his name was *Kole*, but she wasn't sure why he was so concerned about the happenings at her home. Due to the distance and the setting sun, it was hard to read the look on his face. As it was, his dark skin had mostly blended into the shadows on his porch.

Dana rolled her eyes at him and reentered her home. A few moments later, her garage door ascended slowly. She reemerged but didn't look Kole's way as she got into her car. She pulled it into the garage and pushed the clicker to lower the door again.

CHAPTER 15

A FEW HOURS later, the sun had completely disappeared in the western skies; relinquishing its spot to a full moon and thousands of twinkling stars. Neither Dana nor Tariq had gone to bed yet. His excuse was that it was summertime. He didn't have anything going on tomorrow that required an early rise.

Dana didn't discuss it with him, but her reason for delaying sleep was more practical: She was afraid. There was no point in kidding herself.

She had put a Stouffer's lasagna in the oven for supper, but when it was done, neither of them had much of an appetite. Tariq ate a third of his meal and picked at the rest before retiring to his room to play games. Dana put away the leftovers and washed the few dishes she'd used to prepare the meal. When she was done, she wiped the countertops and stovetop, and then swept and mopped the kitchen. She didn't realize she was battling anxiety until she pulled open the cabinet under the sink, in search of a bottle of Mop and Glo.

She caught herself and retreated to her room to change out of her work clothes and bathe. As she passed her son's room, she pushed the door open and saw that he had his headphones on, which effectively muted his television. Dana watched him for a few seconds and then pulled the door closed without him noticing.

The silence in the house was unnerving, but she didn't play any music as she stepped into the shower. She didn't know what she was waiting or listening for, but she felt she should remain alert – just in case.

When someone rang the doorbell a few minutes after midnight, she was startled but not wholly surprised. Her mouth went dry as she sat up in bed, her eyes wide, her heart rattling in her rib cage. She gasped when she saw a movement in her doorway. But as her eyes adjusted to the light, she realized it was Tariq.

"Mama?"

"Yeah," she breathed. She was out of bed by then, crouched next to the nightstand.

"Somebody at the door," he announced, his voice a hush, like hers.

"I heard it."

"Can I turn on the light?"

"No," she hissed. Despite the darkness, she found her handgun right where she had left it. The cool metal felt heavy and powerful when she pulled it from the drawer, but it didn't make her feel *safe*, like she hoped it would. She felt only slightly stronger than she did when she was unarmed.

"Want me to call the police?" Tariq whispered. She could only see his silhouette in the doorway. She heard the fear in his voice.

"Did you see who it was?" she asked him.

"No. Do you want me to go check?"

"No."

Dana approached him, and he stepped aside. Her stomach churned as she marched down the hallway. But her blood was laced with adrenaline now, and her steps were as bold as a lioness. She had no idea who was on the other side of her door, but there was one thing she was sure about: No harm would come to her son —not while she was among the living.

As she neared the front door, her body froze when the doorbell chimed again. She tightened her grip around her pistol and reached with her left hand to cock the weapon. That was something she would normally never do – unless she was positive she was about to pull the trigger. She did not flip the safety off as she inched closer to the door and peered through the peephole.

The man standing on her porch was a stranger. He looked to be in his mid to late twenties. He wore a black tee shirt with dark-colored pants. His hair was shaved low, his face clean-shaven. Despite his clean cut, the first description that came to Dana's mind was *thug*. She hated to stereotype a brother in such a short amount of time, but she couldn't stop her frazzled mind from jumping to conclusions.

She looked back and saw Tariq waiting anxiously, several feet behind her. She saw his wide eyes travel from the gun in her hand and then back up to her face. She started to ask him to look through the peephole and determine whether this was one of the men he and Brendon got into it with yesterday, or if this was the one who came by the house earlier.

She decided against it. Their visitor might hear them speaking, and she'd rather catch him off guard. As far as she could tell, the stranger was unarmed, which put her at an advantage. It was only a slight advantage, but Dana would take whatever edge she could get.

She motioned for Tariq to get out of sight. His eyes registered confusion, but she waved again, and he got the message. He reluctantly backed away and disappeared around the corner.

Dana turned back to the door just as their visitor reached for the doorbell a third time. Except this time he knocked rather than ring it again. Dana had never been more horrified by a gentle rapping at her door. Her features were rigid as she undid the locks with her free hand. She quickly pulled the door open and was happy to see a look of surprise on the stranger's face. She was even more pleased to confirm he didn't have a weapon.

They stood no more than four feet away from each other, with only the glass from the screen door as a barricade. The man looked Dana up and down. She wore pajama bottoms with a tee shirt. Her feet were bare, her hair pulled back and away from her face. She saw that he was tatted-up; with both arms completely filled with lettering and images that appeared random, rather than a uniform sleeve. The stranger had fair skin, small eyes and thick eyebrows. She might have considered him handsome under different circumstances. As it was, Dana found him more spooky than the boogey man.

Behind him she saw a car idling on the curb. It was one of the old-school Crown Vic's the Overbrook Meadows PD once used, before they switched to the Dodge Charger. Dana couldn't tell if the Crown Vic had other occupants. She didn't spend too much time studying the vehicle, because the primary threat was standing right in front of her.

She watched the visitor's eyes settle on her weapon before returning to her face. If he was bothered by the Glock G43, he didn't show it. Dana didn't expect him to run away screaming, but his lack of reaction made him appear ten times more dangerous.

"Is it somebody here that drive a blue Explorer?" he asked.

No *Excuse me, ma'am*, or *Sorry to disturb you* for this guy.

At that moment, Dana knew this was the same person who had come to her home earlier. And she was fairly certain he was part of the group who had attacked her son. Her need to protect Tariq was so strong, she wanted to point her pistol at him before they continued the conversation. But she remembered what the policemen had told her. There was nothing illegal about someone knocking on her door. Regardless of how sinister the creep looked, if she jumped the gun, she would be in the wrong – not him.

But that didn't mean she had to play nice. She narrowed her eyes and bared her teeth before responding.

"What the hell you knocking on my door for at this time of night?"

Once again the stranger was not bothered by her aggression. Not in the slightest. He rolled his eyes slightly before looking down at her gun again and then back into her eyes.

"I ain't trying to argue with you, lady. I just asked a simple question. I'm looking for somebody. I wanna know if he stay here."

Dana wasn't sure where she found the strength to maintain defiance, but her voice barely rattled when she replied. "You ain't got no right to be knocking on my door. I know it was you who came by here earlier today."

"Yeah, it was me," the man admitted. A sneer began to rise on the side of his face. "It was a dude here, but he didn't open the door. Was that him? That the one I'm looking for?"

"Get away from my house," Dana demanded. "We ain't got nothing to do with whatever you talking about."

The man shook his head and stood his ground. "Naw, I think you *do* got something to do with what I'm talking about. I think y'all got *a lot* to do with it."

His boldness shook Dana. She tried to hide it, but she couldn't. "I'ma call the police," she threatened.

He nodded. "Yeah, I know you is." His eyes returned to her pistol. "You gon' shoot me too? Why you ain't shooting then?" He raised his arms, to reveal his hands were both empty. "I'm standing right here. You gon' get to busting, or what?"

Dana's chest began to rise and fall visibly. She looked past him to the Crown Vic idling on the curb. Even if the sun was out, she doubted if she'd be able to see anything past the car windows' dark tint.

Part of her wanted to take the thug up on his offer for gunplay. She was a vulnerable homeowner, and it was after midnight. Surely she could come up with a justifiable reason for ventilating this asshole. But it would be just her luck if one of her neighbors caught the whole incident on a Ring doorbell camera. The police would arrest her for first degree murder, and what would become of Tariq? Dana had grown up in the foster care system. She would never let that fate befall him.

"Get off my porch," she growled through the screen door.

She hoped the thug would make a sudden move or reach to open it. She prayed he'd lunge forward and break the glass. She knew it was wrong to wish for such things, but she couldn't help it. Fortunately (or maybe *un*fortunately) the man remained frozen in place. He slowly lowered his arms.

"*Bitch, you gon' shoot?*"

So many emotions stormed through her chest, Dana's whole body began to tremble. Her heart roared as she sucked in deep breaths. She flipped the safety on her pistol with her thumb, but she did not point it at him.

"We don't got nothing to do with whatever you're talking about!" she screamed.

"You know exactly what the fuck I'm talking about!" the man retorted. "If you ain't have nothing to do with it, you would'a said so by now. You would'a said don't nobody here drive that fucking Explorer!"

"What Explorer?" she fired back.

"Nah, too late for that shit now! Where your boy at? If it ain't y'all, bring his ass out here and let me get a look at him."

She did raise the gun then. She pointed it directly at his chest, knowing it wouldn't take much pressure from her trigger finger to end the man's life and change hers and Tariq's forever.

"*Get away from my house! I ain't gon' tell you again!*"

"Fuck you!" the stranger spat.

Dana almost pulled the trigger when he raised his arm, but she realized he was only pointing at her, rather than producing a weapon of his own.

"*Yo bitch-ass son killed Shank, and he gon' pay for that! You hear me? We know y'all down with them Bideker niggas! That nigga gon' pay for what he done!*"

The stranger's eyes were filled with blind rage; the kind that makes men do outrageous things, without foresight or consideration of the consequences. But Dana saw pain in his eyes too. His turmoil was heart wrenching. There was no doubt he loved the fool Tariq had run over.

She had never heard the name *Shank* before – not that it mattered now. The important thing was she now had proof that her visitor was related to yesterday's incident, and he had officially threatened her and Tariq. Dana wondered if this wasn't enough to shoot him now. Before she made up her mind, the stranger turned and hopped down the steps. Dana kept her eyes and gun trained on him until he approached the driver's side of the Crown Vic and disappeared inside.

The moment she slammed her front door closed, all of the stress and adrenaline from the past five hours took its toll. Dana's eyes filled with tears. A cool fever washed over her, causing her to sweat and shiver at the same time. Tariq rounded the corner and rushed to her.

"*Mama!*"

Noticing her unsteady hands, he reached past her and locked the front door. Dana's head spun. She placed a hand on his shoulder, but it wasn't enough to fight gravity and her sudden weakness. She vaguely realized she was falling. Tariq cried out again. Dana barely heard him. His voice was no more than a muffled echo. She realized she was passing out. That had never happened to her, but she'd witnessed it over a dozen times with patients at the hospital.

She fought to maintain consciousness, but it was like trying to scale the walls of a dark, slippery well. Way up above her, she saw the light of the real world. Making her way to it didn't seem possible.

"*Mama!*"

Tariq knelt beside her. Dana felt like an idiot for losing control of her equilibrium, but in retrospect, her dizzy spell might have saved her life. The first shot rang out before Tariq was able to help her to her feet.

BRAP!

Dana's eyes widened to the size of doorknobs. Her initial thought was that her gun had somehow gone off. She couldn't remember if she'd put the safety back on. But when she heard the second shot, followed quickly by a deafening barrage, everything started to make sense.

BRAP! BRAP!
BRRRRRAT! BRAT!
BRAP!BRAP!
BAT! BAT!
BAT-TAT-TAT-TAT!
"*Shit!*"

She reached up and grabbed the collar of Tariq's shirt. He was already kneeling, but she yanked him down anyway. The boy lost his balance and landed on his mother. Before he could react, she wrapped both arms around his neck and held on with all her might. A moment ago she didn't have the strength to stand. Now she felt strong enough to lift an automobile – whatever it took to save her son.

The fog in her brain dispersed immediately. Dana could see and hear everything clearly. She was far removed from her childhood on the south side of Chicago, but some experiences never leave you.

The gunfire continued. Splinters and sheetrock and glass flew all around them like confetti. Dana knew there were multiple shooters. There was no doubt the man who swore to avenge a fallen soldier named *Shank* was behind it.

Dana didn't realize she was screaming, but she must have been. When the gunfire finally died down and the screech of tires from the getaway vehicle quieted, she heard her own frantic wail in the vacuum of silence. Her eyes were squeezed closed. Her throat felt hoarse. Tears squirted from her closed eyelids. She continued to hold onto her son.

Five seconds after the last gunshot, she still hadn't mustered the nerve to let Tariq go or even ask if he was alright. In the forefront of her mind, Dana understood that she must do both of these things. It was inevitable. But in the back of her mind, she was convinced that everything would be okay if she did neither.

CHAPTER 16

THE POLICE CAME to Dana's neighborhood a second time that night. This time their concern and show of force was evident. Four squad cars converged in front of her home with their lights on, sirens blaring. Fortunately there was no need for an ambulance. Both Dana and her son survived the shooting unscathed.

She didn't have time to fully assess the damage before the police sat her and Tariq on the couch and questioned them about the visitor who came just before the shooting. Dana understood that every bit of information she could give them was vital to the case, but it was hard to remain focused. Her eyes were nearly bloodshot from crying. There were too many holes in her walls to count. Glass from her windows twinkled on the carpet in large shards and many more tiny pieces. The crime scene investigators scoured every inch of her home. They dug bullet fragments from the walls and labeled and bagged them.

Dana sat stoically, with a blanket draped over her shoulders. She held her son's hand firmly, refusing to let go. Tariq was normally against such public displays of affection, but he didn't pull away from her. He wasn't crying, but Dana could tell he was as distraught as she was. His wide eyes darted here and there; following the policemen as they moved about the house. His knee bounced anxiously.

Despite her state of mind, Dana's observations were surprisingly detailed. She remembered that the visitor was tall, over six feet. He had short hair and was clean shaven. His skin tone was fair. He wore a black tee shirt with dark pants. His arms were covered with tattoos, but she couldn't describe any of them in detail.

"Did he tell you his name?"

"No."

"Did he mention any gang he might be affiliated with?" She shook her head. "No."

"Did he know your son's name?"

"No. He never said his name."

"But you know he came looking for Tariq?"

"He said he was looking for whoever drove the blue Explorer. That's my son's car."

"You're sure this was related to yesterday's incident?"

She nodded. "He said it was. He said the person in the Explorer killed his friend, or his *homey*, or whatever."

"He said that?"

"Yeah. He said..." Dana frowned. She closed her eyes and racked her brain for the name he used. "I – I don't remember who he said got killed."

"Shank," Tariq said. "He said it was somebody named *Shank*."

"You saw him too?" the detective asked.

"No," Tariq said. "I mean, yeah, I saw him when he came the first time. The second time I was in the living room, but I could hear him through the door. He said the man that got killed was named Shank."

The cop nodded and jotted more notes.

"Did either of you see who was shooting?"

The mother and son both shook their heads.

"I was on the floor," Dana told him. "I pulled Tariq down with me, to keep him safe."

She looked over at her son, and her eyes filled with tears. She squeezed his hand tighter.

The detective asked a few more questions before concluding his interview.

"So, what happens now?" Dana asked him.

The policeman had pulled a chair from the dining room. He sat across from her and Tariq, while his cohorts continued their investigation inside and outside of the house. This wasn't the same detective who had questioned Tariq at the station, but he was familiar with the case.

"I think you should leave."

Dana had a feeling that was the advice he'd give them, but it hurt to hear it. She looked around her living room. The bullet holes probably didn't look like much from the outside, but in some places they left tennis ball-size holes in the sheetrock after plowing through the walls. Framed pictures littered the floor. There were holes in her television. Holes in the couch she was sitting on. Holes in everything.

But this was still her house. She and Tariq had wonderful memories there. The thought of being chased from the only true home she had ever known made her tear up even more.

"You're gonna get them?" she asked the detective. "You know who they are?"

"Yes, and no," he said. "The man who came to your home tonight... With the description you provided, we should be able to nab him. But neither of you saw him shooting at your home."

"But—"

"I know it seems open and shut," the cop said, cutting her off. "But it's not. Yes, an individual threatened you, and moments later someone shot up your home. I agree with you: It was probably the guy you spoke to. But the DA will want more evidence. The real issue though, is catching that one individual will not be the end of your problems. Have either of you ever heard of *MMG*?"

Dana shook her head, but Tariq said, "Yeah. I have."

"Wh, what's that?" Dana asked them.

"MMG stands for *Murder Meadows Gang*," the detective informed her. "It's the largest street gang in the city. They are very dangerous. I believe these are the people targeting you and your son."

Dana felt like she got punched in the gut. All the air in her lungs escaped. Before she could respond, the cop continued speaking.

"The man who was killed in the accident yesterday is Shakeim Taylor. He's known on the streets as *Shank*. I know your son was cleared of any wrongdoing in that accident, but the gang obviously has a different opinion. Word on the street is Tariq – or possibly the other individual who was in the car with him at the time – is involved with a rival gang called the *Bideker Boys*. MMG believes the accident was gang-related, and it was intentional."

Dana brought a hand to her mouth and stared wide-eyed at the policeman. Everything he said was foreign to her, but at the same time it wasn't. The man who came to her door had mentioned *Bideker*. She still had no idea why anyone would think Tariq was affiliated with a gang, but if they truly believed that, it made sense for them to retaliate in this manner. Tariq felt his mother trembling against him. He wrapped an arm around her shoulder and drew her closer.

"I know all of this sounds bad," the detective said, "but I'm afraid it gets worse. Shakeim, or *Shank*, wasn't just a random member of MMG. His father is Brian Campbell. Brian is known on the streets as *Brass*. He's the leader of MMG."

The cop waited a few beats, to let all of that sink in. But no matter how long he gave them, Dana felt overwhelmed with information. *Brass. Shank. MMG. Bideker Boys...* None of this was part of the life she chose for her and her son. Since leaving

Chicago, Dana had done everything she could to raise her boy right.

Sure, there were times when she longed for a father figure to counsel Tariq with certain issues. But for the most part, Dana thought she had done a good job. Tariq was a good student. He didn't skip school or get high. He certainly wasn't involved with the *Bideker Boys* – whatever the hell that was. For the life of her, she couldn't fathom how one accident had led to all of this.

Tears streamed down her cheeks as she contemplated their fate. If a whole gang wanted them dead, where could they go? It didn't seem like the police could help them – not on a long-term basis.

"How, how did they find us?" she wondered.

She knew the answer to that question wouldn't solve anything. But it was important to her. Unfortunately the detective's knowledge of the situation was not complete. He shook his head.

"I've been trying to figure that out. The problem with MMG – and quite frankly the reason we've never been able to fully eradicate them – is how large and deeply rooted the gang is. They have plenty of street level thugs who are easy to spot. But they also have members who are more low-key. They get regular jobs and infiltrate nearly every aspect of society.

"We've arrested MMG members who were working as correctional officers in the jails. We've found some who had jobs in the courthouse. They work in the hospitals, you name it. The only people who know about Tariq's involvement in yesterday's accident – and would have access to his personal information – is the police. As much as I hate to admit it, there might be a leak somewhere in the force. I don't believe any member of the gang has made it far enough to become a police officer. But honestly, I can't put anything past them."

Dana shook her head as she listened to him. Everything the policeman said reinforced her belief that she and Tariq were doomed.

71

"Do you have somewhere you can go," the detective asked, "until we can get things sorted out and hopefully make some arrests?"

Dana shook her head. She sniffled and reached to wipe the tears from her eyes.

"Don't you have any family you can stay with?"

She continued to shake her head. "I'm, I'm from Chicago. I don't have anyone here."

There was compassion in the detective's eyes. After a moment he said, "What about a hotel? I really think you and your son need to get out of this house, at least for a little while. The likelihood of the gang returning is very high."

Dana made decent money at the hospital, but it wasn't enough to maintain the mortgage at her home and live in a hotel for an extended period of time.

"What, do you think I should quit my job? Move to another state?"

Her hopelessness broke the detective's heart. "Ms. Moore, I am truly sorry. I hope it doesn't come to that. I assure you I'll be working this case nonstop. But in a few hours, all of the police are going to leave, and *you are not safe here*. For now, that's the only thing I know for sure."

CHAPTER 17

THE POLICE CONTINUED their investigation for another hour. They collected spent casings from outside, bullet fragments from inside and took dozens of pictures. As promised, by three a.m. the emergency vehicles began to leave the scene. The detective was one of the last to go. He reiterated his desire for Dana and Tariq to leave the house and stay away for as long as possible, before he hopped in a sedan and disappeared into the night.

Dana knew his advice was sound, and she had every intention of taking it. The Murder Meadows Gang had already proven themselves to be as ruthless and daring as their name suggested. Yesterday they initiated an altercation at an accident scene that wasn't Tariq's fault. They shot at his Explorer in broad daylight. Now they had Dana's address and murder on their mind. She had no doubt they would remain on the warpath until they avenged their fallen soldier.

At a quarter after three, the last squad car backed out of the driveway, leaving Dana and Tariq to fend for themselves. Thankfully they were mostly packed and ready to go. She just had to gather a few more toiletries before they hit the road.

"Hey, have you checked with Brendon?" she called to Tariq from the bathroom.

A few hours ago, Dana didn't think she had the resilience to get anything done. Now she was starting to feel like her old self. She was frazzled and a little war-weary, but she understood that nothing would get accomplished if she sat in a corner and cried her eyes out.

Tariq appeared in the doorway, looking a little worse for wear himself.

"I called him a couple of hours ago," he replied. "He said there's nothing happening at his apartments."

Dana frowned at that. She didn't wish this kind of trouble on anyone, but it seemed a little unfair that Tariq was the only one the gang was after.

"Do you have any idea what the detective was talking about?" she asked him. "That *Bideker Boy* stuff? That's the same thing that man said when he came to the door. Do you know why those people think you and Brendon are in some type of gang?"

"We, uh..."

Dana's eyes narrowed. Her head cocked slowly to the side as she waited for him to respond. She didn't believe her parenting skills were phenomenal, but when it came to Tariq, she almost always knew when he was lying to her.

Before the boy could finish his statement, he was saved by the bell. Literally. Dana and Tariq both got a sudden chill when the doorbell sounded. They turned towards the living room and then locked eyes, each of them thinking the same thing.

No way.

The last policeman had *just* left. Dana didn't think it was possible for MMG to return so quickly, unless they'd been watching the house for the past three hours. But they couldn't do that with all of the police there, could they? It was more likely one of the investigators had forgotten something, maybe a piece of equipment, and had returned to retrieve it.

Either way, Dana wasn't taking any chances. She snatched her pistol off the bed before heading to the front room. Tariq started to say something, but she told him, "Shhht. Stay here until I say it's okay to come out."

When she got to the living room, Dana was struck by an overwhelming sense of déjà vu. The only difference was this time she had no fear of the unknown. If there was an MMG thug standing on her porch, she wouldn't entertain a conversation. She wouldn't ask him what he wanted before she started shooting. After what happened earlier, she didn't think any jury would blame her.

When she checked the peephole, Dana's trepidation transitioned to confusion and then annoyance. The man standing on her porch was not the thug she expected, but the urge to shoot him was just as strong. She yanked the door open and scowled at him through the remnants of her screen door. Most of the glass had broken and fallen away from the frame. She had a clear view of her visitor. She could see that he had no fear of the weapon in her hand.

Kole Stone was her neighbor from down the street. He still wore the dark blue tee-shirt and jeans he had on earlier that evening. Kole's skin was dark chocolate. His hair was shaved low. He sported a moustache and goatee that was always trimmed neatly.

Now that he was closer, Dana could make out the definition of his pectorals and shoulder muscles beneath his tee shirt. His forearms and biceps were massive. Kole's gaze was as steely as ever. He studied Dana's features and looked past her to check out some of the damage to her home.

It had been a long time since the two of them were this close. Dana thought she was past the point of being affected by his nearness, but her stomach tightened. Her heart rate kicked up a notch as she stared at him. Her physical response only served to remind her why she hated this man. Her look of irritation deepened.

She sneered as she asked him, "What you want?"

Kole was not surprised by her icy reception. He did not respond in kind. He continued taking in the scene before his eyes returned to hers. They watched each other for what felt like a long time before he asked, "What's going on over here?"

Dana's pulse raced. Her attitude remained intact. "What it look like?"

Kole's jaw tightened. Dana thought he'd take that as his cue to run away – which was something she knew he was good at – but he didn't leave. He shifted his stance, causing some of the broken glass from her screen door to crackle beneath his shoes.

"Who shot up your house?" he asked.

Kole's voice was deep and domineering. Once again Dana's body reacted to him. This time a spattering of goose bumps blossomed on her forearms. She hated that he still had the power to do that to her.

"I don't know," she said, maintaining as much frustration as she could muster. "What's it to you?"

Kole brought a large hand up and rubbed his mouth, as if he was blocking the response he wanted to give her. Instead he asked, "You really wanna do this now?"

"Do what, Kole?"

"Keep up this old-ass argument. Do this seem like the best time for that?"

Honestly Dana thought *every time* was the best time to keep up her grievances with this man. But he had a point. The police were gone, and the biggest gang in the city had her and Tariq on their hit list. This wasn't a good time to argue with her asshole neighbor.

"Yeah, I got some trouble," she conceded. "You still haven't said what's it to you."

"I'm trying to help you," Kole replied, "if you give me a chance."

"Oh yeah? How you gon' help me?"

"Well, for starters, maybe you could tell me who shot up your house – and why."

"The police already know who did it," Dana told him. "They working on it. What makes you think you can do anything they can't do?"

"I don't know for sure if I can," Kole admitted. "But the police can only do so much. Like, where they at right now? You out here totally unprotected, and they somewhere eating donuts and shit. I'm standing right here offering to protect you. So it looks like I'm already doing more than them."

Dana couldn't deny any of that was true, but, "Just because you standing here don't mean you're protecting me. If them people come back right now, you gon' get shot up, just like me."

"You right," Kole said. "That's why I think we should continue this conversation somewhere safe. Are you leaving? You got somewhere to go?"

Dana didn't think sharing the information would hurt her in any way, but she didn't see how it would help.

"They told us to go to a hotel," she revealed with a sigh.

"And then what?" he asked. "How long you supposed to stay there?"

Dana shook her head with a grimace. Standing there answering questions wasn't getting her and Tariq any closer to safety.

"It's *a whole gang*," she spat. "They don't know how long it's gonna take to get to the bottom of it. All they know is I'm not safe *here*."

Kole's eyes widened for a second. Dana hoped she'd satisfied his curiosity, and he understood that her trouble was much too complex for whatever help he was offering. But he nodded slightly and seemed even more resolved when he told her, "I'm pretty sure I can help you with that a lot better than the police can."

Dana was at her wits' end. "*How*?" she barked. "How the hell you gon' help me?"

Kole deflected her insolence and kept his cool. "I got some connections in the streets." He spoke calmly and assuredly. "I know every gang in this city. If you want me to get to the bottom of it, I will. You ain't gotta run off to no hotel and leave your house unprotected. You and Tariq can go right down the street to my house and stay there till I get things straightened out. You ain't gotta spend no money. But if you wanna let your little attitude lead you in another direction, that's on you. I ain't gon' *beg* you to let me save your life."

Dana wasn't sure how long she stood there considering his offer. Kole had always been a mysterious individual, so she couldn't discount anything he'd said. Back when they were friends, the mystery didn't work out in her favor. But maybe now it would.

The detective had no idea when this would be over, and Dana couldn't really afford to live in a hotel. Plus – if she had to go into hiding – it would be better to do it within eyesight of her home. For all she knew, the thugs would come back and burn the place to the ground. She probably couldn't prevent that, even if she was watching from Kole's house. But at least she wouldn't be holed up halfway across town; with no idea what was happening to her home.

She sighed and pushed the remnants of her screen door open.

"Alright. Come in."

Kole pulled the door the rest of the way and stepped inside. His presence was immediately the largest thing in the room.

Dana turned and saw that Tariq did not heed her instructions to stay in the bedroom. He was standing right behind her.

"Hurry up and finish packing," she told him. "We're going to Kole's house."

Tariq wore the same frown Dana had when she first looked through the peephole and saw her neighbor standing there.

"But Mama–"

She cut him off. "You heard what I said, boy. Now hurry up."

CHAPTER 18

KOLE'S HOME WAS exceptionally neat. It had been for as long as Dana had known him. Stepping in, from the garage to the kitchen, she was struck with a sense of familiarity that was not initially comforting. All of the countertops in the kitchen were bare, outside of appliances that were so clean, they looked brand new. There were no dishes in the sink waiting to be washed. Even the tile floor was free of debris and mopped to a gleaming shine.

"You can bring your bags in here," Kole said to Tariq as he led the way through the dining room to the living room. In each hand, he toted one of Dana's suitcases. She had attempted to carry them herself, but he insisted. From behind, she saw that his back and broad shoulders were rippling with muscles. His strong hands looked as big as cantaloupes as he gripped the handles of her travel bags.

The house was dimly lit. Kole didn't flip a switch in the dining room, but there was enough light from the kitchen to follow him without bumping into anything. When he reached the front room, he left her bags in the hallway before turning on the light. Dana rounded the corner and saw that the living room was as beautifully decorated as she remembered.

His carpet was so plush, Kole left visible footprints with each step, as if he was stepping on snow. His leather couch was long and angled, offering enough seating for five adults. The glass tops of his coffee and end tables were spotless. The bases were solid black, as was his entertainment center and the frames of the few paintings he had on display.

Dana had never known Kole to be flashy, but a cursory glance around the room was enough to reveal his financial superiority. All of his electronics were state of the art. Dana guessed his cherry wood front door cost more than her whole bedroom suite.

The only thing missing from Kole's home was a woman's touch, but she knew that was by design. There were no flowers, no colorful bowls of potpourri, no Glade plug-ins enhancing the house with the scent of rosemary or vanilla. The only scent Dana detected was the rich, leather smell of his couch as she took a seat in one corner. Tariq deposited his bags next to hers before he sat down.

Kole sat in a love seat on the opposite side of the room. He studied the mother and son before leaning forward with his forearms on his knees. Dana found his gaze intimidating. The way his strong jawline always seemed to be clenched added to the effect. She knew he meant them no harm, but her heart skipped a beat when he locked eyes with her. She inhaled deeply and blew the breath out slowly. She looked over at Tariq, who appeared just as uncomfortable as she was.

"Y'all alright?" Kole finally asked. "Y'all want something to eat or drink?"

They both shook their heads, though neither of them had a proper supper that night. It was almost four a.m., but Dana felt more wired than hungry.

"Alright," Kole said. "Y'all feel like talking, or you wanna go to bed?"

"I don't think I can sleep," Dana said with a sigh. She looked over at her son. He didn't say anything.

"Can you tell me why those people targeted you?" Kole asked. When Dana didn't respond, his eyes moved to Tariq.

But then she said, "It, it's all a misunderstanding. The way it started – it's so stupid."

Kole watched her closely. His attention was so fixated, she couldn't tell if he was even blinking. She looked to Tariq again, hoping he'd tell the story from his point of view. But the boy remained mute. Dana couldn't blame him for being shell-shocked or for the way he was reacting to their neighbor.

She took the lead and told Kole everything she knew about the accident and the subsequent incidents at her home. She was still doubtful that he could offer any assistance, but at that point, she had nothing to lose. When she was done speaking, Kole asked the most obvious question.

"Why would they think Brendon's down with the Bideker Boys? It must have been something that happened to make them think that."

Tariq hadn't added anything to his mother's version of events, but with all eyes on him, there was no way he could stay silent. He cleared his throat and rubbed his hands together. He looked down at the coffee table, rather than meet either of their gazes, which felt a little accusatory at that point.

"It was, uh... It wasn't me. It was Brendon. He not in a gang, or nothing like that. But, uh, he had these beads he been wearing. It's a necklace..."

This was Dana's first time hearing about the beads. Her jaw dropped, both out of shock and embarrassment that this was only now coming to light.

Kole shook his head. "Black and yellow?" he asked knowingly.

Tariq looked up at him. He frowned slightly as he nodded. "Yeah."

Dana frowned too as she watched the men. "Black and yellow? What's that?"

"That's the gang color for the Bideker Boys," Kole informed her. "They're based on the south side. It's not a *huge* set, like

MMG. But they got a pretty big crew. They can get rowdy and kick up dust with the best of them."

Dana was surprised by Kole's knowledge of the gang. For the first time, she felt a little hopeful that he could provide a solution.

"Why the hell is your friend wearing their colors, if he's not down with them?" Kole asked Tariq.

"He's like..." The boy shrugged. "I guess you could call him a wannabe. He got some friends that are in the gang, and he say he wanna be down with them."

"Why didn't you tell me about this?" Dana asked, her mama bear claws extending. "I told you I don't want you hanging around nobody that got anything to do with a damn *gang*. I don't care if it's Brendon or whoever the hell else. You *know* I don't want you to have nothing to do with that."

"I know, Mama. And I told him. I told him I couldn't kick it with him no more, if he was gonna get down with them. But he said he was just playing, and the beads didn't mean nothing, unless he got jumped in."

"Well, obviously they do mean something, if them people got so pissed about it," Dana countered. "They were *shooting at you*, Tariq. Don't you think that means something?"

"I know, Mama. Nothing like that ever happened before. We never got into it with nobody about no gang stuff."

"Goddammit boy..." She shook her head in frustration. "You could've been *killed*, Tariq."

The teen looked from his mother's scolding eyes to Kole's critical stare, and his fair skin reddened. His gaze returned to the coffee table.

"Y'all told the police about that necklace?" Kole asked.

Dana shook her head. "I didn't know about it until just now. Tonight the detective was asking why they thought Tariq was in a gang. Him and Brendon been lying to them ever since this happened."

She glared at Tariq, as if she might deliver a slap to the back of the head, but she refrained.

"The man that got hit," Kole said, "you said he was a member of MMG?"

Dana nodded. "Yeah. The police said he was the son of their leader. What'd they say his name was?" she asked Tariq. "Skank, or something like that?"

The boy chuckled. "Naw, Mama. It was *Shank.*"

"You think this is funny?" Dana asked, sneering now.

Tariq lost his grin in a split second. "No, Mama. I was just saying, you got his name wrong..."

"Boy, I don't give a damn what his name is! Ain't nothing funny about what's going on! We just got our house shot up. What part of that is funny to you? Which one of those bullet holes is a joke?"

Tariq was smart enough to keep his mouth closed.

Watching Dana go off on him almost made Kole crack a smile. But he didn't want her venom directed at him. He maintained a neutral expression.

"Okay. I think I got everything I need for now," he said.

"Wh, what are you gonna do?" Dana asked as Kole rose to his feet. Her eyes followed him up, until he reached his full height. She was often taken aback by how tall he was, considering his stout frame.

"I'll talk to some people tomorrow." Kole checked a clock hanging above the couch. "Well, I guess that'd be *today.* I think I'll try to get a few hours of sleep. Are you sure y'all don't want to eat something?"

Dana thought she was okay, but she felt her stomach grumble unexpectedly. Thankfully it wasn't one of those audible growls, or at least she hoped it wasn't.

"No, I'm okay," she replied.

Kole's kitchen was so sanitized, she didn't think he'd be able to sleep until he washed every dish and utensil he used to feed them. She was hungry, but she didn't want to be an inconvenience.

"What about you?" Kole asked Tariq. "You feel like eating?"

He shook his head without looking up. Dana nudged him in the ribs with her elbow, and Tariq's head shot up.

"I mean, no, sir. Thank you, though."

Kole nodded. "Come on," he said. "Y'all can use my guest bedrooms."

He hefted Dana's bags again. Dana and Tariq followed him. Halfway down the hallway, Kole stopped and opened the door on his right. He reached inside and flipped a light switch.

"One of you can sleep in here." He took several more steps and opened another door, this time on the left. "And one of you can have this room."

By then Dana had caught up with him. She paused at the first room. She knew it wasn't the master bedroom (that was all the way down the hall on the left), but the room was big enough to be a master bedroom. It was fully furnished; with a king-size bed, two dressers, and even a desk with a couple of plush chairs.

She told Kole, "We can both use this room. It looks big enough..."

Tariq squeezed next to her and peered into the room. If he objected to sleeping in the same bed as his mom, he didn't mention it. Dana suspected his nerves were just as fried as hers. After what they'd been through, he'd probably prefer to have her as close as possible.

Kole hesitated in the hallway. He turned and walked their way.

"You sure?"

"Yeah," Dana said. She entered the room with the two men on her heels.

Tariq left his bags by the doorway and took a seat on the corner of the bed. Dana saw the fatigue in his eyes. She knew he'd be asleep a few minutes after his face touched the pillow.

"Okay," Kole told them. His frame filled the doorway. He took a few steps inside the room and placed Dana's bags next to the bed. "If you change your mind about eating, I have some frozen dinners in there. You can have whatever you want – just clean up your mess after you're done."

"Thank you," Dana said. "But we're beat. I don't think we'll be leaving this room for the rest of the night."

"You know where the bathroom is..." Kole caught himself, and his eyes widened briefly. He knew Dana knew where it was, but he wasn't sure if Tariq knew that she knew. "It's next door on the right," he added. "I'll check to make sure it's stocked before I go to bed."

Dana nodded. "Thank you." She felt like she should do or say more to show her appreciation. A part of her wanted to hug him, but an even bigger part wanted to do no such thing. Just because Kole came to their rescue didn't mean he wasn't an asshole anymore. Sometimes assholes do nice things for their fellow man. It was rare, but it happened.

She walked to one of the chairs and took a seat. She turned back to Kole when she felt he was still standing there.

"Thanks again," she said, hoping to get him moving. "For everything."

"It's okay," he replied, then, "You bring your burner with you?" In response to Dana's frown, he said, "Your *gun*. You got it, right?"

"Oh, yeah," she said. Dana thought she was familiar with most slang words, but she had never referred to a gun as a *burner* before.

"Y'all need something else?" Kole asked. "Or you feel safe with that?"

"Something else like what?" Dana said.

He shrugged. "I don't know. A shotgun. Another pistol. Something bigger, fully auto..."

Tariq looked like he was about to pass out a moment ago, but his eyes lit up at that. He looked at his mother. She was as surprised as he was.

"Uh, no," she said, wondering why Kole had so much firepower at his disposal. "We'll be fine. Thanks."

"Alright. I'll see y'all in the morning," Kole said and finally backed out of the room. "If you need anything, I'm at the end of the hallway–"

On the left, Dana thought, just as he said it. *Yeah, I know where to find you, Kole.* If she closed her eyes, she could picture the room perfectly. That knowledge took away some of her gratitude. But she knew that wasn't fair.

Her features softened as she told him, "Thanks again, Kole. We really appreciate your help."

CHAPTER 19

"SO, WHAT HE know about a burner?" Tariq asked.

Dana gave him a look, imploring him to keep his voice down, as she crossed the room and closed the door. She went and sat next to him on the bed.

"Maybe I should be asking what you know about it," she finally replied.

"I hear it in some rap songs," Tariq explained. "But he too old to be listening to the same music I listen to."

"He's 41," Dana said. "That's only two years older than me."

"Sounds like he knows a lot about gangs and stuff," Tariq noticed. "And he got a bunch of guns..."

Dana nodded slowly.

"So, what's up with him?" Tariq pressed. "What he got all those guns for? Was he talking like that when y'all was together?"

"We were never really *together*," Dana said. "We just had dinner a couple of times. But no, he never talked guns and things like that."

"What did y'all talk about?" Tariq wondered. "Why you willing to trust him, after what he did to you?"

Dana frowned. She hadn't told her son much about what happened between her and Kole. At the most, Tariq picked up on her mood change after they stopped talking. "Boy, why you asking all these questions?"

"I'm just saying; how you know he can help us? What is he gonna do, shoot somebody?"

Dana frowned at that. "No, he's not gonna shoot anyone. Kole's not like that."

"Then what he gon' do, Mama? How long we gotta stay here?"

Dana saw the agony in his eyes. With so much going on, it was easy to forget the guilt he must have felt for his role in this. Even though he wouldn't admit it, Dana believed the accident left her son traumatized.

"I don't know, Tariq. I can't promise that he can help us. He said he would try, and for now, that's good enough for me. Why? Do you have a problem being here?"

He shrugged. His shoulders were bony and damn near pointy, compared to Kole's. "I just..." His eyes welled with tears. "I'm sorry, Mama. I didn't mean for none of this to happen."

His face crumpled in on itself. Dana pulled him closer and allowed him to cry on her shoulder. "Shhh. Baby, it's not your fault. Even the police said that man ran into the street, and you didn't have time to stop. Wasn't nothing you could do about it."

"Yeah, but, but Brendon. If he didn't have those beads..."

"Even if he didn't have those beads, I'm sure they would've found some other reason to attack y'all. An angry mob doesn't need an excuse to act like animals."

Dana wasn't sure if she believed what she told him, but her words calmed Tariq, and that was all that mattered. After a few minutes, the boy stretched out on the bed fully clothed and turned his attention to his cellphone. His feet were hanging off the mattress, but Dana told him to, "Take off your shoes," and he was obedient.

Despite the late hour, she still wasn't sleepy, so she pulled her laptop from her bag and took a seat on one of the chairs. She searched the internet for *MMG* and *Bideker Boys*. There was scarcely any information. She found nothing at all on the Bideker Boys, but MMG was mentioned in a few articles from the *Overbrook Meadows Telegram*.

Dana didn't learn anything she didn't already know: MMG was a problem, and it was the largest gang in the city. The articles didn't mention *Shank* or *Brass* or any other gang members by name. Dana was sleepy when she shutdown her laptop, so at least it helped with that.

Before she crawled into bed, she had to use the bathroom. She left the room and looked down the darkened hallway, towards the master bedroom. There were a few paintings hanging in the hall, but no family portraits. Dana knew their caregiver fairly well, but she couldn't say if Kole had any brothers or sisters or if his parents were still living. The man had always been ambiguous, from the day he moved to the neighborhood two years ago.

When she returned to the guest bedroom a few minutes later, she felt exhausted, but sleep was elusive. Rather than fret about her home or the gang that was out to get them, it was Kole that overwhelmed Dana's thoughts. She tried to push the memories from her head, but her brain was still racing ten minutes later. Frustrated, she conceded to her mind and allowed her heart to drag her down memory lane.

PART THREE
KOLE WORLD

CHAPTER
20

I think I've found eternal peace
It came from my internal split
Fool me twice, shame on me
Now, I think you get my drift
I think I needed you too much
I know I tried to hold you close
I found eternity in your touch
You chose to simply let me go
Remember when you caused me pain?
That night, through tears I cursed your name
I found our love was just the same
Same situation with different names
You tried to rip apart my soul
Instead you only made me whole

LIKE KOLE, DANA didn't have many family pictures on
display in her home. As far as family, there was only her and
Tariq, as it had always been since she fled Chicago at the age of
twenty-two. She chose to use the word *fled* to describe her
departure from the Windy City, because there was no doubt she
was running away. She fled her upbringing in the foster care
system. She fled Chicago's turbulent south side, which was
starting to pile up bodies on a daily basis, even back then. She fled
Tariq's father, who knocked her up during her senior year of

college and started seeing other women when her belly began to protrude.

The only good thing Dana took from Chicago was a bachelor's degree in imaging science. Her skills had always been in demand. After a little research, she accepted a position at Jackson Memorial Hospital in Overbrook Meadows, Texas.

When she first arrived, she and Tariq lived in a small apartment on the north side. It took a few years to save up enough to buy a home, and a couple of weeks to find the perfect neighborhood. Willard Street was beautiful and tranquil, with late model cars in every driveway, and best of all no hoodlums hanging on the corners after dark.

The area had a nice mix of cultures and an award winning grade school and middle school nearby. Dana cried when she signed the last pages of her contract and the realtor handed her the keys to the house. For the first time in her life, she had her very own HOME. She vowed that Tariq would never know what it was like to be shuffled from family to family or hear bullets buzzing by his window at night. In the past 17 years, her son had grown into a handsome, intelligent young man. Dana was proud that she'd raised him so well without a father figure or even a constant mentor in his life.

Two years ago, when a moving truck backed in the driveway of the vacant property across the street and three houses down, Dana didn't try to hide her curiosity – especially when she saw that all of the movers were young, black men, and her new neighbor had been ripped from the pages of GQ Magazine.

To say that Kole was *fine* was an understatement. The first time Dana saw him, he wore jeans with a white tee that began to cling to his frame more and more as the summer day wore on. By the time the movers brought the last of his things inside, Kole had accumulated enough sweat to make his dark skin glisten like a moonlit sea. It took an extreme amount of willpower to keep Dana away from his house for the first few days. On the fourth day, she baked a tuna casserole and strolled across the street to welcome him to the neighborhood.

Kole answered the door wearing a Nike jumpsuit. The way the black fabric blended with his skin tone made Dana's stomach tighten. He stared down at her with a perplexed expression. His gaze was intimidating, even back then. Dana had been a bundle of nerves since she started baking the casserole. Now that she was standing before him, her palms were so sweaty, she was glad she slipped on a pair of oven mitts before bringing the dish over.

She smiled uneasily and told him, "Hi. My name is Dana. I brought you this – to welcome you to the neighborhood."

And then Kole smiled at her for the first time, and that was all it took. Dana's heart fluttered, as did her eyelashes. Kole took a step back and held the door open for her.

"Thank you. Would you like to come in?"

She hadn't expected that. She thought he'd ask what she brought him and accept it through the doorway. But it would've been impolite to turn down his invitation, wouldn't it? Dana was glad she had dressed for the occasion. She wore her hair down, in loose curls. Her sun dress was short and flirty. Her smooth legs had a fresh coat of cocoa butter lotion. Her sandals exposed toenails that were painted fuchsia; which matched her dress.

She felt Kole's eyes on her as she crossed the threshold into his home. He continued to look her up and down when she stopped in the living room and turned to face him. His eyes were keenly focused, like a lion stalking his mate. Dana felt a flurry of butterflies in her belly that made the hairs stand on the back of her neck.

"You, um, you have a nice home," she commented.

Kole grinned and continued to take in her physique. She was a foot shorter than him with smooth curves. Long legs with full hips and thighs. Her breasts weren't enormous, but her pushup bra did wonders. Her cleavage was enticing. Her eyes were innocent, her lashes full.

"Here, let me take that," he said reaching for her dish.

So caught up in his gaze, Dana almost handed it to him. She caught herself at the last minute.

"Oh, wait. It's still a little hot."

She tried to draw back, but he took hold of the casserole anyway.

"No, it's fine."

Her eyes widened as she looked down at his hands. They were so large, they looked like bear paws. She noticed a few old scars on his knuckles, but his hands didn't look calloused enough to withstand the temperature of the dish.

"Are you sure?"

"Yeah. Come on," he said and continued walking through his home.

Dana had no idea where he was leading her, but she was obliged to follow.

Kole's dining room was one of the nicest she'd ever seen. The table was large enough to seat six. It was completely bare. It looked as if it had been recently polished. A glass chandelier glistened overhead. A curio in the corner displayed fine china and a few expensive vases.

Kole told her, "Have a seat," as he stepped into the kitchen.

Dana wasn't prepared for any of this. She hesitated, not wanting to touch anything. She knew he had just moved in, but his home didn't have the feel of a place where someone actually *lived*. It felt more like a show house that was still on the market.

Kole reappeared a moment later. "Oh, I'm sorry. I didn't ask if you were gonna eat with me."

Dana's eyes widened once again. "Oh, well, I didn't think..."

His head tilted slightly as he watched her. "You didn't expect me to eat all of that by myself, did you?"

"You, um... Well, I was just being neighborly. I wasn't sure if you lived alone, or if you had a family..."

Dana hadn't seen anyone but him at the house in the past few days, but that didn't mean he didn't have a wife tucked away somewhere. She hoped she hadn't made it obvious that she was questioning his marital status.

He shook his head. "No. It's just me. What did you say your name was?"

She smiled. "Oh, I'm Dana. Me and my son live across the street."

"I'm Kole," he said, reaching for her hand.

The rush of energy Dana felt when she shook it made her eyes sparkle. By the look in his eyes, she could tell Kole noticed.

"Do you have time to eat with me, or would your husband mind?" he asked, looking down at her bare ring finger.

Dana was too nervous to eat. But she had nothing to do at the time. She was off that day, and Tariq wouldn't get out of school for a few hours. And of course there was the fact that she had never dined with a man as fine as Kole. Even as she stood in his dining room, their encounter had the shimmering feel of a fantasy.

"I'm not married," she revealed.

His smile deepened. "Good. Then let's eat."

CHAPTER
21

OVER LUNCH, DANA told him a little about her life in Chicago and her move to Texas, where she knew absolutely no one. Kole seemed to marvel at her story.

He told her, "I don't think I've ever met a woman as independent as you."

Dana was curious about the occupation that led to his lifestyle.

"I flip houses," he told her.

"What does that mean?"

"I buy houses that need work done, do the work and then sell them at a profit."

"You work on the houses yourself?"

"I used to. Not anymore. I have a good group of guys."

"You must be doing really well," Dana said, once again admiring the dining room.

"It took a while," he said. "As with any success story, my beginning was very modest."

Dana was impressed by his dialect, his home, and she was floored by his looks. She could tell he enjoyed her company, but she didn't think she actually had a shot at being with him. But as fate would have it, Kole was just as attracted and intrigued by her.

It took three weeks of dating before he completely rocked her world. He invited her over for dinner one evening. The delectable aromas hit her the moment she entered his home. When he led her to the dining room, Dana was shocked to see that he had personally prepared a three course meal. His dinner consisted of filet mignon with crab cakes and salad on the side.

Dana moaned audibly when he told her, "I made a cheesecake too, for dessert."

A brother who was fine, had his own place and could cook too? *Damn.* She felt like she'd hit the lottery!

She started sucking his lips in the kitchen, before he had a chance to serve their plates. Kole matched her intensity and upped the ante. He let her back him into the counter before he reached and grabbed her ass with both hands. Dana's skirt was not too short, but it rose up her thighs when she reached to caress his neck and chest as they kissed. She wasn't sure if Kole pulled it the rest of the way up while they were making out, or if it just happened. But she felt the air between her legs at the same moment she realized Kole's hands were on her bare cheeks. She soaked the crotch of her thong as he caressed her. Her breaths were hot and moist. His eyes were dark and demanding.

Her head was spinning so fast, she scarcely remembered him taking her to the bedroom. But she remembered everything that happened there. When she first laid eyes on his dark piece, both sets of her lips moistened in anticipation. Kole didn't reach for a condom – not right away. He laid her back on the bed and slowly pulled her panties off. Dana was so wet, he left a trail of her essence glistening on her thigh.

Standing on the side of the bed, he stared down at her before spreading her legs wide. Dana's heart thundered while she watched him. He reached and titillated her clitoris with his fingers before submerging the longest one. Dana threw her head back and moaned loudly. She arched her back as he caressed her for several mind-numbing minutes. She hadn't cum solely from being fingered in so long, she didn't think it was possible. But soon the throbbing in her clitoris surpassed her heart rate.

"*Shit*," she breathed, lifting her head so she could watch him.

The look in his eyes as he pleased her took her over the threshold. She squealed with delight, and her trembling thighs snapped closed on his hand. He spread them patiently and continued to stroke her while she thrashed about on the mattress. Just as her orgasm began to ebb, he removed his hand and replaced it with his lips. Dana gasped and immediately rolled into another climax. She passionately rode the second wave, using his face as a surfboard.

When he rose to his feet, she was so satiated, she forgot that he even had a dick. But there it was, thick and throbbing. Kole didn't wipe her juices from his face before he slipped on a condom and joined her in bed. Despite the Niagara Falls between her legs, he had to take it easy with his first thrust. The burning sensation Dana felt as he stretched her walls made her cry out, but once he was fully submerged, there was only pleasure.

Kole made sure to give her a third orgasm before he sought to please himself.

CHAPTER
22

BUT AS DRAMATIC and spontaneous as their lovemaking was, Kole flipped the script just as quickly.

The following weekend Dana called to see if he wanted to catch a movie.

"No, sorry. I can't."

"Oh," she said. "Okay. Maybe I can see you later next week. I'm off Tuesday through Thursday."

After a long pause, he said, "I'm sorry, Dana. I think you're a beautiful woman. An awesome lady, but..."

Dana's heart dropped all the way to the floor before he finished the sentence. The cloud of dread that enveloped her made every one of her internal organs shut down momentarily.

"I gotta stop seeing you," he continued. "It's nothing you did. It's not you, it's me."

Dana's mouth hung open. Tears filled her eyes and nasal cavity.

It's not you, it's me? What the fuck was that shit? The man had given her the most glorious lovemaking of her life less than a week ago. What could've possibly happened since then to make him do this? Was he using her? If so, what was his goal? He had more money than her, and he could've gotten more sex by simply being nice and taking her to a goddamned movie!

99

BACKSLIDE

She simply said, "Alright," and hung up the phone before the first tear fell.

CHAPTER 23

THAT WAS ONE year ago. Dana had purposefully avoided her *asshole-love-'em-and-leave-'em-no-good-good-for-nothing-heartbreaking-**ASSHOLE**-neighbor* since then. She was poised to continue ignoring him for the rest of her life, or until he moved far away, whichever came first. But as fate would have it, she found herself inside his home once again.

This time she had her son with her, her house had been shot up, and out of all people, Kole believed he could solve her problems. Dana felt like a fool for trusting him, but desperation causes people to do strange things.

She didn't realize she was crying until she felt a tear roll down her face, towards her ear. She rolled to her side and watched her son sleep soundly, until Mr. Sandman finally paid her a visit as well.

CHAPTER 24

You wanna see my ghetto groove?
First, take off your red and blue
Now come on, hop inside my ride
First we rolling to the south side
You see them niggas with them tools?
You see that gangsta wearing blue
You see them bangers wearing red?
They 'bout to make that blue boy dead
You see them red boys pull they guns?
You see the way that blue boy jumps?
You see the way his body moves?
That boy got the ghetto groove!
Now his girls come running out
You see the way them black girls shout?
Damn, I love those soulful hymns
When the groove takes over them!

A FEW HOURS later, the sun was on the rise above Overbrook Meadows. It was Sunday, but Kole didn't dress for a house of worship when he rolled out of bed at 8:30 a.m. He took a shower and pulled on a pair of black jeans and a black tee. He completed the outfit with a pair of dog tags that hung around his neck on a ball chain.

He left his bedroom and noticed the door to the guest bedroom was closed, but not all the way. He hesitated at the entrance and could hear light snoring coming from inside. He did not push the door open to check on his guests.

In the kitchen, he turned the stovetop on and made eggs with breakfast sausage while it heated. When the oven was ready, he slid a sheet of biscuits inside. He didn't hear anyone moving about his home, but when he went to the living room to check on his neighbor's house, he found Dana doing the same thing.

She stood at the window with the curtains parted slightly, her finger lifting one of the blinds. She leaned forward as she peered across the street. She wore the same clothes she had on when Kole invited her over last night. He hadn't expected her to put on a nightgown, but he was surprised that she had slept in jeans. She didn't notice him approaching until he cleared his throat before speaking.

"I made breakfast, for you and Tariq."

She looked back at him, her soft eyes showing signs of stress. Kole doubted if she had gotten more than a few hours of sleep.

She turned towards him and said, "Thank you."

They stood watching each other for a moment.

"Did you see anything?" he finally asked.

She shook her head. "Can't see too much from here. No strange cars, or nothing like that. The house is still standing. I guess that's something."

"I'll ride by and check it out when I leave," Kole offered. "I'm gonna take off in a minute."

She looked him up and down. Kole had a quiet energy about him. But his eyes and physique revealed the raw power bubbling beneath the surface.

"Where are you going?" she asked. "I mean, are you gonna look in to my problem today?"

He nodded. "I'm gonna ask some questions. See what the streets are saying."

"You know people – like, who are involved with gangs?"

After a second he nodded slowly.

Dana continued to stare at him. Judging by his house, she knew Kole was living comfortably. He'd told her he was a house-flipper, and she had no reason to doubt that. Nothing in his bio would put him around gangs or gang associates, but she had to admit that she didn't know him very well. Kole's background was one of many mysteries surrounding him.

"Do you, what do you think it will take to get them to leave us alone?" she asked.

"I would always prefer to talk it out," he commented. "If I can get in touch with the right people."

Dana was curious how he'd go about that, but she didn't question him.

"Do you have to work today?" he asked.

She shook her head. "I work tomorrow, but I'm thinking about taking the day off. How long do you think this will take?"

"No telling," he said honestly. "Hopefully I'll know more when I get back."

"You... You want me and Tariq to stay here while you're gone?" Dana sensed that was the plan, but she felt a little uncomfortable about the arrangement. Kole had no reason to stick his neck out for them or trust them in his home alone.

"If you want me to take you somewhere, I can do it now," he replied. "But I definitely don't think you should go home – even to pick up anything. I don't want anyone to spot you on the street or find out where you're holed up. Is there something you need? I could bring it for you."

She shook her head. "No." She didn't want to be a burden, even though Kole didn't seem to view them as such. "We don't need anything."

"If the police call while I'm gone," he said, "and they want to meet with you again. Call me, and I'll come and take you. You still have my number, right?"

She wondered if he noticed the momentary angst and embarrassment that clouded her vision. This was as close as he had come to acknowledging they had once dated. Dana's soul never stopped yearning to know why he aborted their love affair. But she didn't feel this was the time to ask.

Despite the anger and betrayal she felt a year ago, she had never deleted his number from her phone. She nodded.

"Okay. I'll be back in a second," he said. "The biscuits should be ready in a few minutes."

Kole returned to his bedroom. Inside his walk-in closet, he parted a row of dress shirts to reveal a hidden arsenal mounted on the wall. His breaths came slow and hot as he looked over the weaponry. He had small arms as well as assault rifles with extra large banana clips. There were ten pieces in total. All of the guns were legally registered to him, but Kole's pulse quickened as he selected a Beretta 9mm. He checked the clip to verify it was full before tucking the weapon into a concealed holster on the small of his back.

He moved the shirts back into position and locked a deadbolt he had installed on the closet door. His bedroom door only had a turn lock, which he secured as well when he left the room. He returned to the living room, but Dana was no longer there. He found her in the kitchen, removing the biscuits from the oven. She placed the baking sheet on the counter and turned his way.

She asked, "Are you going to eat before you leave?"

"I was gonna take a biscuit sandwich with me."

She stepped aside as he approached the counter. The biscuits were still smoking, but he grabbed one without hesitation. He split it open and jabbed a couple of sausage patties with a fork. He put them on the bottom half of the biscuit and slapped the top back on.

Dana had seen the type of dinners he produced in the kitchen and was surprised by his rough man meal.

"You don't want any cheese or jelly?"

He shrugged. "I guess it wouldn't hurt..."

"Here. Give me that."

She took the sandwich from him and placed it on a saucer. Kole backed away while she spiffed it up for him. He did not stare at her backside while she worked, though she looked mighty fine in those jeans. He only allowed himself a few approving glances.

She returned his sandwich with a few paper towels and a bottle of orange juice she found in the fridge.

"Here."

Kole took it and headed for the back door that led to the garage. "Thank you."

"No, thank you." She stood quietly as he exited the kitchen. She made it back to the living room in time to see Kole roll out of the garage and disappear down the street.

CHAPTER 25

DANA TOOK A shower and put on a fresh outfit before she woke Tariq up for breakfast. They ate together at the kitchen table. The dining room seemed too fancy for such a small meal.

When he was almost done eating, Tariq asked, "Where's Kole?"

Dana sat across from him. She rested her elbows on the table and brought her hands together. "He went to ask a few questions, see what people on the streets are saying about what happened."

"Ask a few questions? Who's he gonna ask?"

Dana sighed. "I asked him that too. He didn't say."

"What's he gonna do when he gets his answers?" Tariq wondered.

Dana shook her head. She brought her hands to her mouth, watching him over her interlocked fingers. "I don't know."

"But you think he can help us?"

She continued to shake her head. "Tariq, I don't have all the answers. He said he can do more than the police. I don't know what he meant by that. But, I mean, if the police catch the people that shot at us, that's only three or four guys. MMG is a big gang. I don't think they'll leave us alone if only a few of them get locked up."

She realized her statement only served to introduce more questions. What could Kole, a sole individual, do against a gang that large? Thankfully Tariq didn't ask.

Instead he said, "So, y'all back together or something?"

She frowned. "What makes you say that?"

"Why else would he be offering to help us?"

"He's a neighbor, and he's a friend. I don't need more explanation than that. I'm glad someone wants to help. I don't care who it is."

Tariq rolled his eyes slightly. "Are we supposed to stay here till he does whatever he's supposed to be doing?" He looked around the beautiful kitchen as if it was a roach motel.

"Are you saying you wanna go to a hotel?"

He frowned. His brow furrowed when his eyes returned to hers. "Mama, I don't know why you wanna be here, after what he did to you."

Dana's heart sank. She rubbed a tense spot near her temple. "What do you think he did to me?"

"I know y'all were going together. You say you weren't, but I know you were. You used to get dressed up and go out on dates. And then one day you were upset, and y'all didn't talk anymore. You used to smile every time you went outside and saw him. And then you started rolling your eyes at him."

Dana was glad she was never specific about her and Kole's problem. But she wasn't surprised Tariq had picked up on her nonverbal cues.

"Now he say he wanna help," he continued, "and you come running right over here, like nothing ever happened."

His statement cut Dana to the core. She tried not to let on, but once again Tariq read her like a book.

"I'm sorry, Mama," he said, in response to her sullen features.

Dana's eyes watered. She was determined not to cry in front of him. "No. It's okay. You're right. If you don't wanna be here, we can leave right now. We'll go to a hotel. I'll call Kole and let him know."

Tariq turned away, looking towards the front of the house. When his attention returned to her, he said, "No. That's alright. If he thinks he can help, we might as well let him. I just don't want y'all to get back together."

Dana thought that prerequisite was obvious. She told him, "That's fine. Why don't you call Brendon to make sure everything's alright on his end."

"He don't wake up this early," Tariq said as he rose from the table. "But I'll give him a call."

CHAPTER 26

WHEN HE HIT the road, Kole called an old friend he hadn't spoken to in a couple of months. Benjamin Cummings, better known as Moon, answered after a few rings.

"Kole! Always good to see your name on the caller ID." Moon had a deep, gruff voice, like an idling 18-wheeler.

"What's been up, man?"

"Business as usual. How 'bout you? How's the retired life treating you?"

"It's gravy."

"Yeah, I know it is. Must be nice."

"You know you could do the same."

"Nah. I'd miss the game too much. Don't have no hobbies. Can't stand fishing."

"I dig. I know you'll slow down when you're ready."

Moon chuckled. "What's on your mind? I know you didn't call to talk me into getting in your lane."

"No, you're right," Kole said. "Got an issue I need to discuss."

"What kind of issue?"

"Where you at?" Kole asked.

"At Brenda's. Where you need me to be?"

Kole knew Brenda was one of Moon's long-time girlfriends. She didn't live too far from his nightspot, so he said, "Can you meet me at the club?"

"I can be there in fifteen," Moon said. "How far away are you?"

"I'll get there a couple of minutes before you."

"A'ight. See you in a few."

CHAPTER 27

THE OLD NEIGHBORHOOD was as grimy as it had always been. At half-past nine, there wasn't much automobile or pedestrian traffic, which left more time to observe eyesores that had been there so long, everyone in the community expected them to be there forever.

At Davis and Evans, Kole noticed an abandoned auto shop that still bore the damage from an accident that occurred four years ago. The driver of a box truck lost control of the vehicle and careened into a crowd of young boys who had chosen to loiter there; some selling dope, others just chilling. Most scattered out of the way in time, but a thirteen year old was pinned between the truck and the building. Rumor had it Timothy Riddell had time to cry and scream for his Mama before his crushed internal organs notified his brain that he was deceased.

Eight blocks down the road, on Glen Garden, Kole could still spot holes in a brick storefront from one of the most nonsensical slayings the south side had ever experienced. Six months ago, two thugs hanging out at the store accosted a provocatively dressed customer. They resorted to calling her a bitch and a ho when she rejected them. The woman ran home to her boyfriend, who returned with three goons and two assault rifles. The first two guys didn't stand a chance, just as the killers stood no chance against the legal system. Despite each one snitching on the others, all four of them got life sentences.

Kole pulled into the parking lot of *Moonlight* at Berry and Riverside. The lot was mostly empty, outside of a Cadillac Moon kept there for personal use and another vehicle belonging to his nighttime security guard. Kole exited his vehicle and admired his friend's club as he approached the entrance. The huge building was once a skating rink, back in the 80's. It had been abandoned and left to decay for more than a decade before Moon bought the lease and embarked on a massive remodeling project.

Today the Moonlight was one of few bright spots on the south side. Every Thursday, Friday and Saturday night it was packed with patrons from eight p.m. to two a.m., with nary a shooting or stabbing reported in the fifteen years it had been in operation. Considering the neighborhood, that was quite a feat.

Moon's security detail played a part in the club's squeaky clean reputation. But the main reason patrons refrained from violence was because of Moon and the nefarious group he lorded over. If anyone got drunk enough to let off a few shots in the parking lot of Moonlight, the police would be the last thing they had to worry about.

The front door of the establishment was locked. Kole didn't bother knocking, because unless the guard was standing nearby, no one would hear it. He assumed he was being watched on one of dozens of cameras that surveilled the premises, and he was right. In less than a minute, he heard the locks disengage. One of the doors pulled open, revealing a grizzly bear of a man standing in the dimly lit lobby. Hootie was all chest and arms, with a big, bald head sitting on top. He barely had a neck, which made him look like a football player in full gear.

Hootie's disposition matched his appearance, but he had known Kole for years, so he offered him a half smile.

"What's going on?"

Hootie did not step aside until Kole walked towards him. "What's up, Hootie? I'm meeting Moon here in a few."

If it was anyone else, Hootie would've hit them with a mean clothesline the moment they took a step into the club. But Kole warranted as much respect as Moon did, even if he was out of the game.

Kole headed for the bar and took a seat on one of the stools. He occupied himself with his cellphone until he heard Hootie unlock the door for another visitor. Even though it was his boss this time, Hootie was not jovial as he greeted him.

"Yeah, he at the bar."

A moment later Kole's eyes brightened when his childhood friend rounded the corner. Moon was a slightly smaller version of his henchman. He was a tall man, with dark skin and a bald head. He had always been stout, but he was in his early-forties now, and he had a bit of a gut to go along with his massive chests and arms. Despite the extra weight, Kole knew his friend could still throw down with the best of them.

But it was Moon's brains that propelled him to the top of *The Organization* and allowed him to maintain a stronghold on the many criminal activities they dominated for the past twenty-five years. Moon often gave Kole credit for teaching him the game, but Kole always knew his friend was a force to be reckoned with on his own. He just needed Kole to step aside, so he'd have a chance to shine.

The two men embraced fully, like brothers. When they backed away, Moon looked him up and down, smiling.

"Good to see you, bro. You been hitting the gym? I thought you'd have a belly like mine by now."

He jabbed him playfully in the stomach. Kole's six-pack was so rigid, he barely felt it.

He shook his head, grinning. "Don't need no gym. Still doing push-ups and sit-ups every night. Run a few miles every other day. I ain't gotta pay nobody for that."

In other circles, the comment may have come off as *cheap*, but Moon knew Kole could afford a membership at any gym in the country. Hell, Kole could buy the whole building, if that was his wish.

The men returned to the bar and took a seat on the stools.

"Man, it's good to see you," Kole told him. Looking around, he said, "I miss this place."

"You should come by more often," Moon responded. "Just because you doing the straight-and-narrow now don't mean you can't hang out with us crim-*nals* every now and then."

Kole laughed at the way he pronounced the word. "Yeah, you right," he replied. "I wouldn't mind stopping by sometimes."

"Got you a lady friend yet?" Moon asked. "If so, you should bring her. I'll set y'all up in VIP. Free bottles all night. If you let me know when you coming, I'll bring in one of those R&B cats; make sure to get her panties wet before you take her home."

Kole was all for that plan, but he shook his head. "Ain't got no woman to impress."

"That's cool. I can still get Trey Songz to sing for you," Moon joked.

"You gon' get his skinny-ass whooped," Kole replied, and they both laughed.

"So what brings you out here?" Moon asked. "If you wanted to shoot the shit, we coulda did that over the phone."

"You right," Kole said. His smile ebbed. "What's up with those MMG cats?"

Moon's smile went away too. "What you mean what's up with them? They still causing as much ruckus as they was when you was here – except now it's prolly more of them, and they make a lot more noise."

"They ain't giving y'all no trouble?"

"Hell naw," Moon said with a frown. "They stay in they motherfucking lane, like they supposed to. You know I don't fuck around with them clowns. Why you asking?"

"They giving a friend of mine some trouble," Kole replied. He told Moon about Tariq's accident, the necklace Brendon wore and the subsequent harassment and shooting at Dana's house.

When he was done, Moon asked, "What that got to do with you?"

"They was shooting on my street," Kole repeated. "It's a quiet neighborhood. I don't need shit like that so close to my doorstep."

"Sounds like that bitch needs to move," Moon suggested. "Them young niggas been acting reckless for the past couple of days. I heard Shank got killed, but I didn't know he got ran over like that. You know they rode on them Bideker niggas last night..."

"Word?"

"Yeah. I think they ran through two or three times. Lit 'em up like the Fourth of July."

Kole was disturbed but not surprised to hear that. If MMG sent soldiers to shoot up Dana's house, of course they would take the fight to Bideker Street as well. Unfortunately for the Bideker Boys, they were completely innocent. They probably had no idea why their rival had targeted them.

"Anybody killed?" he asked.

Moon shrugged. "Maybe."

Kole shook his head. "Sounds like they trying to make a statement."

"That was Brass' son who got killed," Moon said. "What you think they gon' do, turn the other cheek?"

"But he got hisself killed. And Bideker didn't have nothing to do with it."

"What that got to do with anything? You know MMG ain't never sat down and thought about nothing rationally. They OG's son is dead, and it look like Bideker did it. As far as they concerned, that's enough reason to heat up the burners."

Kole sighed. "So, what you think it'll take to end this? Maybe if I talk to Brass directly..."

Moon's eyebrows bunched together. "You wanna talk to Brass? For what, man? This shit ain't got nothing to do with you."

"I told you they going after my neighbor. I can't have this going on on my street."

"They'll quit once they get her, or the boy. Shouldn't take too long."

Kole didn't appreciate his friend's callousness, but he couldn't blame him for speaking so bluntly. The Organization and MMG didn't necessarily get along, but they had maintained a mutual respect for years. One of the key requirements of the armistice was to stay out of each other's business. Kole hated to be the one to go against the grain, but he didn't see a way around it.

"You think you could set up a face-to-face with me and Brass?" he asked again.

Moon's look of confusion deepened. "I'ma ask you again; why you wanna do some shit like that? We ain't got no reason to communicate with them niggas."

"The neighbor I'm telling you about, her name is Dana," Kole revealed. "Last night I took her and Tariq in."

"In *where*?"

"In my house," Kole said. "They under my protection."

Moon brought a large hand to his face. He rubbed his cheek and then his forehead. "Now why you wanna do some fool-ass shit like that?"

"I care about this woman. I'ma look after her."

"You fucking her?"

Again Kole was agitated by his friend's crassness. His nostrils flared before he responded. "I'm not fucking her, but I do know her. She a good woman, and her boy don't get in no trouble. I ain't finna watch a pack of wolves tear them to pieces, just because Shank was dumb enough to run out in the middle of the street. I'm gonna help this woman, and I need you to help me."

His last comment was a statement, not a question, so Moon gave up trying to talk him out of it. Ever since Kole retired, Moon was the sole leader of The Organization. But prior to that, he'd been answering to Kole for decades. If Kole needed help with something, he had the full weight of The Organization at his disposal, starting with the man at the top.

117

"A'ight," Moon conceded. "I'll talk to some people and see if I can set up a face-to-face with you and Brass."

"I appreciate that."

"In the meantime, you want me to send some guys over to watch your place? Don't you think they gon' find out where that lady's hiding?"

Kole agreed there was a possibility MMG would learn that he had Dana and Tariq tucked away, but he declined his friend's offer for protection. "Nah. We'll be alright."

Kole felt like that might not be the best decision, but he knew the guys Moon planned on sending would be armed to the teeth. If possible, he wanted to settle this matter without bloodshed – on his side and MMG's.

"Alright," Moon said. "Your call. But if this shit gets any closer to your doorstep, you ain't gon' have a choice in the matter."

"Yeah, I know," Kole said somberly. He stood and gripped his friend's hand and pulled him in for a bro hug. "Thanks, man. I appreciate it."

CHAPTER 28

It's time to see some northern parts
A quinceañera's about to start
The girl's as pretty as a picture
Her uncle's drunk off half-priced liquor
You see the way that big man dances?
He got the groove in his big pants
Did you hear someone say, "disgrace?"
That drunkard slapped his sister's face!
And now three cousins take the flo'
Yeah, these big boys can rock and roll
Now uncle's dancing best of all
He takes a beating fo' he falls!
Man, I love the way he moves!
North side's got that ghetto groove!

RATHER THAN HEAD straight home after his talk with Moon, Kole piloted his Jeep Renegade to Bideker Street, which wasn't too far from the club. As far as streets go, this one wasn't very long. The majority of it branched off the east side of 287, with only four more blocks extending from the west side of the highway.

Likewise, the gang that bore the street's name wasn't large. Last Kole heard, they had fifty bangers in the neighborhood and twenty or so more who were incarcerated. The Bideker Boys also recruited members who did not physically live on the street, but their OG (leader), and most of their high-ranking G's were born and raised on Bideker.

Kole felt tension in the air the moment he exited the freeway. The street was quiet at that time of day, but it was by no means sleepy. As he drove deeper into the neighborhood, Kole noticed some of the cars sitting in the driveways were occupied by two to three goons. They eyed Kole suspiciously as he passed them. Kole recognized them as lookouts, and he knew they were armed. Not only would they give a heads up to their comrades further down the block if someone blazed down the street with a shooter hanging out of the window. They would also give chase and hopefully murder the offenders before they did any harm.

There were no police in the area, but Kole noticed a couple of houses with crime scene tape stretched around the front yard. The familiar scene made his stomach tighten, even though he wasn't responsible for it – this time. Tariq wasn't responsible either, but Kole felt sorry for the role Dana's son played in this. Based on what Dana had told him, Tariq was a good kid, an A/B student who didn't get into fights, skip school or experiment with weed or cigarettes. He didn't deserve to have blood on his hands – especially victims he didn't even know.

When Kole stopped in front of a two-story home that looked substantially better than the other houses on the street, the show of force was more prominent. Kole counted five goons sitting on the porch as he put his car in park and killed the ignition. Before he exited his vehicle, three of the men left the porch and walked purposefully down the walkway. They all sported the gang's colors; either in beaded necklaces or their clothing.

Kole understood why street gangs chose to represent their set and show solidarity in this manner, but he always felt it was one of their dumbest trademarks. The soldiers in The Organization avoided such foolishness. They had no official colors or style of dress. Dressing like a gang member not only tipped off the police to your affiliation, but it tipped off your enemies as well. The Bideker Boys could step out of a convenience store and get blasted by a complete stranger, simply because the gunman was an enemy of the set, and he was instructed to murder black and yellow on sight.

The men approaching Kole's SUV were all armed, toting pistols and small assault rifles in broad daylight. Texas was an open-carry state, but that didn't apply to convicted felons. If the police rolled through, they could put a case on each one of them, but desperate times call for desperate measures. Kole did not reach for his own weapon as he lowered the window on the passenger side.

The bangers stopped a safe ten feet away from his vehicle.

"Fuck is you?" one of them called. He was short, in his mid-twenties, with an old scar than ran across his throat, from ear to ear. The wound looked like it should've been fatal, yet there he was, standing as tall as ever.

"I'm Kole," he said, ducking a little so he could look the boy in his eyes. "Popcorn here?"

The speaker gave his cohorts a look before his gaze returned to the stranger. His look of contempt was as intimidating as it was unwarranted. Kole's expression remained neutral.

"Who the fuck *is* you?" the boy asked again.

"I done told you who I am. My name's Kole. If Popcorn's here, go tell him I'm out here. He know who I am."

None of the men budged. Kole looked from one to another, hoping they had enough sense to do as he'd asked.

"Where you from?" the short one asked.

Kole thought the question was asinine. He wasn't going to give them any more information than he already had. Even if he was with MMG, it would be completely idiotic to say so, while he was clearly outnumbered and outgunned.

He looked past the boys when the front door of the house opened and a familiar face stepped onto the porch. Popcorn was a large man; more fat than brawny, but he had a good deal of muscle

121

stacked on his 320 pound frame. He had a medium-size afro that he rarely attempted to tame, either with a comb or cornrows. He had big lips and a pudgy nose that had been broken a few times. Popcorn's skin was fair, his arms emblazoned with his gang affiliation, among other things.

At 39, Popcorn was close to retirement age, but he was still putting it down for his squad. His gang distributed everything from dope to firearms and women. Kole had known the man for more than fifteen years. The Organization never had beef with the Bideker Boys. The groups stayed in their own lanes and rarely had cause to communicate, let alone argue over something as trivial as turf.

Popcorn ambled down the sidewalk, and his crew made way for him. They continued to mean-mug Kole as their leader peered into the vehicle.

"Nigga won't say who he is," the short one reported.

Kole didn't call him on the lie.

He and Popcorn locked eyes, and the big man said, "*Kole*. What the fuck you doing over here?"

"Stopped by for a little powwow." With the gang leader there, Kole finally felt comfortable enough to unfasten his seat belt.

"You shoulda called first," Popcorn said, looking up and down his street. "This ain't a good time for no visit. Some shit might go down."

"That's what I wanna talk to you about," Kole informed him. "I know a little something about the trouble you having."

The larger man's eyes narrowed, as did his cohorts'. "What you know about it?" Popcorn asked.

"I know I don't wanna be sitting out here in the open if they *do* run through here again," Kole stated. "Can a nigga come in or what?"

"Yeah," Popcorn stated. "Come on in."

Kole exited his vehicle and attempted to follow him inside, but one of his soldiers continued to block the walkway. Kole could've walked around him. But stepping onto the grass would've been a show of weakness.

To some it may sound childish, but on the streets, respect means everything. Kole didn't consciously decide he was willing to die, rather than step around the man. But his body language delivered that message. He stepped to the thug and stared him down. The banger sneered back at him, and his grip on his weapon tightened.

Popcorn looked back and was quick to admonish his soldier.

"Say, move out the way, nigga. Don't be eyeballing that man like that! Do you know who that is?"

The flunky stepped aside but didn't fix his face right away. Kole gave him a pass. His features softened as he told Popcorn, "Don't even worry about it. I don't expect these young cats to know me."

"Well they should," Popcorn said. "My nigga Kole is a *motherfucking street legend*. Got more bodies than he got hotties. This man been putting in work since the eighties. Y'all lil' niggas need to show some *respect*!"

Popcorn's soldiers wore curious expressions now, but Kole wasn't necessarily appreciative of the endorsement. Unlike the typical gangster, he didn't need or want his reputation to glorify him.

Then again, sometimes having a legacy is necessary. When Kole followed Popcorn up the steps, everyone made way for them.

One of the thugs said, "Say, I know who you is. You run The Organization."

Kole looked him in the eyes before shaking his head. "Naw. I'm retired."

He didn't offer any additional information before he and Popcorn stepped inside the house.

CHAPTER 29

THE LEADER OF the Bideker Boys lived like a king, with all of the amenities one would expect for a man in his position. His home was laced with designer furniture and all the latest electronics. The house was old, had been in his family for generations. But looking around, it was hard to put an age on it. The windows were all new. The carpeting and paint job were new as well.

Popcorn's house wasn't as clean as Kole's, but that was because of all the traffic from his minions and the fact that Popcorn was raising his family there. He lived with his wife and four children. In Kole's opinion, that was a mistake that could end tragically. At forty-one, Kole's preoccupation with safety had left him single and childless.

Popcorn led the way to the den, which was quiet and spacious and thankfully deserted. He took a seat on one of the sofas. Kole selected a leather executive chair. He rolled it to the center of the room, so he could sit across from the OG.

"What's up with you, Kole?" Popcorn asked him. "So it's true what I been hearing? You done traded in your pistols for golf clubs?"

Upon mention of his gun, Kole felt the firearm sitting snugly on the small of his back.

"I don't know about no golf clubs," he replied. "But yeah, I gave that shit up over a year ago."

"Why?" Popcorn asked him. "Y'all was doing it big."

"They still are. Just because I stepped down don't mean the train stopped rolling."

"Moon took your spot?" Popcorn wondered.

Even though Kole didn't consider the Bideker Boys a rival, he wouldn't say they were allies either. Even if they were, he wouldn't feel comfortable discussing The Organization in Popcorn's home. For all he knew, the feds had the place bugged.

"If you need to get in touch with somebody, you can holler at me," he said. "I'll pass the word to the right people."

Popcorn was accustomed to the secrecy surrounding Kole's group, so he didn't press for details. He nodded and then said, "So what you know about the shit going on around here? You say that's what you came to talk about...?"

Kole nodded. "Yeah. I heard MMG been giving y'all the business."

Popcorn frowned. "Them pussy-ass niggas rolled through last night, making a lot of noise. Ain't really do shit, though."

"Anybody got hit?" Kole asked, thinking about the crime scene tape he saw on the way to the OG's house.

Popcorn's sneer intensified as he nodded. "They hit a few cats. Only one was a homey, though. Other two was just some kids from the neighborhood. Them bitches run through here three times. Coward-ass niggas. Ain't got the nuts to hop out and take care of business. That's alright, though." He brought a hand up and stroked one of his chins. "We got something for that ass. Bet they won't come through here no more. If they do, they damn sure ain't gon' make it off this block. I guarantee you that."

"I'm sorry that happened to you," Kole said sincerely. "You know anything about what it's about?"

"We heard somebody killed that nigga Shank," Popcorn replied. "Run his ass over on Lancaster. But what that got to do with us, I got no idea. I'm glad that motherfucker dead, but it ain't like none of us was driving the car that hit him." The OG stopped rubbing his chin, and his eyes narrowed. "You say you know something about it?"

"I do," Kole said. "And you right, it ain't got nothing to do with y'all."

He told him about the accident without mentioning Tariq or Brendon's name. He told them about the beads Brendon was wearing and how they sparked a near-riot while Shank's body lay crumpled on the street. Popcorn became visibly agitated as he listened.

"It ain't just y'all they going after," Kole explained. "They after the boy that was driving too. They shot up his mama's house last night."

"What about the one was flaunting our beads?" Popcorn asked. "Sounds like *that's* the one they need to be getting at. You know who he is?"

Kole nodded. "I do."

"Where he at? If that nigga ain't down with the set, he ain't got no business wearing our colors, bringing this shit down on us. He gon' get his ass skinned up for that. Maybe worse."

"Ain't happening," Kole said with a shake of his head.

"What you mean it ain't happening? You see what the hell going on over here?"

"Yeah, I see it. That's why I came to talk to you."

"You ain't got no business interfering with the way we handle ours. That nigga done brought a lot of trouble our way. He got one coming. You know that."

"I know what you saying," Kole conceded. "He got one coming from you and MMG. But I still ain't handing him over – to you or them."

"He some kin to you?"

Kole shook his head.

"Then what you got to do with it?"

"I'm doing a favor for a friend," Kole said simply.

The two men stared at each other for a few seconds. Kole knew the OG would back down. He had no choice.

"Alright, well, we still gon' ride on them MMG niggas," Popcorn stated. "I don't care if it was a misunderstanding. This shit's personal now."

Kole sighed and shook his head again. "Naw, man. I need you to stand down. Let that shit go."

Popcorn's eyes widened. "What? I know I heard you wrong."

"If you ride on them, it's gon' be an all-out war."

"*A war they started*!" Popcorn's voice boomed.

"A couple of drivebys ain't gotta start a war," Kole countered. "I'm asking you to chill, at least for a few days. I'ma have a sit-down with Brass, try to talk some sense into him. I'ma tell him Shank got hisself killed, and y'all didn't have nothing to do with it."

"That ain't gon' take away from what they already done to us!"

"You said ain't nobody got killed. Can't you charge it to the game?"

"Hell naw!" Popcorn continued to frown as he shook his massive head. "Young niggas out there ready to put in work. And I don't blame 'em. Them niggas brought that shit right to *Bideker Street*. This as personal as it gets."

"Do you really wanna go to war with MMG? I told you; I'ma take care of this. This ain't got nothing to do with y'all."

Kole knew Popcorn had an image to uphold. But from a logistical standpoint, Kole's offer was the best thing going. MMG outnumbered the Bideker Boys four-to-one. Popcorn's crew would get slaughtered if they tried to go head-to-head. But if he told his gang The Organization had intervened and implored them to chill for a minute, the weight would be off his shoulders. He could save face, and even better, he could save lives.

"I'll *think* about it," the OG replied.

All things considered, Kole found that response acceptable.

CHAPTER 30

ON THE WAY home, Kole called Dana's cellphone. She answered right away.

"Hey."

"It's me," he said. "How y'all doing?"

"We're fine," she breathed. "Just a little cabin fever. What about you? Did you find out anything?"

"I did," he said. "But I'm still working on it."

After a pause she asked, "Is it something you can talk about?"

"Yeah. I'll talk to you when I get there."

"Are you on your way home?"

"Yeah."

Dana wasn't sure why she was so happy to hear that. It wasn't like he'd been gone for very long.

"Have you been checking on your house?" he asked. "Any more visitors?"

"No. Not that I've noticed. Everything's fine."

"Haven't seen any unfamiliar cars?"

"No."

"Tariq's friend, what'd you say his name was?"

"Who, Brendon?"

"Yeah. I wanna go see him. Can you or Tariq take me to his house?"

"Sure," Dana said, then, "I mean, why do you want to see him?"

"I been talking to people," Kole said, "offering them a version of events based on what Tariq told me. But the things that are going on are too deep for me to take your boy's word for it – no offense. I need to look Brendon in the eyes and let him tell me for himself what those beads mean to him. Plus it might be some trouble coming his way. I wanna make sure he's aware of it."

"Okay," Dana said. "I can take you by there. Tariq will probably want to come too. Is that alright?"

"Yeah. That's fine. I'll be there in twenty minutes."

PART FOUR
KOLE'S FURY

CHAPTER 31

Oh, now you wanna get out my ride?
First we grooving to the west side
Just sit yourself inside that chair
It's at the light, we almost there
Did you know my car's got 'draulics, fool?
I got a bad-ass system too
A lot of niggas want my ride
Like these gangstas at the light
They got a shotgun to your heart
Yo ghetto dancing's about to start
Wait till you see the moves you do
You really got that ghetto groove!

DANA WAS HAPPY to get out of the house when Kole arrived to pick them up. He instructed her and Tariq to sit in the backseat of his Jeep, where the tint was darker. If they passed any unfamiliar or angry faces before they left the neighborhood, it was unlikely they'd be spotted from there.

Dana was excited to hear that Kole had made a little progress that morning. But the good vibes didn't last long. On the way to Brendon's apartment, Kole delivered dreadful news that would've made her clutch her pearls if she owned any.

"Them boys out for blood," he said, occasionally watching his outcasts in the rearview mirror. "They rolled down Bideker

Street a few times last night. Shot some people. Their leader said nobody died, and only one of them was actually a member of the gang. The other two were just kids from the neighborhood."

Dana's eyes were wide and fretful. Her son's were too.

"They did *drivebys*?" she asked.

Kole nodded. "Yeah. It sounds like the same as what happened at your house, except the folks on Bideker weren't as lucky."

"They're trying to kill people," Dana said, mostly to herself. "Don't they know it was an accident? Those people they shot, they don't have nothing to do with it."

"I think they honestly believe Tariq ran into that man on purpose," Kole stated. "Right now they're hot, full of venom. Revenge is the only thing on their mind. But once everything cools down, and more facts come out, I'm hoping they'll let it go. I talked to the OG on Bideker; asked him not to retaliate for the shootings. I think they'll be cool, until I have a chance to talk to Brass."

Dana squeezed her eyes closed, struggling to keep up. "Who, who is that again? Sorry, I can't..." She looked up and locked eyes with Kole in the rearview mirror.

His attention returned to the road as he told her, "That's alright. There's a lot of people involved, and it is kinda confusing. Shank is the man that got killed; the one Tariq hit. Brass is his father. Brass is the leader of MMG."

"Okay," Dana said, nodding. "What, did you say you're gonna talk to him?"

"That's the plan. I don't know if he'll sit down with me, but I don't see why he wouldn't. I think he wants answers as much as everyone else."

Dana shook her head, her brow still furrowed. "You... These people, you know them?"

Kole could tell she was having a hard time balancing the back story he'd given her with the moves he was making today. He wasn't sure how much of the truth he wanted to tell her. With Tariq in the car, he'd have to keep her in the dark for now.

"I know the guy from Bideker. But I've never met Brass. I hope I get to meet him very soon."

"How are you gonna get in contact with Brass?" Dana wanted to know.

After a pause, Kole said, "I know some people that should be able to make it happen."

Sensing she wouldn't get anywhere, Dana held on to the rest of her questions for now. She took a few moments to stare at Kole's smoky eyes in the rearview mirror when his gaze returned to the road. Who was this man? She had to admit that she didn't really know him at all. She looked over at Tariq, who was as perplexed as she was. He hadn't said anything since they got in the car. He remained silent and brooding for the rest of the ride to Brendon's apartments.

CHAPTER 32

BRENDON LIVED ON the southeast side. His home school should've been Langford, based on his address, but he was living in the Finley High zone during his freshman through junior years. Despite moving, the principal allowed him to finish his high school career at Finley.

Tariq was glad for that, but Dana sometimes had misgivings, especially on days like this. If Brendon wasn't going to Finley, she wondered if Tariq would've made other friends who were more in line with the lifestyle she expected from him. Then again, Tariq was old enough to make his own decisions about who he wanted to hang out with. Odds are he and Brendon would've remained homies, regardless of how far away he lived.

Their bond was evident from the moment Brendon's aunt Victoria opened the door and invited everyone inside. Brendon gripped Tariq's hand and pulled him in for a hug.

"Yo, what up, man? How you doing? That was some messed up shi–" Brendon looked around and caught himself. "That was some messed up stuff that happened at your house last night," he said.

"Yeah, it was," Tariq said, following him inside the apartment. The boy hadn't cracked a smile all morning, but with

Brendon, he was beaming. "I can't believe they didn't come after your dumb butt."

"They already tried that," Brendon said. He shrugged his shoulder, reminding Tariq of his gunshot wound to the arm. Brendon's facial injuries hadn't healed much over the past two days, but he was able to open his black eye fully.

"Whatever, man," Tariq said. "You only got grazed. Why you still wearing that bandage? You know it ain't bleeding."

Tariq poked the fresh gauze. Brendon slapped his hand away.

"Fool, you better watch out, 'fore you catch these hands!"

Brendon looked past his friend and acknowledged the other two visitors for the first time.

"How you doing, Miss Dana?"

"I'm fine," she said with a smirk.

"Who is this y'all brought with you, your bodyguard?" Brendon asked Tariq.

"Naw. That's my neighbor I was telling you about."

"Damn this fool *swole*!" Brendon exclaimed. "What up, G?"

He brought a hand up to give him dap, but Kole's arms remained by his sides. His expression was disapproving.

"Aww! He left me hanging," Brendon said, turning back to Tariq.

"He don't like you," Tariq deduced.

"That's alright. I got enough friends," Brendon said. "Say, you get that text I sent you?" he asked, changing the subject.

"I didn't know what that was about," Tariq replied.

"I told you it was from that shorty," Brendon said, leading him to the other side of the room. "I showed you her picture, right?" He dug his phone from his pocket. Tariq leaned closer to check out whatever woman he was talking about.

"How you doing?" Dana asked his aunt, who was standing near the doorway.

"I'm fine," Victoria said. She was talking to Dana, but her eyes were glued to the man accompanying her. "Who'd you say this was?"

Kole knew she was talking about him, but she wasn't talking *to* him, so he didn't bother to respond.

"This is my neighbor, Kole," Dana explained. "He helped us out last night. We're hoping he can talk to those people and get them to leave us alone."

"*Kole.*" Victoria said it as if she was tasting his name. "Where you from? You look familiar."

He looked down at the woman and ignored the lust in her eyes.

"No, I don't think I know you."

"You live in Overbrook Meadows all your life?"

He nodded.

"What kind of work you do?"

"I'm retired," he said, looking away now.

"What kind of work you *used to* do?" Victoria asked, totally oblivious that her flirting was going nowhere.

Kole didn't respond this time. Dana followed his gaze to Brendon and Tariq. The boys didn't seem to be doing anything out of the ordinary, but Kole appeared perturbed by what he was seeing. Before Dana could ask him what was wrong, he walked away, taking slow, purposeful steps towards the friends.

"What the hell is so funny?" he asked, speaking directly to Brendon.

The boy turned and the smile dropped from his face. "Huh?"

"What's so funny?" Kole asked again. He nodded towards his phone. "Show me. I been having one hell of a day. I need something to laugh at."

Brendon's smile returned partially. He looked at Tariq with a confused expression.

"Yo, is he serious?"

"I'm standing right here," Kole stated. "You got something to say, you can say it to me."

The whole house went quiet while Brendon's smile slipped again. Attracted by the conflict, one of Victoria's daughters appeared in the hallway with another rug rat right behind her. Dana could never remember the youngest one's name. The children were as confused as everyone else was by the sudden turn of events. Kole said he wanted to talk to Brendon, but no one expected him to confront the teen in this manner.

"It, it's nothing," Brendon said, putting his phone away. "I was just showing Tariq..." He trailed off, taking in Kole's full size and posture. Despite the fact that Kole had the strength to wring his little neck, Brendon had home field advantage, so he felt comfortable enough to ask Tariq's neighbor, "What's your problem?"

"I'm glad you asked," Kole said, taking another step towards him.

His large hands weren't balled into fists, but Brendon felt uncomfortable enough to take a step back.

"My problem is you strutting around with your little gunshot wound like you hard or something. You think you hard now? Getting shot make you hard?"

Kole's voice was booming. Everyone's eyes grew larger by the second. Victoria knew her nephew was a screw up, but she jumped to his defense.

"Hold up, um, *sir*! You can't come up in my house yelling at him like that!"

Kole ignored her. His eyes were focused solely on Brendon. From the back, his muscles looked massive. Dana prayed he wouldn't lay hands on the boy.

"Are you hard or what?" Kole demanded. "I see you got your beads on. I thought they snatched that shit off your neck? What, you got you a new one?"

Brendon's look of guilt was so extreme, it was almost comical. Dana looked and saw that he did in fact have another black and yellow Bideker necklace. Suddenly furious, she didn't feel half as bad about the way Kole was speaking to him.

"I – I uh..." Brendon reached nervously and scratched his head.

"Speak up!" Kole barked. "I asked about your necklace. Tariq said the one you was wearing got ripped off. Either you was at the scene of the accident picking up beads off the street, or you got you a new one. *Which is it?*"

"Hold up, Dana. Who is this man?" Victoria wanted to know.

"I, I already had this one," Brendon managed. He looked like he was about to piss his pants. Dana thought she might too, if Kole had advanced on her like that.

"You had another one?" the dark behemoth asked.

Brendon nodded. "Ye, yeah."

"Where you have it at?" Kole asked. "In your jewelry box? You throw them beads on the same way you'd sport a ring or a bracelet?"

"I..."

"*Are you down with Bideker Street or what?*" Kole demanded. "Somebody put you down, or you out here perpetrating?"

Brendon shook his head. He looked around for someone to intervene. Victoria was the only one legally required to do so, so she took a few timid steps in their direction. Kole turned on her, as if he could *feel* someone sneaking up on him.

"*Back off!* Don't try to get involved now. If you was paying half as much attention to him as you are now, none of this shit would've happened!"

Victoria was stunned stiff. Her mouth fell open. Somehow her eyes grew even larger. Despite her brain telling her that this was her apartment, and she most certainly *did not* have to back off, her body felt differently. She took three quick steps back, until she and Dana were side by side.

Kole spun back to Brendon, who by then realized he was up shit creek. Even Tariq began to cower away, leaving his friend to fend for himself.

"*Are you down with Bideker Street or not*?!" Kole asked again.

Brendon shook his head fiercely.

"Have you ever been to Bideker Street? You know who Popcorn is?"

Brendon continued to shake his head, but then he nodded. "I, I been over there. I don't – I don't know Popcorn. *I heard about him, but I don't know him!*" The boy's voice was shrill. His eyes glistened. He looked like he might start bawling. How gangsta would that be?!

"Then why the hell you wearing those beads? You think this a game? I talked to Popcorn this morning! You know what he wanna do to yo skinny ass? You know what MMG wanna do to you?"

"No. No, sir!"

"You know how many bullets flying around this city because of *you*?! People is getting shot in these streets, 'cause yo dumb ass wanna wear a necklace! You think it make you look cool? How cool you feel now? Somebody's in yo face charging you up about your goddamn necklace! How cool is it? Huh?" Kole stepped even closer, until there was but a breath of space between them. "How cool is it, Brendon?! You almost died over this! Tariq and Dana could've died last night! And you still over here perpetrating! Nigga, *gimme that shit!*"

He reached suddenly and snatched the beads off Brendon's neck. The boy didn't know what to expect when he saw the big hand coming his way. He flinched and almost screamed. But Kole only had the necklace gripped in his fist when he withdrew his hand. Black and yellow beads fell to the floor and bounced before rolling to a stop.

Kole's chest heaved as he sucked in deep breaths. He stared at Brendon for a few more seconds, his nostril's flaring. He didn't mean to get so upset, but it was too late to take it back. He turned back to Dana, wondering if she was spooked as well. From the look in her eyes, he knew she thought he was a monster.

He told her, "Let's go," not sure if she would follow him out of the apartment. He yanked the door open and didn't wait for her.

She didn't catch up to him on the breezeway, but halfway down the stairs Kole heard Dana's voice behind him. She said, "Come on, Tariq. Let's go."

Kole wasn't sure why he was so relieved to hear that.

When he got to his Jeep, he had half a minute to cool down before Dana and her son joined him. They both sat in the backseat again. This was what Kole instructed them to do on the way to Brendon's, but now he couldn't help but feel as if they were trying to put as much distance between them as possible.

He sighed as he started the SUV and rolled out of his parking spot.

CHAPTER 33

HE DROVE IN silence for five minutes, until he felt calm enough to address his behavior at Victoria's apartment.

"I'm, uh..." He cleared his throat. He kept his eyes on the road, rather than meet their faces in the mirror. "I'm sorry I yelled at that boy. Sorry y'all had to see it. That's not me. I'm not usually like that..."

The silence in the car made it clear they didn't believe him. Kole didn't blame them. His transformation in the apartment came too naturally to be a one-time thing.

"I'm *trying* not to be like that," he clarified. "But the way your friend was acting all happy-go-lucky... I wouldn't have minded too much, but he had those damned beads on again. It's like, he has no idea how much trouble he's caused."

Still no response from the backseat.

Kole sighed. He checked the mirror briefly and saw that his passengers were both staring at him. They looked freaked out, but not as much as they were in the apartment.

"I did what I did because I care about y'all," Kole told them. "Tariq, you gotta understand people like that can get you killed. You should know that by now, after what happened the other day. I know you not a bad kid. And I don't think Brendon is either. But right now he's acting like a *stupid* kid – like there ain't no consequences for nothing he's doing. The people that's after y'all will put a bullet in his head without even thinking about it. If you with him at the time, you'll get one too.

"I said I was gon' protect y'all, and that's what I'm doing, even if it don't look that way. You got threats on the street that are easy to spot. But you got threats on the inside too. I ain't saying you shouldn't be friends with Brendon. But you gotta think real hard about the trouble he can get you in. You gotta pay attention. If you see him doing something you ain't cool with, you gotta be man enough to say, 'Nah, homey. I ain't with that,' and go your own way."

Kole realized he was rambling. Even worse, he was giving fatherly advice to a boy who probably hated him.

Tariq surprised him by saying, "It's okay. Everything you saying is right. Brendon, he need somebody to talk to him like that sometimes."

Kole didn't expect that at all. He was even more surprised by the warm comfort Tariq's approval gave him. He looked to Dana. She remained silent, so Kole couldn't tell if she shared her son's sentiments.

"Well, um, I guess we'll go back to my place," he said. "I'm still waiting to hear if Brass will talk to me."

"What happens if he won't?"

Dana had been so quiet, Kole had forgotten how sweet her voice sounded.

He looked her in the eyes and said, "I got some ideas, but it would be better if we don't have to go that route. For now, I think we should wait to hear from my peeps."

CHAPTER 34

BACK AT KOLE'S house, the mood was tense. Although the talk with Tariq on the way home had gone well, he couldn't shake the feeling that Dana and her son were a little wary of him now. He'd lost his cool and nearly assaulted a teenager. Brendon was a jackass, but he probably didn't deserve that.

Rather than chill in the living room, kitchen or den when they returned, Tariq and Dana retreated to the bedroom they shared. Kole went to his own room and gave them some space.

Six hours later the clock struck seven, and the sun began its descent in the western skies above Overbook Meadows, taking most of the day's heat with it. By then everyone in the house was restless. Dana and Tariq had gradually migrated from their rooms, but there was little communication between them and the man of the house.

Dana had resumed her vigil at the living room window. From that distance, her home looked as perfect as the day she bought it. She couldn't see the bullet holes. It was almost possible to convince herself that they weren't there. But every time she thought about returning, her mind would replay the horrific scene from last night; when she and Tariq cowered on the floor with what sounded like Vietnam erupting all around them.

Tariq had an easier time being stuck in Kole's house. He'd packed his PlayStation, so all he needed was a TV and WiFi connection to feel like he was home. But even his games started to get boring after so many tedious hours.

He was all for it when Kole emerged from his bedroom and asked Dana, "Y'all wanna go out for dinner?"

She and Tariq were both in the front room at the time, watching Denzel's new movie. Dana looked up at him, surprised by the request.

"You wanna go out?"

Kole shrugged. "I got some stuff in the fridge, but I'm getting a little bored being cooped up all day. Aren't y'all?"

"I am," Tariq said. He looked to his mother, hoping she'd agree.

"Do you think it's safe for us to be outside?" Dana asked.

Kole had been trying to subdue the feelings he once had for her. But as she looked up at him, with her large innocent eyes, he was struck by how beautiful she was. He wanted to tell her how far he'd go to protect her, but he was afraid he'd freak her out more than he already did at Brendon's apartment.

"We'll go somewhere out of town," he offered.

"Out of town? Like where?"

"I don't know. Arlington's not far away, but I don't think we'll run into any gangbangers at the Cheesecake Factory."

Her eyes lit up. "You wanna take us to *Cheesecake*?"

Kole knew she'd appreciate that. Back when they were dating, he loved that Dana wasn't afraid to *eat* when she was around him. Somehow she maintained a knockout figure and a dainty personality.

"Yeah," he told her. "You down?"

"Heck yeah," she said, rising to her feet. "When are we leaving? Do I have time to change?"

"Yeah. Take your time. I think I'll change into something different myself..."

CHAPTER 35

KOLE'S NEW OUTFIT consisted of khakis with an untucked button-down. His shirt was maroon-colored, matching his loafers. Without a tee-shirt underneath, Dana couldn't help but notice the top portion of the smooth crease that divided his pectorals. She'd seen him naked, so her imagination easily filled in the rest of the picture.

She wore a skirt that extended almost to her knees with a sleeveless blouse that didn't show any cleavage. Even still, she had a lot of chocolaty flesh on display. Kole took his time devouring her with his eyes when they met up in the front room. His gaze singed her skin as he looked her up and down. Despite their past, Dana was flattered. She hadn't felt that way about him since they were dating.

Tariq emerged from the guest room wearing jeans and a tee-shirt. He stepped between the adults, totally oblivious to the chemistry he was disturbing.

He looked from Kole to his mother and said, "Dang. Am I underdressed? I didn't bring a lot of clothes over here."

"No, you're fine baby," Dana told him. She put an arm around his waist and walked him towards the kitchen.

"You still want us in the backseat, right?" she asked, looking back at Kole.

She thought he looked ravenous, and not necessarily for what was on Cheesecake's menu.

"Uh, yeah," he said, looking into her eyes. "I think that's for the best."

CHAPTER 36

THEY DIDN'T SEE any goons creeping through the neighborhood when Kole rolled out of his garage, but he wanted to look around a little more before he headed for the restaurant. After crisscrossing the area for a few minutes, he was confident MMG had not returned.

"Do you think they gave up on us?" Dana asked from the backseat.

"I don't see why they would," Kole replied. "By now they know they didn't hit anyone when they shot up your house. Even if they don't come back tonight, I wouldn't let my guard down so soon."

"That man you're trying to get in touch with, still no word?" Dana asked.

Kole shook his head. "Not yet. But I got people working on it. Don't worry. I'll keep you in the loop."

At the restaurant, the threesome was able to forget about their worries for a little while as they feasted on succulent dishes that were packed with calories but well worth it. Kole was mostly finished with his meal when his cellphone rang. He excused himself from the table when he saw Moon's number on the Caller ID. He answered on his way to the lobby.

"Yeah, what's up?"

"Got some news." Moon's voice was as gruff as ever.

"Good or bad?"

"Bad. Brass said it's a no-go on the meeting."

Kole was disappointed to hear that. "You talked to him?"

"Naw. He wouldn't talk to me. Got that message from a runner."

"What did he say exactly?"

"You don't wanna know."

"Yeah, I do."

Moon sighed roughly. "He said, and I'm quoting the runner, 'Gimme the driver or the passenger, and let my boys run a train on the bitch, and we'll call it even.'"

Kole's peripheral vision was suddenly shaded with white, hot rage.

"You there?" Moon asked.

It took Kole another couple of seconds to unclench his jaws. "Yeah. I'm here."

"Hey, I know you said you had your reasons for helping this lady out. But are you sure you don't wanna let it go?"

"I'm sure."

"What about the passenger?" Moon asked, "the one who was wearing them beads? Can you hand him over?"

As much as Kole hated Brendon's insolent ass at the moment, he was Tariq's best friend, therefore he was an extension of Dana's family. If he allowed harm to come to him, he'd feel as if he'd failed Dana.

"Naw. They can't have the passenger either. Them niggas ain't finna get revenge on some people who didn't have nothing to do with that fool getting run over. Shank is the only person responsible for Shank's death," he said, for what felt like the hundredth time. "They gon' have to come to terms with that."

Moon grunted. "Alright. I hear ya. So what's the next move?"

"Not sure," Kole said.

"Brass is talking shit right now 'cause his son just got killed," Moon guessed. "I think if we give him a few days, he'll come around."

Kole doubted that but said, "Maybe."

"Everything still looking good around your place?" Moon asked. "Now that Brass knows you wanna talk to him about this, he might try something over there."

"You think he'll try to get at me?"

"That'd be stupid," Moon said.

"Colossally," Kole agreed.

"But MMG's filled with hotheads who don't think things through," Moon reminded him. "Look at all the dumb shit they doing."

Kole nodded. "True."

"You still don't want protection?"

Kole turned down his offer the first time, and he hadn't changed his mind. Protection meant armed men. Even though the soldiers in The Organization were a lot more disciplined than MMG's squad, they would shoot first if a threat presented itself. So far no one had been killed but Shank. Kole wanted to keep the body count there, rather than add to it.

"Nah, man. I'm good."

"Alright," Moon said. "If you change your mind, you know my number."

"For sure," Kole said and disconnected.

He tried not to dampen the mood when he returned to Dana and Tariq, but she sensed something was amiss when he sat down. Kole's jovial mood was gone, and he looked down at his plate, rather than make eye contact.

"What's wrong?" she asked. "Did you hear something about that guy you're trying to meet with?"

Kole was taken aback by how well she could read him. "Yeah, but we don't have to talk about it now."

Dana's heart sank. Her eyes were suddenly filled with concern. "I guess it wasn't good news."

Kole shook his head. "Brass won't meet with me. He still wants to get revenge."

The worry lines on Dana's forehead deepened. "On who?" She looked to her son and reached to hold his hand.

Kole nodded. "Him and Brendon."

"But – doesn't he know it was an accident?"

Dana was near tears. Kole hated that their dinner had been ruined by talk of murder and bloodlust.

"I don't know if he knows," he told her. "I wanna give him the benefit of the doubt. I don't think he'd let all of this go down, if he knew what really happened."

Dana brought a hand to her face and shook her head woefully. Her grip on Tariq's hand tightened.

"Don't worry," Kole told her. "I'm not gon' let nothing happen to y'all."

Dana wasn't sure why he'd go through so much to protect them, but she didn't question it. So far Kole had made her feel much safer than the police did. She hadn't gotten any updates from them, but somehow Kole received a message from the head of MMG.

"I'm sorry," she said, wiping her eyes. "I didn't mean to ruin dinner."

"It's not ruined," he said. "We haven't checked out the cheesecakes yet. I'm sure they got something over there that will put a smile on your face."

Dana followed his eyes to the bakery and grinned. "I think anything with caramel would do the trick."

Kole smiled. "A lot of their desserts have caramel. That's my favorite too..."

CHAPTER 37

WHEN THEY GOT home, the trio had a surprise waiting on their street. Kole was the first to spot them.

"We got visitors," he told Tariq and Dana. "Get down, away from the windows."

In the darkness of the car, Dana's eyes were wide with fright. "What? Who is it?"

"Maybe the same crew from last night," Kole said. His voice was as calm as it was when he spoke to their waitress at the restaurant. "I'm about to drive by them."

"Really?" Dana's voice was laced with dread. She wanted to see for herself, but she was mindful of Kole's warning. She remained hunkered down. She reached for Tariq's hand across the seat. He was as anxious as her.

Kole slowed to 15 miles per hour as he rolled towards his house. The unwelcomed car was parked directly in front of Dana's home. It was a Mustang – not the same vehicle from yesterday, but the dark faces huddled inside were definitely not from their neighborhood.

The Mustang's windows were down. Kole locked eyes with the driver for a moment before he continued on his way. The man looked to be in his late twenties. His stare was meant to be intimidating, but Kole smirked and muttered, "Bold sonofabitches," under his breath.

"What happened," Dana breathed.

"They're damned near in your driveway," Kole reported. "Look like they're waiting for you to get home."

Dana's fear kicked up another notch. Her voice shuddered when she asked, "Wh, what are we gonna do? Call the police?"

Kole had made it to his house by then. He jabbed the clicker, and his garage door rolled up slowly.

"What's the point in that?" he asked as he parked his Jeep.

Dana waited for the doors to close behind them before she felt safe enough to sit up. "What do you mean?" she asked. "We need to let them know they're back over here, don't we?"

Kole shook his head as he exited the vehicle. He didn't respond to her until all three of them had made it to the kitchen. His eyes were dark and focused, his voice still calm.

"Running them off won't do any good. They got a hundred more to replace them."

"Then what are we gonna do?" Dana wondered. Her heart hammered so hard, she felt her arms trembling.

"I'm gonna talk to them," Kole revealed.

"What?" Her eyebrows rose even higher. "What are you–"

"Trust me. I told you I'd take care of this."

"But, you can't – *Kole!*"

She gave chase when he turned and headed to the front room. She caught up with him before he made it to the door. She grabbed his arm, turning him around. The terror in her eyes broke his heart. It reminded him of her innocence and steeled his heart against the men threatening her.

"It's okay," he promised. "I'm just gonna talk."

"*They just shot up my house*," she pleaded. "You can't talk to them."

"I'm gonna talk to them," Kole said definitively. "I'm gonna try to, until they make it clear talking won't work. Then I'll do something different."

Dana was going crazy trying to wrap her mind around this man. With anyone else she would've described him as cocky to the point of *stupidity*. But there was more to Kole than met the eye. He was more than just a house-flipper, of that much she was sure.

Against better judgment, her hand fell away, and she allowed him to turn back to the front door.

Before he exited, he looked back and told her, "Step into the hallway for a second. When I leave, you can watch through the window if you want. If something goes wrong, lock the door, and I guess you can call the police."

"What?" Did he say *If something goes wrong*? Did that mean he had doubt about what was going to happen?

Before Dana could drill him again, Kole unlocked the door and looked back to find her still standing there. "Step into the hallway," he repeated.

Dana was so afraid, her eyes filled with tears. She grimaced. A whimper escaped her as she turned and hurried to the hallway. Tariq was there waiting for her. She took hold of his hand, which may have been shaking as badly as hers. They both listened intently as Kole opened the door and stepped out into the night.

CHAPTER 38

THE MUSTANG WAS parked facing Kole's house, so the occupants had plenty of time to prepare for him before he made it to their vehicle. That was fine. His goal was not to get the jump on them. He was armed, but he assumed they were too. If there was gunplay, he wouldn't stand a chance, but he was fairly sure it wouldn't come to that. MMG was filled with hotheads, but they weren't known to shoot civilians with no cause or provocation.

He strolled to the car casually, as if he was out for a moonlit promenade. He walked in the middle of the street. His footsteps on the pavement were the only sounds in the quiet neighborhood. He felt Dana and Tariq's eyes on his back. He felt the glare from the goons mean-mugging him. He counted three occupants in the Mustang. Smoke drifted from the back window. The driver kept his hands concealed as Kole approached on his side.

"What's going on?" he asked when he was close enough to speak without raising his voice.

Everyone in the car had dark skin. The front two wore black tees with black pants. The one in the back had a white shirt with black Dickies. These were MMG's colors. Now that he was closer, Kole recognized the smoke coming from the back as marijuana, rather than tobacco.

Fucking amateurs.

No one in The Organization would lose their focus by getting high before or during a stakeout, if that's what this was. Then again, no one in The Organization would pull such a silly intimidation tactic. If these clowns really wanted Dana or Tariq dead, they should've been waiting inside her home, with no vehicle in sight. That's the way Kole would've done it.

"Who the fuck is you?" the driver growled.

Kole peered into the vehicle but still couldn't see his hands. The passenger was unarmed, but he couldn't tell if the one in the back was packing.

"Neighborhood watch," he told them. "Y'all got something to do with this lady's house getting shot up last night?"

The driver looked to the one riding shotgun and chuckled. He looked back to Kole and told him, "Man, you better get the fuck outta here, 'less you want yo house shot up too."

"I don't want no trouble," Kole told them. "Just need you to move around – and deliver a message for me."

"Move around?"

"Nigga gon' call the *po-lice*," the one in the back predicted.

"How 'bout we fuck you up right now," the driver offered, "give you something to call the police for?"

"How about you deliver my message," Kole said. Before any of them could make the wrong decision, he told them, "Tell Brass he need to holler at me. My name's Kole. He know how to reach me. Tell him ain't shit going down with that lady or her son until he holler at me first. Think you can remember that?"

Kole watched the driver's eyes as he processed the information. Not only did the neighborhood watch guy know exactly what was going on, but he knew their OG's name, and he wasn't afraid to reveal his. He wasn't even worried that they knew where he lived. The driver didn't know how to respond before Kole began to back away from the car.

"You need to go deliver that message," Kole said. "It ain't safe for you over here."

The driver couldn't hide his confusion. He couldn't come up with a snappy comeback before Kole turned and headed back to his house.

Dana unlocked the door and retreated to the hallway as he climbed the porch. She rounded the corner when she heard him enter and secure the locks again, but Kole continued down the hallway without stopping to explain what had happened.

"I'll be back in a second," was all he said.

In his bedroom, Kole pulled his cellphone from his pocket and called his childhood friend. Moon answered after a couple of rings.

"You good, bro?"

"I'm good," Kole told him. He took a seat on the corner of his bed. "Got a little problem out by my house, though."

"What kind of problem?"

"Some of them MMG cats parked on my street, in front of that lady's house."

"No shit?"

"No shit."

"What they doing?"

"Flexin'," Kole said. "I guess they call theyself waiting for her to come back."

"Goddamn amateurs," Moon grunted. "She still with you, her and the boy?"

"Yeah. I'ma keep 'em here, till we get this resolved."

Moon blew out a slow breath but didn't question him this time.

"I talked to them," Kole informed him.

Moon chuckled. "Oh yeah?"

"Told them to tell Brass to get at me."

"Hmph. You think they gon' deliver the message?"

"Why wouldn't they?"

"I guess they know where you stay now... You okay with that?"

"You think they want an all-out war?"

156

"Shit. Guess we gon' find out."

"Can you get a crew ready? I might have to run these clowns off my street."

"For sho'. Want 'em to come in blazing."

"Naw," Kole said right away. "They just flexin', so let's hit 'em with the same. I need three cars; four deep. I'ma give 'em ten minutes to move around. I'll text you if they don't bounce. Tell the guys I don't want no shooting, unless they get shot at first."

"Bet," Moon said and disconnected.

Back in the living room, Dana and Tariq were as confused as they were anxious. The boy stood peeking through the curtains, while Dana sat on the couch rubbing her hands together. They both turned and stared at Kole when he appeared in the hallway.

"They still out there?" he asked Tariq.

"Yeah. They haven't moved."

"What happened?" Dana asked. *"Please, tell me what's going on."*

Kole took a seat across from her and told them about his conversation with the thugs. "If they're still there in ten minutes, I got some men coming through to escort them out."

Tariq and Dana were seated together now. Their eyes asked a million questions. Dana reiterated the first one, which still hadn't been answered thoroughly.

"Kole, what is going on? There's, it's something you're not telling me."

"I'll talk to you later," he said.

"Who's coming over here? Who's gonna chase them away."

"I'll talk to you later," he repeated. "I promise."

Dana wasn't sure if he was withholding the information because of Tariq, or if he planned to maintain his shroud of mystery *forever*, but she piped down and let things play through at his pace.

After ten minutes, he asked her, "They still out there?"

Dana had been standing at the window, her eyes on the Mustang. "Yeah. They're still there."

Kole texted his friend, waited for a response and then put his phone away. "My guys will be here in fifteen minutes," he told her.

Dana knew he wouldn't explain any further, so she didn't bother asking. The three of them remained in the front room while they waited, with Dana and Tariq checking the window at intervals. At the appointed time, it was Tariq who first saw the crew arrive.

"They here," he announced. "It's two, no, *three* cars..."

Dana rushed to the other side of the window to see for herself. Kole rose casually and peeked out of the second window.

Moon's men arrived in three nondescript vehicles. From that distance, Kole couldn't see who was inside, but he knew each car had two guys in the front and two in the back. He knew all of these men personally. No one from his side attempted to communicate with the occupants of the Mustang. As instructed, this move was only a show of force. The first car moved into position behind the Mustang. The other two pulled to a stop on the opposite side of the street, directly across from the target.

"Those are *your* guys?" Tariq asked excitedly.

Kole nodded without looking his way.

"*All of 'em?*"

Kole didn't respond this time.

Regardless of how many weapons the MMG crew had, they had to know they were surrounded and outgunned. Kole grinned, wishing he could hear the conversation inside the Mustang. He prayed none of them would do anything stupid that would lead to a bloodbath, and his prayers were answered.

He watched the Mustang's headlights come on when the driver started the car. The Mustang pulled away from the curb, and Moon's team got right behind it. Dana's eyes were disbelieving as all four cars rolled smoothly past Kole's house and out of sight.

She immediately looked to Kole, but he only gave her a nod before stepping away from the window and returning to his room.

CHAPTER 39

You think the teardrops in your eyes
Go unnoticed when I see you
I know a part of you despises me
For the grief I put you through
Shards of regret slice my memories
My past is punctuated with pain
What does a woman like you
See in a man like me?
What have I done to make you stay?

AT ELEVEN P.M., Kole emerged from his bedroom. He still had on the khakis he wore to the restaurant, but he'd replaced his button-down with a white tee. He checked on Dana and Tariq as he made his way down the hallway. Neither of them had changed or gotten ready for bed yet.

Tariq was at the bedroom window, looking to see if the MMG goons had returned. Kole didn't have a window in his room that faced their house, so he asked him, "Everything still cool?"

"Yes, sir," Tariq said, looking back at him. "They haven't come back."

Kole nodded and turned his attention to Dana, who was sitting at the desk with her laptop. He asked her, "You work tomorrow?"

"I called-in," she told him.

She didn't look sleepy, but Kole could tell the stress was taking a toll on her. For him, everything that had happened in the past two days was child's play. But for a *normal* person like Dana, it was enough to cause PTSD.

"I was thinking about cracking open that cheesecake," he said, referring to the caramel pecan turtle dessert they brought from the restaurant. "Want some?"

Dana was still full, but she sensed Kole was luring her to the kitchen for their long-awaited talk. Plus, who can turn down cheesecake?

She nodded and closed her laptop. "Yeah, that sounds good."

"I want some," Tariq said as she rose to her feet.

"We're not gonna eat the whole cake," Dana assured him. "I promise to save you at least one slice."

She offered him a half-smile. Tariq was smart enough to pick up on the cue that she and Kole wanted some time alone. He fished his cellphone from his pocket and took a seat on the bed.

"Okay. I'll get some later."

CHAPTER 40

IN THE KITCHEN, Kole brewed two cups of coffee with his Keurig to go along with the cheesecake. Dana didn't think she was hungry, but the cake was delicious, and it paired well with the coffee. They sat across from each other and ate quietly for the first few minutes. Kole broke the silence with a declaration that immediately made the mood awkward.

"I miss this."

She looked up at him with a frown. "You miss what?"

"Eating with you," he said. He stared into her eyes, as if he didn't feel any of the shame he should've felt.

Dana's heart shuddered. She fought to keep her eyes from tearing up. A full year had passed. She was over him. They were never in a real relationship anyway, just a few dates. One night of passion. So what if he broke up with her for no reason at all? It wasn't like she was in love with him. It might have felt like love, but it wasn't.

"I take it you don't feel the same," Kole said, noticing her discomfort.

Dana lowered her gaze. She thought they were going to talk about the men he called to chase the gangbangers off their street, not this shit.

Kole put his fork down and leaned back in his chair. "I'm going to tell you some things you'll probably find uncomfortable," he said. "Some of it has to do with what happened with me and you."

When he didn't speak for a few seconds, Dana looked up and realized he was waiting for her to respond. But she didn't know what to say.

"I'm not a bad person," Kole stated. "I used to be. I have done things that were *very bad*; some things I really don't want to share with you. If you'd like to remain unaware and simply let me do my thing and take care of your problem with MMG, I understand. That would probably be your best bet. But if you want to know who I am and why I make certain moves, I'll tell you."

Dana felt a chill roll down her body as she stared at him. She took a sip of coffee. The hot brew didn't make her feel any warmer. Her cup trembled visibly as she returned it to the table. It was a wonder she didn't spill any.

Finally she told him, "I wanna know."

Kole expected that response. Dana was fiercely independent. It was a trait he'd always admired. She wasn't the type of woman who would allow things to happen around her without wanting to be involved or at least fully understanding what was going on. He leaned forward and rested his massive forearms on the table. She did not back away from him.

"Have you ever heard of *The Organization*?" he asked.

She frowned and shook her head.

"That's good," Kole said. "Unlike the fool's harassing you, The Organization prefers to stay low-key. We'd like it if no one knew about us at all – other than the people we have direct dealings with."

Dana cleared her throat. "We?"

"Technically I'm not with them anymore," Kole revealed. "I founded The Organization twenty-five years ago, when I was sixteen. In the beginning, it was just me and my best friend. Today the group is 200 strong."

Dana's mind raced as she listened to him. "What – is it like a gang?"

"On the contrary," Kole said. "The Organization is the *anti-gang*. When me and my partner started it, we only wanted to defend ourselves from a group of knuckleheads in our neighborhood. They were Crips; I forget which set they were claiming. They had targeted us for recruitment, and we weren't having it. Me and my partner – I'm purposely withholding his name – got jumped plenty of times.

"After a while we learned the Crips didn't pick fights as often when we were together. They started even less shit if there was three of us. When we got our numbers up to five or six, they didn't mess with us at all."

He paused to see if she had any questions or comments, but she didn't. Kole took a sip of his coffee before continuing.

"I called our group *The Organization* for a couple of reasons," he said. "First off, we weren't a *gang*, and I didn't want to be associated with any gang. In my mind, even when our numbers were low, we were better than any gang in the city. We were on another level. Also I wanted us to be more organized. The mess that's been happening at your house, that's not organized. The men that came and chased them away tonight, that's what organized looks like. That's a tier above those MMG clowns. That's The Organization."

The hairs stood on Dana's arms as she stared at him. The man sitting across from her was the same Kole she'd always known, but he didn't *feel* the same. The way he talked about his group wasn't boastful, but there was no denying the pride he felt. She could feel the power radiating off his dark skin.

"As with most groups that start with humble beginnings," Kole went on, "we began to dabble in criminal activities. At first we would only target the Crips and other gangs who had been terrorizing our neighborhood. We'd rob the dope boys; shut their houses down for a little while. We'd actually take their crack and *destroy it*." Kole chuckled, thinking back on those early days.

"No telling how much money we could've made," he mused. "But selling crack was not something we wanted to be a part of. I'm not saying we were only doing good. We never considered ourselves Robin Hoods. But destroying our community with crack was not on our agenda.

"When we started selling drugs, it was only weed at first. Later, when we graduated to cocaine, we either sold it to the Mexicans or drove it uptown, to the white folks. It didn't take long to realize some of the dope we distributed was making it back to our street. So we stopped trying to protect the dopefiends in our neighborhood. If you can't beat 'em, join 'em, you know?"

Dana still didn't know how to respond to the things he was telling her. She was glad that question was rhetorical.

"Over the years," Kole stated, "as we settled into a groove and became more focused, we made peace with the gangs we'd been robbing. We didn't appreciate them, and they certainly didn't like us, but beef leads to bloodshed. And bloodshed put us on the radar. It's impossible to maintain anonymity when every gang in the city is out to get you. We'd done enough damage to let them know we weren't no punks, and we would handle our business if they stepped on our toes, and that was all we needed."

Dana noticed a hint of regret when Kole said, "I led The Organization for a long time. We were involved in every money-making venture you can imagine. With so much cash on the table, from time to time we had altercations with other factions. Each time they tried us, we laid 'em down."

Kole's jaws clenched. He stared at her so intently, Dana's pulse began to race.

"A body count is inevitable, when dealing with the type of people we were dealing with," he explained. "At the end of each incident, The Organization solidified their position at the top of the food chain. But there will always be those who want to test us. Every champ has to defend his title."

Dana noticed how he was going back and forth with his involvement in the group. Sometimes it was *them*. Other times he said *us*. She considered how easily he'd summoned a crew to her house that evening. All she saw him do was send a text message.

"I stepped down from my position for a few reasons," he told her. "First, I'd amassed enough personal wealth to live more than comfortably for a few lifetimes."

With each sentence, he filled in another piece of the puzzle. Dana had wondered about his home, his furniture, his *retired* status.

"Second," he said, "after getting away with the same thing for twenty-five years, I knew it was only a matter of time. At some point I *had* to get arrested or murdered. No one does the things I've done and lives happily ever after. It's not in the script. I got tired of tempting fate. I knew it was time to get out, while the getting was good."

Dana took a deep breath. She blew it out slowly.

Kole brought his hands together and sighed when he said, "The other reason I chose to step down is because of all the blood on my hands."

Dana wondered if he was aware that he started to rub his hands together when he said that.

"We never went out looking for trouble," he told her, "not since the early days. But it's impossible to operate on the scale we did without killing. People try to get over on you. There's always someone who thinks you're not what you say you are – or their crew is bigger and badder. Every time one of them bucked up, we had to lay 'em down."

Kole's deep voice almost slipped into a growl as he spoke.

"It don't matter if it was one of them, five or twenty. We laid 'em down," he repeated. *"All of 'em.* Every time."

Dana's breaths were hot and shallow. The man sitting across from her was the neighborly Kole she had always known. But now that he'd shed his sheep's clothing, she could see him for the wolf he really was. It was terrifying. Even if the wolf was on her side, he was still a wolf; big and black and bloody.

"The last one," Kole said, "was a cat fresh out of prison. He was a member of Tango Blast, which is a pretty big deal in Texas. He also had the backing of the Mexican Mafia. He did fifteen years and didn't get the scoop on what we'd been up to while he was locked up. He messed around and killed one of my soldiers over five pounds of weed."

Kole's voice changed again as he spoke. Dana could feel his pain and embarrassment over the loss.

"After the murder, he went home to his wife and kids, like nothing had happened," he told her. "That night they woke up to a house fire." Kole's eyes were dark and unblinking when he said, "When they ran outside, we laid 'em down. All of 'em."

Dana couldn't help but gasp. She brought her hands to her lap to hide her trembling fingers. Kole noticed the move but didn't acknowledge it. Dana could've sworn she saw the house fire burning in his wolf eyes. In the vacuum of silence, she faintly heard the family's screams.

"It had to be done," Kole said. "But that doesn't mean I don't have regrets. You'd have to be a monster not to. In the end, everyone who needed to get the message got it. Tango Blast didn't retaliate, and neither did the Mafia. They knew the guy got what was coming to him. As for his family, every gangster knows loved ones are fair game when it comes to war, especially if you're stupid enough to live with them. That's why I've been single all these years. Ain't got no kids either. The more people you love, the more opportunities your enemies have to hurt you."

Dana's eyes welled with tears. She wanted to ask how old the gangster's children were. Old enough to run into the barrage of gunfire they faced, or still in diapers, mowed down in their mother's arms? She wanted to know, but she didn't want to know. She took a deep breath. A tear rolled down her cheek.

"I had to leave it alone after that," Kole said, ignoring her grief. "That and the other reasons I gave you. I stepped down and let my partner take over. Thought I could retire, get me a house in a nice neighborhood, enjoy the fruits of my labor. Finally settle down. All of my money has blood on it, but I'm going to hell either way, so I might as well enjoy it."

Dana was no longer surprised by anything he said – not even his nonchalant attitude about going to hell. She felt like she was in a trance. She couldn't eat, drink or even rise from her seat. All she could do was sit there and listen, as she'd been doing for the past ten minutes.

"That was around the time I met you," Kole told her. "I knew I should've held off a while longer, before pursuing anything. But from the day you brought me that casserole, I was all messed up in the head. I thought you were beautiful, a hard worker, very independent... I don't think I've ever fallen in love before. As old as I am, I never let nothing like that happen. Couldn't. But you came along at a time when I thought I could let my guard down."

The flattery gave Dana conflicting emotions. This was still the wolf who had gunned down a whole family, but his voice softened when he spoke of her. His eyes did too.

"Problem was," Kole went on, "I still had some issues I hadn't accounted for. I thought I was ready for retirement, but I got pulled back in when I found out some people were gunning for me. Obviously they didn't get me. They got laid down, just like the others. But before they got what they got, they brought trouble all the way to my doorstep. They rolled by my house one night while you were here."

Dana's eyes widened. During the brief time she and Kole dated, danger was the last thing on her mind.

"I broke it off to protect you," he explained. "It's like I said, your enemies will use your loved ones against you. I know me and you were just starting out, but I cared enough about you to want you to keep on living. You have a good job, your own house, a son to look after. I would've went on a rampage for real if something happened to you because of me. I would've explained this to you at the time, but I would've had to tell you *everything*, and I wasn't ready to do that. I'm sorry that I hurt you."

For more than a year Dana had been wondering why he left her high and dry. Never in her wildest dreams did she imagine the answer was so dark and convoluted.

"For the record," Kole said, "a few months after I broke it off, I tried to come back to you. I came to your house and offered to mow your lawn. You basically told me to get the hell on."

Dana remembered that. Her exact words had been, *No I don't need your help. I been doing it just fine by myself!* But what did he expect? He broke up with her for no reason and didn't speak to her again for three months. He was crazy if he thought she'd accept him with open arms.

"You been awfully quiet," Kole noticed. "Is there anything you wanna say or ask me about any of this?"

Dana felt mentally drained. Her brain was moving a mile a minute, but none of the questions made it through the fog. She sighed and shook her head.

Surprised, Kole said, "Um, okay." He watched her for a second and then told her, "I know this is a lot to take in. I fully understand if you don't want anything to do with me. If you want to take Tariq to a hotel, or anywhere else, I can..."

Despite her misgivings, Dana finally understood what Kole had been telling her all along: Compared to the police, he was definitely in a better position to help with the trouble MMG was causing. She was worried about how far he'd go to keep her safe, but the gangbangers had shot up her house. They were out for blood. She'd be a fool to value their safety over her own.

She shook her head and looked the big, bad wolf in the eyes. "No," she muttered. "We can stay here."

Kole watched her for a while longer, wondering if she'd change her mind. Finally he stood and left her alone with her thoughts.

Tariq, who had been in the hallway eavesdropping, ducked back into the bedroom before Kole rounded the corner.

CHAPTER 41

A FEW MINUTES after one a.m., Kole was alerted to a disturbance in his guest bedroom. He hopped out of bed wearing black jeans with a black tee. Normally he would've gone to sleep wearing only boxers, but tonight he knew to be war ready. He wasn't formally at war with MMG, but running the goons off his block was the first skirmish. He expected some type of retaliation.

He ran into Dana and Tariq in the hallway. They had both dressed down for the night. Dana was not surprised by Kole's outfit or the pistol in his hand. He noticed both of his visitors were alarmed, their eyes wide with fright.

Before he could ask, Tariq announced, *"They finna get Brendon! They outside his apartment, yelling for him to come out!"*

Kole nodded. "They call the police yet?"

"Yeah," Tariq reported. "They're supposed to be on their way, but something might happen to him before they get there!"

The boy's concern was palpable. Regardless of how Kole personally felt about his nincompoop friend, he couldn't ignore the threat.

"Want me to go get him?"

Before Tariq could respond, Dana said, "You wanna go over there? Wha – what are you gonna do?"

"I'ma go get him," Kole decided.

He left them standing there and returned to his room. A minute later he emerged with his sneakers on, laced up tight. His pistol was now concealed. Dana and Tariq were waiting in the hallway.

Rather than question his decision, Dana urged him to, "Be careful," as Kole stormed past them.

CHAPTER 42

AT BRENDON'S APARTMENT, two squad cars were in the parking light with their lights flashing. As far as Kole could tell, the MMG goons had fled the scene. Two of the cops were downstairs, questioning the neighbors. Kole wasn't sure how much ruckus the gangsters had stirred up, but there was an abnormal amount of people outside for 1:30 on a Sunday night.

Kole encountered more residents on the stairway leading up to the apartment. When he got there, he spotted Brendon's aunt Victoria on the breezeway with the other two officers. Brendon stood in the doorway of their unit. He looked more spooked than he did when Kole snatched the beads off his neck earlier that day.

Everyone on the second floor had a reaction to Kole. The children looked up at him in awe. Some of the women had lust in their eyes. The men were mostly wary of his hulkish figure. The one thing they all had in common was reverence. Even if they didn't respect each other, they knew better than to disrespect this man.

Aunt Victoria looked past the cops, and her eyes flashed annoyance.

"What *you* want?"

The cops followed her gaze, unsure if this was something they needed to get involved with.

"I come for the boy," Kole said. His deep voice silenced the entire breezeway.

"What?" Victoria's face twisted up. "What you mean you *come for the boy*? Who the hell are you to be coming around here talking about *taking* somebody?"

With so many eyes on him, Kole remained civil. "Look, I'm sorry for raising my voice when I was here earlier. I wanna take Brendon to be with Dana and Tariq; to keep him safe. I think he should come."

One of the cops reached for his holster. He asked Victoria, "Is this one of the men who was here earlier?"

"Naw," she said with a sneer. "He ain't one of *them*."

Growing frustrated, Kole turned to Brendon. He looked him in the eyes and told him bluntly, "You ain't gotta go. I'm here to help you. Come with me, if you want to live."

The boy looked from his aunt to the cops, and then his eyes returned to the dark knight, who seemed more formidable than all of them. The weight of his decision had him trembling.

"I'ma, I wanna go," he told his aunt.

She couldn't believe it. "You wanna go with *him*?"

Brendon nodded. "Yeah. Can, can I?"

"I don't care," she said with a shrug of dismissal. "You eighteen years old. You don't need my permission. Lord knows I don't want them fools to come back here looking for you."

"Go get whatever you wanna bring," Kole told Brendon. "You got *one minute*."

The boy nodded and ducked inside the apartment.

"Y'all through talking to him?" Kole asked the cops while they waited.

They looked at each other and shrugged, much like the aunt had.

"Yeah. He can go if he wants," one of them said.

"Where you taking him?" the other asked, "in case we need to talk to him again."

"She can call his cellphone," Kole said, nodding towards Victoria.

An awkward silence ensued. Thankfully Brendon rushed out of the apartment thirty seconds later.

"Alright. I'm ready."

Kole turned and headed down the stairs with Brendon right behind him.

CHAPTER 43

I hold you close and kiss your lips
Those lips
So full
I can't resist
I taste your scents
Suckle your throat
Remove your clothes
Inhale your soul
Your body pressed so close to mine
The moonlight
Finds us intertwined
A kiss
One kiss
Your lips
Those hips
So full
So soft
So sweet
So deep

ON THE WAY home, Kole called Dana to let her know he had Brendon.

"Is everything okay?" she asked. "Did anyone get hurt over there?"

"No," Kole told her. "I'm not sure what the hell they were doing. Doesn't sound like they meant business, though. We'll talk more when we get back."

"Okay," Dana said and disconnected.

Kole looked over at the teen in his passenger seat. Brendon still hadn't accepted that he was safe. He looked around furtively, checking the side mirror, as if someone was following them.

"What the hell happened over there?" Kole asked him.

"I – I don't know," Brendon said.

He turned Kole's way but was unable to look him in the eyes.

"I guess when they got there," Brendon said, "they didn't know what apartment I was in. But they knew I lived somewhere in the complex. They started asking around, and somebody told them what building I was in. They was knocking on doors. They knocked on our door, but my auntie wouldn't answer. *I was scared*," he said, cringing. "I thought they was gon' kick the door in and kill me."

The panic in his voice made Kole's skin crawl. He glanced over and saw the boy was crying.

"You know it was MMG?" Kole asked.

"Ye, yeah. They said it. They was down there for like, thirty minutes. Throwing up signs. Threatening people. They, they knew my name. I didn't never..." His voice shuddered. "*I didn't do nothing to them*," he bawled.

It looked like the kid had learned his lesson, but Kole was still upset with him for bringing danger to Dana's home.

"That's what happens when you play around with gangs," he said coldly. "Some of these niggas out here will blow your brains out without a second thought."

"*I know*," Brendon cried. "I'm not gon' do that no more!"

"I thought you would've learned your lesson after you got shot," Kole said. "But you had those damn beads on earlier today. Maybe it'll take another incident before you *really* get the picture."

"No, no sir," Brendon said, shaking his head. "I got the picture now. I don't wanna be in no gang. I don't want nothing to do with them!"

Kole decided he believed him. "Good. 'Cause I don't wanna waste my time trying to save a fool who ain't worth saving."

Brendon was quiet as he considered that. "Where are you taking me?"

"To my place."

"That's where Tariq and Miss Dana at?"

Kole nodded.

"Yuh, you not scared they gon' come messing with you?"

Kole kept his eyes on the road and didn't respond.

"You think you can help us?" the boy asked. "I don't think they gon' leave us alone."

"I wouldn't have picked you up, if I didn't think I could help."

Brendon didn't have any more questions.

They were ten minutes away from their destination when Kole's cellphone rang. He answered when he saw it was Dana on the other line.

"Yeah."

"Where are you?" Her voice was anxious.

Kole was immediately on edge. "About ten minutes away. What's wrong?"

"Somebody came here," she reported. "They knocked on the door."

The hairs stood on Kole's arms. His voice didn't change when he asked her, "Did you get a good look at him?"

"I did," Dana said. "I watched him through the peephole. It wasn't the same guy that came to my house. He looked older. He had cornrows, some tats on his arms and neck, but I couldn't read them. He wasn't dressed like the others, but I think he was with them."

"Alright," Kole said. "Did you see what he was driving?"

"A black Cadillac. It looked new."

176

"Was he by hisself?"

"Yeah, I think so."

"Is he still there? You checked the windows?"

"Yeah. Tariq is checking now. He drove off after we didn't answer. Is it somebody you know?" she asked hopefully.

"Naw," Kole said. "Nobody visits me without an invite. Listen, I gotta make a quick detour. Gonna take me twenty minutes. Y'all alright? You got your piece?"

Dana wasn't hip to a lot of his slang, but she knew what he was talking about this time. "Yeah. I got it in my hand now."

"There's a shotgun in the hallway closet," Kole told her. "Give it to Tariq, if you think you need it. It's loaded. All he has to do is cock it and take it off safety."

"Okay. Do you, where are you going? Do you think we should leave?"

"If you feel the need to call the police, go ahead. But you already know how I feel about that."

"I know," Dana said. "That's why I called you first."

"Alright. I'll be there in a bit."

Kole disconnected and took the next freeway exit. He made a U-turn under the bridge and hopped back on the freeway in the opposite direction.

"Is everything alright?" Brendon asked him.

"Doesn't sound like it," Kole replied. "You'll be fine. I'ma drop you off somewhere different and then go get Dana and Tariq. We should be back in about an hour."

Brendon didn't appear to like that plan, but he wasn't in a position to complain. He piped down as his protector drove them to a hotel on the outskirts of town. Kole purchased two rooms across the hall from each other. He stayed long enough to walk Brendon to one of them before he hit the road again. He was only a few minutes away from home when Dana called again.

"He's back," she said, her voice more harried than the last time.

"What's he doing?" Kole asked, "just ringing the doorbell?"

177

"Yeah," she said, her voice hushed. "I looked at some of his tattoos this time. It says MMG on his right arm, in big, black letters. It's them. *They found us.*"

"I'm almost there," Kole told her. "I'll be there in two minutes."

"Do you want me to say anything to him? Do you think we should leave?" she asked again.

"I got us a couple of hotel rooms," Kole explained. "I already got Brendon squared away. I'm gonna pick you and Tariq up and take y'all over there. Get your stuff together, so we can leave when I get home."

"Okay," Dana breathed. "Are you almost here?"

"I'm in the neighborhood. Is he still on the porch?"

After a moment, she said, "No, he's walking away... He got back in his car, but he's not driving off."

Kole took a deep breath and blew hot fumes from his nostrils. "Go ahead and get packed, so y'all will be ready."

A year ago, or even a month ago, Dana couldn't imagine taking orders from Kole. Now she literally trusted him with her and her son's life. "Okay." She got off the phone and did as she was instructed.

When Kole rounded the corner onto his street, he was disgusted to see the black Cadillac parked in front of his home. He quickly debated how he wanted to approach the situation. MMG had been pulling amateur moves for the past two days, but things felt different this time.

He pulled to a stop directly behind the Cadillac, rather than pull into his garage. He left his headlights shining on the car as he exited his vehicle. Kole drew his pistol and brought it up in a shooting position as he flanked the side of the Caddy, much like the police would. When he reached the driver's side, he saw the window was rolled down. The occupant was familiar. Kole still considered him a threat, but not an immediate danger. He lowered his weapon as a sign of respect but kept his finger in the trigger guard, just in case.

Ice was an upper level member of MMG. Kole didn't know his real name, but he believed he was a close relative of Brass, the gang's leader. Kole hadn't spoken to Ice in years, because their factions rarely did business together. They weren't friends, but they weren't necessarily enemies. Both Kole and Ice were powerful enough to bloody a whole neighborhood with one phone call.

Ice had fair skin and no facial hair. He was as tall as Kole, but not as fit. With hazel eyes and a cleft chin, most women found him attractive. He appeared unfazed as Kole stepped into view. He brought both hands up and placed them on the steering wheel.

"I ain't packing," he announced, looking down at Kole's gun. "Ain't no need for that."

Kole didn't put his piece away, but as a concession, he removed his finger from the trigger guard. Ice seemed okay with that. He lowered his hands into his lap. His car was dimly lit, but Kole was pretty sure he didn't have a weapon there.

"Long time no see," Ice said, looking him up and down. "I heard you was out the game. This where you decided to settle down?"

He may not have meant that as a threat, but that's the way Kole perceived it. He didn't mince words when he responded.

"Fuck you doing over here?"

It had been a while since someone spoke to Ice that way. He couldn't hide his displeasure. "Didn't you tell somebody you wanted to holler at Brass?"

"Yeah," Kole acknowledged. "But you ain't him."

"No, I ain't. He sent me – to see if we can handle this with some diplomacy."

Kole was surprised anyone from MMG knew the meaning of the word.

"You called that crew earlier?" Ice asked, "to run my niggas out from round here?"

"Yo niggas ain't have no business over here," Kole said. His voice was dark and intimidating. His eyes were the same.

"That's *your* opinion," Ice said. "What you know about what's going on?"

"I know Shank ran out in the street and got his ass run over," Kole informed him. "And for some reason, y'all trying to take it out on the boy who was driving. Done shot up his mama's house for no reason."

Ice's eyes narrowed. "You know Shank was OG Brass' son? He was my nephew."

Kole did not know Ice and Brass were brothers. He said, "Don't change nothing."

"You know one of them dudes in the Explorer is down with Bideker?" Ice asked.

Kole shook his head. "No, he ain't. That punk's a wannabe. I talked to Popcorn myself. They ain't never heard of him."

"He had them black and yellow beads on," Ice replied. "All the homies saw it."

"I ain't say he wasn't a fool," Kole said. "He's that for sure. But he ain't banging Bideker. Even if he was, he wasn't the one driving."

Ice shrugged. "All he had to do was look over and tell his partner to run Shank over. He didn't have to be driving to do that."

"Yeah, maybe if the driver was an idiot like him," Kole conceded. "But he ain't. The boy that was driving is a good kid. Don't make nothing but A's and B's on his report cards. Don't smoke or drink or none of that. Damn sure ain't in no gang."

"Oh yeah? How you know that?"

"Them my neighbors," Kole explained. "I know that lady, and I know her son. They good people. This shit y'all putting them through..." He shook his head. "It ain't finna go down like that."

Ice frowned. "What's it to you?"

"What you mean? Y'all brought this shit to my street."

"But ain't nobody fucking with you. Why you care what happen to them people?"

"I'm supposed to let y'all murder my neighbors for no goddamn reason?"

"*You* say we ain't got no reason. Even if we is wrong, it ain't like you ain't never spilled no innocent blood."

In the back of his mind, Kole saw a house fire. He saw a family escape the inferno, only to be gunned down in the front yard by members of The Organization. He wished he could say that was the *only* innocent blood he had spilled.

"I did a lot of things in my past," Kole told him. "But we ain't talking about the past. We talking about what's happening right now."

"So what you saying?" Ice asked. "You gon' keep trying to protect this neighbor lady?"

"I ain't gon' let y'all murder her and her son for nothing," Kole confirmed.

Ice shook his head in disappointment. "What it's gon' take for you to back down?"

"I ain't backing down."

Ice stared at him for a few seconds and considered the weight of his next question. "You willing to go all the way with this?"

"All the way like what?" Kole asked. He too considered the consequences of his words. "You mean like *war*?"

Ice's brown eyes became steely. He clenched his teeth and then relaxed his features just as quickly. "You talking war with *you* or war with The Organization?"

Kole's blood ran ice cold. He'd left The Organization because he no longer had a taste for blood. He'd vowed to never kill again, unless it was self defense. If MMG launched a full-scale war against them, there would be plenty of body bags.

Kole wanted to believe his decision was based on righteousness, but if there was one person he always kept it real with, it was himself. He'd fallen in love with Dana a year ago.

Despite the way she treated him since then, his feelings for her had never changed.

He told Ice, "Me and The Organization are one in the same. You know that."

Ice sighed. "That's a big decision. I hope you know what you're doing."

"Y'all the ones doing it," Kole snapped. "This shit can be over right now, if you go home and leave these people alone."

"You got 'em under your protection?" Ice surmised.

Kole didn't respond to that.

Ice looked past him, at his front door and asked, "Is they in your house right now?"

"You'll have to kill me to find out."

Kole's pulse quickened. He considered taking care of this particular problem right then – with two to the body and one to the head. Ice had solidified his place as a new ENEMY. Every general knows you don't leave an enemy behind on the battlefield. You don't let them retreat and regroup.

But Kole held out hope that cooler heads would prevail once Ice delivered the message to his camp. Surely Brass would decide a war wasn't worth it. Both sides had too much to lose and virtually nothing to gain.

Kole raised his gun when Ice raised his arm, but it was only to put his car in gear. The MMG chief drove away slowly without another word.

CHAPTER 44

KOLE PULLED INTO his garage and didn't waste time explaining the situation to Dana and Tariq. They had both been watching him and Ice through the front windows. Kole told them they'd have to wait until they were on the road before he could give them an update. If MMG made the foolish decision to attack Kole at his home, he figured he had at least thirty minutes before they returned. That was enough time to pack a bag for himself and grab as many weapons as he thought he'd need before returning to his Jeep.

As they drove to the hotel, Kole relayed the conversation between him and Ice. When he was done, Dana couldn't hide her frustration.

"Are they serious? They don't even care that it was an accident?"

"Not right now they don't," Kole told her. "But he just got killed a couple of days ago. Wound is still fresh. And I haven't talked to Brass directly. If I can get through to him, he can make all of this go away in an instant."

"Are you really going to war with them?" Dana watched his face in the rearview mirror, afraid to hear the answer.

"I don't think it'll come to that," Kole said.

"But things have already gone so far," she pressed. "People could get hurt. Why are you doing all of this for us?"

Kole didn't respond to her question right away. He certainly wasn't going to tell her he loved her. "It's the right thing to do," he offered. "Maybe I need a little good karma coming my way."

Dana didn't appear to buy that, but her eyes were grateful now. "Thank you," she told him. "This is..." She shook her head. "I can't imagine anyone else helping us like this."

"We're the only black families on the block," Kole said, hoping to lighten the mood. "We gotta stick together, right?"

His joke fell on deaf ears. Not even Tariq, who was the goofiest of the three, felt comfortable enough to crack a smile.

CHAPTER 45

WHEN THEY GOT to the hotel, Brendon was ecstatic to see that Kole had not left him there to fend for himself. Kole saw the chemistry between the best friends when Brendon and Tariq hooked up and started chatting and even laughing, despite their circumstances.

The rooms Kole purchased were identical; with large bedrooms that had two beds. In the front room, the sofa had a pull-out bed. Kole stayed with the group for a while, before fatigue started to get the best of him. By then it was nearly three a.m. None of them had slept yet.

Before Kole retreated to his room, he told Dana, "My room's got as much space as this one. If you wanna use one of the beds, I'll sleep on the couch."

Dana looked back at her son and Brendon. They had already claimed the two beds. She would've taken Kole up on his offer, but she didn't want Tariq to get the wrong idea about them. Plus her sofa bed was adequate.

"No. I'll stay here with the boys," she told him.

Kole nodded. He went to the front room and pulled the bed out for her before he left.

"If you need anything, you can call my room or just come over and knock," he told her.

Dana thanked him again and secured the locks on the door when he was gone.

CHAPTER
46

KOLE DID NOT expect the worst when he heard a knock on his door less than an hour later. The knock didn't sound urgent. It was more of a light rapping, as if the visitor didn't want to wake him and wouldn't mind if he didn't answer.

Kole had been asleep, but he always slept with one eye open when he was at war. He left his bed and answered the door wearing black Dickies with a clean, white tee. If Dana was curious about his *pajamas*, she didn't mention it. She wore an oversized tee-shirt with leggings.

On the surface, there was nothing sexy about her outfit. But Kole's eyes dilated as he looked her up and down. She was barefoot, her hair pulled back in a ponytail. Her lips were full and luscious. The swell of her breasts were the only curves the tee-shirt highlighted, but that, along with her bare feet, was enough to raise Kole's temperature.

"Everything alright?" he asked.

Dana wore her uncertainty awkwardly. It appeared she had to force herself to look him in the eyes. "The boys are still up, a little rowdy," she said. "I don't think I'm gonna get much sleep in there."

"Oh, well you know my offer's still open," he told her.

He took a step back, and she entered his room quietly.

"I was using one of the beds," he told her. "But the other one is fresh. You can have that one, and I'll take the couch."

"You don't have to sleep on the couch," she said.

She stepped past him, heading for the bedroom. Kole turned off the light in the living room before following her. There were no lights on in the bedroom, but they were eight stories up, so Kole didn't have the curtains fully closed. There was a sparse amount of illumination from the lamps outside. He was confused when Dana approached the beds and then stood between them, as if she couldn't tell which one had been used.

"I was sleeping over here," he said. "You can have that one."

Dana still seemed hesitant. It was too dark to read her features. Kole took a seat on his bed and she approached the other one. He lay back on his pillows wondering if she was going to stand there all night. Dana surprised him by sitting on his bed. She didn't speak as she reclined next to him.

Kole was by no means a novice when it came to women, but his body grew tense. He stared up at the ceiling, wondering if he should say or do something.

Dana was the first to speak. Her voice was soft – not necessarily sultry, but it sounded as sweet as honey to him.

"Why are you doing this for us?"

Kole thought he'd sufficiently avoided the question on the way to the hotel. He closed his eyes and sighed softly.

"Because it's the right thing to do."

He felt her shift positions. He opened his eyes and looked her way. She was lying on her side now, facing him. It had been so long since they'd been in this position, Kole didn't know how to react. He was glad he'd taken the time to bathe. He would've felt even more unsure of himself if he had B.O. to worry about.

Dana's gaze was unflinching. Despite the darkness, the power of her stare was unnerving.

She said, "From what you told me about your lifestyle, doing the right thing is not high on your list of priorities."

Tired of feeling like she had the upper hand, Kole rolled to his side and faced her fully. His dark skin was nearly one with the darkness, but Dana could feel every bit of him.

"I told you I retired," he said.

"Just because you retired doesn't mean you have to run around saving people."

"I'm not running around saving people," Kole stated. "I'm trying to help a neighbor; someone I consider a friend."

"You consider me a friend?"

He nodded. "I do."

"After the way I've been treating you for the past year..."

"I understand why you treated me that way. I deserved it, after what I did to you."

"So, is this your way of trying to make it up to me? Because you did that already. You told me why you broke it off. That's enough."

"I'm not sure what you want me to say."

She closed her eyes. When she opened them, Kole thought her orbs were glistening, possibly with tears, but he couldn't be sure. Rather than speak again, she took a deep breath and slowly moved towards him. Kole sensed she was about to kiss him, but he was blown away when their lips actually touched. She gently sucked his bottom lip and sighed. Her breath on his mouth was warm and sweet.

Dana's heart thumped so hard, she thought she felt the bed shaking. She kissed him again before Kole reciprocated. He kissed her back and brought a hand to her side. His touch made her shudder involuntarily. She sucked air between her teeth as his paw caressed her tenderly, sending tingles through her rib cage. He watched her reaction as he cupped the side of her breast. His hand then moved down until it rested on her hip.

Dana opened her eyes. Kole's eyes were darker than the darkest shadows in the room. She felt the heat and hunger radiating off him. She kissed him again and whispered, "Tell me why you're doing this for us."

He swallowed and moistened his lips. She kissed him again, urging his tongue to make an appearance. She pushed his shoulder back and moved a leg over him in one smooth motion. Kole rolled to his back with her straddling him.

He looked up at her and asked, "Why? Why do you keep asking?"

Dana sat up and rested both hands on his stomach. She slipped her hands under his tee-shirt and pushed it up, revealing a toned six pack. His muscles hardened as her hands moved upwards, towards his chest.

"*Jesus,*" she whispered when she had one of his pectorals in each hand.

Kole was built like a comic book hero. His upper body was massive, every muscle toned and pronounced. She felt his powerful heart thudding beneath her hands. His nostrils flared as he filled his lungs. Even his inhalation was strong enough to make Dana feel like she was riding a wave.

"You said you didn't want to break up with me," she recalled. A stream of heat flowed down her body as she massaged his chest.

Kole said, "I didn't."

"I was falling in love with you," Dana revealed. "You broke my heart."

From this position, the scant light caught her face, and Kole could see she was crying. Her tears pierced his soul. Everything he had ever done to her was either to put a smile on her face or protect her.

"I'm sorry. That wasn't my intent."

"Is that why you're helping us? Is this your way of trying to make it right?" she asked again.

Dana sensed he wouldn't tell her that he was falling in love with her too, but she desperately wanted to hear it. A year ago she had poured her heart into their burgeoning relationship. Although his reason for pushing her away was adequate, appropriate even, she needed to know that it was hard for him too.

"I'm helping you because I care about you," he said. "I don't want anyone to ever harm you. If I have to go to war to keep you safe, then I'll go to war."

Dana was never the type of woman who needed or wanted a man to fight for her, but Kole's declaration touched her, all the way to the core. She reached to wipe the tears from her eyes, and then she scooted down, towards his thighs. From the moment she straddled him, she had felt how badly he wanted her. She knew he had to be uncomfortable, because of the pants he chose to sleep in.

She unfastened the Dickies and slowly pulled the zipper down. Kole's chest continued to rise and fall rhythmically as he watched her. His manhood was pinned next to his thigh. She reached with one soft hand and freed it. Kole's eyes narrowed. She pulled his boxers down, until his piece was totally uninhibited.

Dana had seen his manhood before, over a year ago. Despite knowing what to expect, she couldn't help but marvel at the length and width. She caressed it with both hands as she stared down at him. Kole's breathing became audible. She squeezed his piece and brought his pre-cum to the tip. She couldn't see it, but she ran her thumb over the top and felt it. She imagined what it tasted like.

He began to throb in her hands as she fondled him. The warmth flowing down Dana's body was an inferno now. The heat settled between her legs and was drowned in a river of her essence.

"Do you have a condom?" she breathed.

Dana realized she should've asked sooner when he shook his head. Never had she been more disappointed by that response. She wanted him so badly, she could almost feel him penetrating her oasis. She was so desperate for him, she nearly shed another tear.

But this wasn't all about her. She had brought Kole to an optimal state of arousal. She would feel guilty if she did not give him a release.

"I'll be right back." She crawled off of him and left the bed.

Kole looked after her curiously as she slipped into the bathroom. She turned the lights on and scanned the sink until she found one of the complimentary bottles of lotion the hotel left for its guests. She snagged a washcloth before returning to her dark knight.

She did not turn off the bathroom light and could see him more clearly now. The sight of his erection pointing skyward gave her pause. She stopped to stare at it, without realizing she had done so. Her clitoris pulsated, causing her legs to wobble slightly when she got moving again.

Kole didn't speak as she climbed back into bed, straddling his thighs again. Initially he scoffed at the idea of a hand-job, as he watched her squirt lotion on her palm. But the moment she wrapped her hand around his meat, he realized the pleasure she produced was much more than satisfactory.

Dana watched his expression as she caressed him, stroking him all the way down and all the way up. His body responded when she used both hands. His reaction was even stronger when she concentrated her efforts on the sensitive spot at the base of the head. Kole's stomach tightened. He began to thrust his hips, flowing with her rhythm. After a couple of minutes, he started to grunt and mutter expletives that made Dana's clitoris throb even harder.

"*Damn.*"

"*Shit.*"

"*Shiiiit.*"

She knew he was close when his whole body tensed. She stroked faster, until the cum exploded from his shaft with the force of a volcano. Dana's eyes widened as she watched the beauty of his biology in action.

Oh wow.

His explosion was more potent and copious than she expected. She felt the heat of the ropy rivulets flowing over her hands. She continued to please him until he was completely spent – until his toes uncurled, and his head fell back on his pillows.

Sweat glistened on his forehead. The rise and fall of his chest gradually ebbed as she cleaned him with the washcloth.

She had to return to the bathroom for a slightly bigger towel, half of which she dampened and applied a little hand soap, before she got him sufficiently clean.

When she returned to the bed a third time, she saw contentment in Kole's eyes. He pulled the sheet back and made room for her to snuggle against his hot body. When she was settled, he rolled to his side and draped a protective arm around her.

Despite all that had transpired and the uncertainty of what tomorrow would bring, Dana didn't think she had ever felt more safe.

PART FIVE
SMOKING THAT WET

CHAPTER 47

THE NEXT MORNING, Kole felt fully rested when he sat up in bed at nine a.m. It was Monday, the start of the work week for most. Kole was retired, but he also had business to attend to.

He didn't wake Dana when he left the bed, but she was up when he exited the bathroom after his shower. The sight of him with nothing but a towel draped around his waist jolted her like a shot of espresso. Dana was even more impressed when he shed the towel and crossed the room to where he'd left his suitcase.

She felt a little guilty as she watched him fish out a clean pair of boxers, because Kole hadn't acknowledged her. It was almost like she was peeking through someone's window. Back when they were dating, she didn't notice how perfect his ass was. And his manhood, even in a flaccid state, was remarkable.

He pulled on a pair of jeans and a tee-shirt before looking her way.

"How'd you sleep?"

"I slept good," she told him. "Are you leaving?"

"Yeah. I gotta check on a few things." He took a seat in one of the chairs and bent to put his sneakers on.

Kole had never been forthcoming with whatever he was doing on the streets, but Dana didn't see any harm in asking.

"What are you gonna do?"

"Nothing," he promised her. "Just ask a few questions; see what I can find out about what we're up against. I'm not sure how big MMG has gotten over the years. They seem unorganized, but I wanna make sure before we do anything drastic."

Dana could only imagine what *drastic* steps he might take.

"Do you think you can take care of this with no violence?"

Kole had been wondering the same thing. He shrugged.

Dana waited, hoping for more of a response. She didn't get one.

When he got his shoes laced up, Kole stood and returned to his suitcase. He tucked a pistol inside a holster that was concealed on the small of his back.

She wished he didn't feel the need to tote the gun. The last thing she wanted was for him to get arrested for something he did while protecting her. But she knew Kole was careful. He had led a criminal organization for decades and had never made any mistakes that landed him in prison.

Even still, Dana had a sinking feeling in her gut when she rose from the bed and followed him to the front room. Kole gave her his keycard and told her, "I'll call you when I'm on my way back. Don't leave the hotel. You can order room service for breakfast. If I'm not back for lunch, order that too. If there's an emergency, you got my number."

"Wait," she called as he approached the door.

When he turned, she hurried to give him a kiss before he left. "Please be careful."

Kole nodded and exited the room without another word.

CHAPTER
48

ON THE SOUTH side, he met up with Moon, who didn't mind meeting with him at any hour. He and Kole had been friends since they were teenagers. There was no telling how many times Kole had saved his ass over the years.

The men greeted each other before taking a seat at the bar in the empty club. The only other occupant was a massive goon named Hootie, who served as a security guard and bouncer.

"How are things going with your little problem?" Moon asked. He sat with his forearms on the bar.

Kole sat on a stool facing him. He told his friend about the latest developments. He wasn't surprised that Moon had new information of his own.

"I talked to that dude Ice," he informed Kole. "He must've come over here before he headed your way."

"Yeah?" Kole knew the gangster was ballsy because of the way Ice sat in front of his house last night and didn't flinch when Kole trained his pistol on him. "Why you ain't tell me?"

"Shit, I didn't think he was headed to your place." Moon's bald head looked like a giant Milk Dud. "When he showed up, I thought he was gon' tell me Brass agreed to the sit-down. Instead he come up in here asking questions; trying to figure out why you sticking your neck out for that neighbor lady. I told him to move around with that shit, and holler at me when Brass wanna talk. He left, and I thought that was the end of it."

"You know that's Brass' brother?" Kole asked him.

Moon's eyes brightened. "Oh. So Shank is Ice's nephew. Okay," he said, nodding. "Now this is starting to make sense. Say, I got some more information about that accident..."

"What'd you hear?" Kole asked.

"Word on the street is Shank was smoking that wet when he got killed," Moon stated. "He been fucking with it for the past few months. They say he got so zooted one time, he forgot how to walk for a couple of days. He was laid up in the hospital shitting on hisself."

Kole couldn't hide his surprise. "*What?*"

Back in the day, *wet* was a cigarette or joint soaked in PCP. With the decline of PCP, users found they could get a similar high by dipping the cigarette in embalming fluid. The high was psychedelic, like LSD. But with embalming fluid, it was a lot less predictable. Nearly every time the Overbrook Meadows' police encountered a nude, irrational junkie roaming the streets, wet was the culprit.

"They say his crew was trying to get him to calm down, right before he ran out in the street," Moon reported. "But they couldn't get through to him."

Kole's mouth hung open as he listened to him. "You mean to tell me them niggas know Shank got hisself killed, and they still wanna start shit with the boy that was driving and Bideker Street?"

"I heard Brass is in denial," Moon told him. "He ain't trying to hear that his boy was a crazy-ass dopefiend. When they told him about the passenger wearing them beads, he latched onto that shit. Honestly, at this point I think they trying to save face."

"This some *bullshit*," Kole growled. "They gon' save face by killing folks who didn't do nothing?"

"I can't say for sure if that's where Brass' head's at," Moon replied. "This is just what the streets is saying."

Kole shook his head, growing angrier by the second. "How he gon' be the leader of *a whole fucking gang* and be making dumb ass moves like this?"

"He hurt," Moon said. "He loved that boy. Brass got two other kids. They both girls. Shank was his only son."

"I don't give a fuck about that sentimental shit!" Kole belted.

Moon chuckled.

"The truth is the *truth*," Kole went on. "I been saying since day one that *fool got hisself killed*. Now you telling me they been knowing it, but they still wanna pull this ho shit. I had some respect for Brass. Now I don't know what to think about that nigga."

"So what's next?" Moon asked. "Want me to put out word that we still wanna holler at him?"

"Naw," Kole said, shaking his head. "We tried that. I looked Ice dead in his eyes last night and told him what the deal was. Brass got till sundown to get in touch with me. If they wanna be ignorant, I think we need to show 'em how real gangstas get down."

"That's the Kole I know," Moon said, grinning. "What you got in mind?"

"Take a ride with me," Kole told him. "Got somebody I wanna talk to."

CHAPTER 49

ON BIDEKER STREET, Kole did not receive an icy reception like he did the day before. The two soldiers posted on Popcorn's porch remembered him, and they knew Moon from his night club. One of them ducked inside to let the boss know he had visitors. The soldier reappeared a moment later and invited them inside.

Rather than the den, the leader of the Bideker set received his guests in the kitchen, where he was enjoying a breakfast so greasy, Kole could see the diabetes glistening on his lips.

Popcorn sent his wife away, telling her, "Keep them kids outta here while we talking." He turned his attention to Kole and Moon and asked, "Y'all want something to eat?"

"Not gon' be here that long," Kole said. "Just got a couple of questions."

"What's up?" Popcorn asked, not bothering to swallow the food in his mouth before speaking.

"You having any more problems with MMG?" Kole wanted to know.

"Not really," Popcorn said with a sneer. "They came to the Rainbow talking shit last night. Caught a couple of the homies slipping, but they didn't shoot nobody."

Rainbow was a corner store where a lot of thugs in the area hung out and sold rocks. Graffiti on the side of the building designated it Bideker Boys territory.

"Thought you was supposed to be taking care of them," Popcorn said to Kole. "The only reason we haven't rode on them niggas is 'cause you told us to chill."

Yeah, that and you'll get slaughtered if you try to stand up to MMG, Kole thought. "I'm working on it," he said. "That's what I came over here for. I wanna hit some of their dope spots tonight. Since you and MMG operate in the same areas, I was hoping you could have somebody point 'em out."

Popcorn frowned. That sounded a lot like snitching. But Kole wasn't the police, so maybe it would be alright. He looked away from them and shouted down the hall.

"Charlotte!"

A few seconds later his wife stepped into the kitchen. She was a voluptuous woman, a Little Debbie or two away from being fat like her husband.

"What's up?"

"Where Half-Dead at?" Popcorn asked her.

"He in the den."

"Go get him."

She frowned. "Why you didn't just call him yourself?"

"Bitch, go get him!"

Up until that moment, Kole's opinion of Popcorn was neutral. But hearing him speak to his wife that way left a bad taste in his mouth.

Charlotte left the kitchen with a roll of her eyes. Thirty seconds later a wounded warrior took her place. Kole didn't know Half-Dead, but his moniker was appropriate. At some point in his life, the banger had taken a shotgun blast to the left side of his face. Kole supposed the man was lucky to have survived, but *damn*. It took a good deal of discipline to look him in his good eye without grimacing.

"These men wanna know where some of MMG's dope spots are," Popcorn told him. "Roll with 'em and point 'em out."

"Alright," Half-Dead said without questioning him. He turned, heading for the front door. He looked back and said, "Come on."

CHAPTER 50

OVER THE NEXT couple of hours, Popcorn's henchman pointed out more than two dozen MMG dope houses on the south, east and west side of the city. He didn't ask Kole or Moon why they needed the addresses. When they dropped him off, Kole gave him a few hundred bucks and an ominous warning.

"Y'all niggas might wanna stay off the streets tonight."

Kole hadn't informed his friend of his plan, so Moon was eager to hear it as they returned to the club.

"Tonight, I wanna shut down as many of those spots as possible," Kole told him.

"Shutdown how?" Moon asked, knowing that could entail anything from torching the houses to murdering everyone inside.

"Robbing them," Kole clarified. "Duct tape and zip ties."

"What about the spoils?" his friend asked, referring to the weapons and drugs they'd recover. "We keeping that, or holding it for a bargaining chip?"

"I was thinking we'd hold on to it, see how bad Brass wants it back."

Moon nodded. "If you wanna get Brass' attention, that'll work. I'll get the crew ready. What time you talking?"

"Around midnight," Kole said, knowing each house would be fully stocked with inventory at that hour.

203

"You trying to do this without killing nobody?"

"That's my preference. But if it come down to it, we gotta do what we gotta do."

As he spoke, a dark pulse of electricity flowed through Kole's body.

Moon knew about his vow to never take another life. He also knew Brass' dealers would be (or *should be*) ready to defend themselves against a robbery.

"You wanna get some lunch?"

It was after one p.m. Kole wanted to get back to the hotel to check on Dana, but neither her nor Tariq had called, so he figured everything was okay.

"Yeah, let's do that," he told his friend.

CHAPTER 51

KOLE HADN'T RETURNED by five. Dana was growing restless at the hotel. The urge to call and check on him had been nagging her fiercely. The boys had their phones and PlayStation, so they were content with being confined in the room. But Dana couldn't stop her mind from racing as she tried to pass the time.

She'd spent most of the day in the boy's room. She ducked into Kole's room a few times, thinking she needed respite from their incessant chatter. But she found no peace there. Even though they were right across the hall, she worried she might fall asleep and not be there for Tariq if something went wrong.

She didn't realize she was in a daze as she stared at the television, until Tariq called her a second time. He took a seat next to her.

"Mama."

"Hmm?" She turned and blinked at him curiously.

"What's wrong?" he asked. "You daydreaming?"

"Yeah, I guess so."

"You alright?" he asked, his expression concerned.

"Yeah," she said and forced a grin. "What's up? Everything okay?"

"Yeah." He leaned back on the sofa and sighed. "What's, um, what's up with you and Kole? Y'all back together?"

Dana looked past him to the bedroom. The door was open, and she could hear Brendon speaking on the headset he used to play games. She was sure he couldn't hear them.

She didn't think Tariq had noticed that she spent the night in Kole's room, because he was asleep when she returned to their room in the morning. She guessed he had gotten up in the middle of the night to check on her.

"No," she said. Then, "I don't think so."

"You still like him?" Tariq asked. He answered the question before she could reply. "I saw the way y'all were talking when we went to the Cheesecake Factory. Since then, y'all seem pretty close."

Dana wasn't sure how to respond. She knew he didn't like Kole because of what happened when they were dating.

"I heard y'all, the other day," he revealed.

Dana frowned. "When?"

"When we were at his house. He was telling you about that stuff he used to do. *The Organization*." Tariq didn't look too sheepish about eavesdropping. "I heard what he said, about why he had to break up with you back then."

Dana was upset with him for snooping, but she was more interested in knowing how he felt about what he'd heard.

"I understand why he did what he did," Tariq continued. "Do you? Did you forgive him?"

Dana continued to frown as she shook her head. "I don't know, Tariq. I don't know how I feel about any of that."

"I was just gonna say that if y'all *do* get back together—"

Someone knocked on the door. Dana's heart raced as she turned towards it. In her mind, it could've been anyone from housekeeping to an MMG hitman.

But a deep voice announced, "It's Kole," and her dread was replaced with relief and (though she wouldn't admit it) elation.

She left the couch and opened the door. Kole stood tall and dark on the other side. Dana's body heated when he stared into her eyes. She stepped aside to let him in, but he did not enter the room.

Kole looked around, locked eyes with Tariq for a moment and then asked Dana, "Everything good?"

She nodded. "Yeah, we're fine. How about you?"

"Y'all eat lunch already?" he asked, ignoring her question.

"Yeah, we're fine," she breathed.

He nodded. "Alright. I'll be over here for a while," he said, gesturing towards the other room. "You got the keycard?"

"Yeah." Dana retrieved it from the dining table.

She gave it to him, and Kole stepped across the hall and unlocked the door. Dana told Tariq, "I'll be back," before she followed him.

Kole's room was chilly and quiet. It was completely clutter free, in stark contrast to the mess the boys were making. Dana's heart thudded when she closed the door, and Kole turned to face her.

"Are you okay?" she asked again. "Did you – any news yet?"

"Yeah. I learned some things."

He stepped to the couch and took a seat. Dana was increasingly anxious as she sat next to him.

He told her about Shank's drug use. Dana had the same questions he had, wondering why the gang was pursuing this if they knew the truth about the accident.

"So they're gonna keep pushing it?" she asked. She was losing hope that they'd ever resolve this. She wasn't sure how many more personal days she could take off work before they asked her to document whatever problems she was having.

"I got some stuff to do tonight," Kole informed her. "By tomorrow, I'm sure Brass will wanna talk to me."

Dana's heart shuddered. She knew he wouldn't tell her what his plans were. She didn't want him to leave again, but if his actions brought them closer to a resolution, she wouldn't complain.

"What time are you leaving?"

"At eleven." His tone was even, his expression calm. "Y'all wanna go out for dinner in a couple of hours?"

Dana checked the clock. Kole would be with them for six hours before he embarked on his mission tonight. She was grateful for every minute. She couldn't explain why tears glistened in her eyes as she nodded.

"Yeah. That, that would be nice."

CHAPTER 52

We congregate in this parking lot
Though unfamiliar cars are creeping near
If I die crumpled on this block
Then I'm immortal
So there's no fear
Tinted Crown Vics are slow and mean
When their windows spit
Our bodies are lifted
Sometimes slugs go through smooth and clean
We still flash signs with missing digits
Sometimes I contemplate my fate
Bullets that miss stay on my mind
Fuck all the fame
I just want wealth
But fame and wealth are intertwined

AT ELEVEN P.M., Kole was ready to leave the hotel. Dana had sat on the couch in the front room while he dressed entirely in black. When he emerged from the bedroom, she thought he looked as dark and ominous as a nighttime tornado. His features were hard and unreadable, in stark contrast to the Kole who took her and the boys to Dave and Buster's a few hours ago. That Kole had smiled as he chatted with everyone. He even challenged the boys to a game of hoops in the arcade room.

This new Kole was determined and formidable. He had told Dana that he stepped down from his role in The Organization because he didn't want any more blood on his hands. She feared he'd backslide tonight, and she'd be somewhat responsible.

Part of her wanted to tell him to back off. She'd rather take her chances with the police, than allow anything to happen to Kole. If it wasn't for Tariq, she would've gone that route. She wasn't too concerned about her own fate, but she couldn't allow her son to become another homicide statistic if it was in her power to prevent it. If that meant siccing Kole on her adversaries, then so be it.

He paused in the front room and turned to face her. Dana didn't bother asking what his intentions were. Not only did she not want to know, but she knew he wouldn't tell her. She did ask him, "Do you know when you'll be back?" as she rose to her feet. But Kole didn't have an answer for that either. He shook his head.

Dana approached him quietly and embraced him fully. Kole wrapped his strong arms around her and squeezed her close to his chest. When they separated, he didn't speak before turning and exiting the room.

CHAPTER 53

AT THE MOONLIGHT, Kole was pleased to see over a dozen cars in the parking lot. The club wasn't open on Monday nights. He knew all of the vehicles were there for the business at hand. Kole surveyed the cars as he slowly drove past them. They all appeared to be in good shape; good tires, good tags. He knew the men had already checked to make sure the headlights and blinkers were in working order. Only an amateur would risk getting pulled over for a busted taillight while on their way to or from one of the robberies they'd planned.

Inside the club, nearly fifty soldiers greeted Kole as if he'd returned from war. Kole had never been power-hungry, but the love and respect he received from his comrades made him feel invincible. He knew that if he were to die tonight, retaliation would be brutal and extensive. His men would flood the streets with MMG blood. His legacy would be elevated with every body that hit the ground. With that in mind, he had nothing to fear.

Moon gathered the crew near the dance floor. They stood in a semi-circle with Kole and Moon in the center. All of the soldiers were dressed similarly in all black. They would complete their ensembles with ski masks and assault rifles when they reached their destinations.

The men were accustomed to taking directives from Kole, but he gave Moon the responsibility, because he was the head honcho now. Not surprisingly, Moon took a step back and told his friend, "Go 'head, bro."

Kole looked upon the crowd of disciplined thugs with a sense of familiarity. He couldn't count how many times he'd sent them into battle to protect or progress the interests of The Organization. This time was different because they had nothing to gain from this conflict. But Kole's poise and leadership was the same. The soldiers quieted when he began to speak. Prior to this moment, they had no idea why they'd been gathered or who they'd be pointing their guns at.

"Tonight, we're going after MMG," Kole announced.

No response.

"We have the address of twenty-six dope houses," Kole continued. "We're hitting all of them. Each team will be at least three deep. If you have to kick the door, make sure you got somebody at the back. I recommend finding a dopefiend to gain entry. I want to coordinate the attacks, the first wave at least, so they won't have time to warn the others. But if everything goes well, they won't have time either way.

"When you get in, restrain the workers with zip ties and duct tape. It's okay to rough them up, but I wanna try to do this with no killing. Be smart with the duct tape. If you bust a motherfucker in the nose, you know he gon' suffocate if you tape his mouth.

"Once you get everybody in the house secured, we're taking all the dope, guns and money. If they try to hold out, you can cut off a finger or two to get 'em talking. But don't take it too far. Getting the dope is not a priority. Don't spend too much time in them houses. You need to be in and out in ten minutes. Each crew's gonna hit two houses and then meet back here. If we start at midnight, everybody should be back by two.

"When you got them niggas tied up and paying attention, give 'em this message," Kole said, "'*Shank got hisself killed. Leave that boy and his mama alone.*'"

No one had expressed doubt or confusion until that moment. Kole knew the request was odd, but it was crucial that they got it right.

"*Shank got hisself killed,*" he repeated. "*Leave that boy and his mama alone.* Everybody got that?"

The men nodded.

"We 'bout to roll out," Kole said. "If any of you niggas got a question, ask it now."

No one questioned the message they were instructed to deliver, but a killer known simply as *G* said, "I don't think we gon' pull this off without wetting somebody."

Several others nodded their agreement.

"Maybe not," Kole conceded. "But I'm asking you to try. Obviously, if they got a weapon aimed at you, and it's either you or him, you gotta do what you gotta do. But murder ain't on the agenda tonight. That shit would be counterproductive to what we trying to accomplish. Any more questions?"

No one else spoke up.

CHAPTER 54

ONE OF THE lieutenants helped organize the men and give them their assignments.

"Commit these addresses to memory," Byrd told each crew. "Don't write nothing down."

When he was done, and the club was mostly empty, Byrd returned to Kole and Moon.

"Hey, did we bring enough guys?" he asked them. "I think we're one crew short."

Byrd was in his mid-twenties, tall and lanky with a mouth full of gold teeth.

"Naw, we got everybody," Kole told him.

"We got two addresses left," Byrd informed him, "and nobody to assign them to. You want me to go with Earl and them, right?"

"Yeah, that's right," Kole said. "Those last two houses are for me and Moon."

Byrd's eyes narrowed.

Kole chuckled. "What, you didn't think us old-heads could get down no more?"

"Naw, it's not that. I just didn't expect y'all to get your hands dirty with this kinda work."

Moon laughed. "Been getting my hands dirty for years," he said to Kole.

"Me too," Kole replied. He looked back to Byrd, grinning. "Matter of fact, I been getting my hands dirty since you was learning to use the potty."

Byrd chuckled. "A'ight. I feel you. You want me to roll with y'all? I'd be the fourth man on Earl's crew. If I go with y'all, we'll both have three."

"Nope," Kole told him. "Gone and handle your business with them. We don't need another gun over here."

"*Okay*..." Byrd said doubtfully. "If that's the word, then I guess we're through. Everybody's ready. Some of the guys are already moving into position."

"Let's be out then," Moon said. He gave Kole a pat on the back as they headed for the exit.

CHAPTER 55

TEN MINUTES LATER, Kole found himself basking in nostalgia as he and his old friend headed for the west side of town. Back when The Organization was in its infancy and it had no official name, he and Moon were on a mission to shut down the crack houses in their neighborhood *just because*. They didn't profit off the drugs they confiscated in those days.

Kole and Moon took many twilit trips to the bridge that ran over the Trinity River and tossed the crack into the murky water. They used to joke that they were either killing a large population of fish or getting them *hella high*! It didn't take long before they got over their lofty *Save the World* ambitions and began to redistribute the drugs they pilfered.

They drove with the radio off, Moon riding shotgun, each man lost in his own thoughts. From experience, Kole was aware of the risks involved when forcibly entering someone's home. The potential for bloodshed was even more prevalent if the residence was a dope house. He wasn't surprised when his friend broke the silence by asking him, "So, you banging this chick or what?"

Kole frowned as he looked over at him. Moon stared back at him unblinking. The darkness in the car was broken intermittently by streetlights as Kole drew closer to their first target.

"I'm just asking," Moon said. "Ain't like I'm gon' call this shit off if you say yes. Matter of fact..." He checked his watch. "Shit's already going down. I'm just asking you, man-to-man."

Kole's sighed as his eyes returned to the road. "Naw, man. We had a thing – back in the day. But it didn't work out."

"Back when you first moved over there?"

Kole nodded. "I had to cut her off. You remember when them Houston cats came down here, trying to set up shop?"

Moon nodded. "That ugly nigga, what was his name?"

"Turkey," Kole recalled.

"Hmph. Yeah, that nigga looked just like a *turkey*, ol' ugly ass! That's the one tried to bring some heat to your place."

"I was with Dana one night when he rolled through," Kole said. "Only way to protect her was to take her ass home and tell her I didn't want her no more."

"Damn," Moon said with a grin. "That's cold, blood. Even for you."

"She been hating me ever since," Kole told him. "I see her all the time, 'cause you know I likes to sit on my porch."

"Like somebody's goddamn grandmama," Moon joked.

"Always cutting her eyes at me," Kole continued, as if he hadn't heard him. "I wanted to tell her I did that shit to save her life, but I couldn't. So I just left it like that."

"You get your little heart broke?" Moon asked, grinning. "Ain't that one of them, uh, what you call it? *Unfulfilled love stories*?"

"Man, what the hell kinda movies you been watching?" Kole asked him. "Get the fuck outta here with that shit!" He laughed.

"Hey, laugh all you want," Moon said, "but you the one ready to go to war over some broad. Was the pussy that good?"

Kole's smile fell away. Normally he was cool with this type of locker room banter, but he felt it was disrespectful to speak about Dana that way. She wasn't just a piece of ass. She was a hardworking woman; a single mother who was doing the best she could.

"Uh oh," Moon said. "Sounds like I hit a nerve. You got real feelings for this woman," he noticed.

Kole didn't respond.

"Y'all banging again?" Moon pressed.

Kole thought about last night. He didn't think that counted. He shook his head.

Moon smacked his lips. "You know I don't believe that shit! But it's all good. I ain't gon' tell the homies you in love."

"Glad to see you can still laugh one minute and stick a gun in somebody's face the next," Kole said.

"Yessir," Moon agreed. "Hell, I can do *both* at the same time."

CHAPTER 56

BY THE TIME they reached the Como neighborhood, the conversation in the Altima had died down. It picked up again when Kole turned off Horne Street to Lovell Avenue.

"Damn, it's popping over here," Moon noticed.

Kole agreed. It was after midnight, but the street was populated; mostly with dopefiends and hookers, who were often one in the same. There were a handful of dope boys hanging out, some riding bikes, others chilling in front of a convenience store that was closed for the night.

"Hope it's not like this at our spot," Moon said, his eyes on the night life.

"Why?" Kole asked with a chuckle. "Back in the day, you didn't care if it was a party going on. You'd still run up in there and tell everybody to hit the floor."

"That was back in the day," Moon said. "I didn't have nothing to lose back then."

"Being a millionaire makes you see things differently," Kole stated.

"True. But I don't see no change in you," Moon said. "You still the same grimy goon."

Kole didn't take offense to that. "Here we go," he said as they neared their destination.

The MMG house on the left didn't look any different than the other houses in the neighborhood. There was no one loitering outside and no vehicles in the driveway. The porch light was on, but Kole couldn't tell if there were any lights on inside the house.

"You sure this the one?" Moon asked as he peered out of the window.

"You was sitting right next to me when the man pointed it out," Kole reminded him.

"Yeah, but what if he was wrong?" Moon asked. "That nigga only had one eye. He prolly don't know what the fuck he was looking at!"

Kole laughed at that. He drove past the house without stopping. "I guess we'll find out when we pick up our key."

They found their *key* around the corner. The prostitute actually flagged them down, which was very convenient. Kole stopped in the middle of the street. The whore's bug eyes became wary when she approached his window and saw two men in the car.

"Oh, my bad. I thought you was somebody else," she said and started to back away.

Kole brought up his pistol, and Moon told her, "Bitch, get in the car."

She fell apart right before their eyes. Kole thought she was ugly before her meltdown. Crying and begging for her life pushed her over the threshold of *hideous*.

"*Please! Please leave me alone!*" she wailed. "*I don't mess with nobody! I gotta get home to my daughter! Ain't nobody watching my baby!*"

"*Get in the fucking car!*" Kole demanded.

"*I got AIDS!*" she shrieked. "*If y'all rape me, you'll get AIDS!*"

"Don't nobody wanna rape yo nasty ass," Kole said with a grimace.

"Man, shoot that bitch," Moon said nonchalantly. "That ho is way too uncooperative."

"*No! No! Please! I'll get in! I'll get in!*"

The hooker hurriedly hopped in the back seat of the car. Both of the front windows were down, but her stench filled the cabin immediately.

"*Aw hell naw!*" Moon complained. "We need to find somebody else."

"Fuck it," Kole said. He got moving again. "She already here."

"*Please don't rape me!*" the woman yelled.

In his rearview mirror, Kole thought she looked like a Halloween mask.

"Ain't nobody gon' rape you," he said. "We just need you to get us in a dope house. Gon' chuck you a little change too."

Hearing that, her crocodile tears stopped immediately. "Oh. How much?"

"Fuck no," Moon said. He turned towards his window, trying to avoid inhaling her funk. "Don't pay her *nothing*! Bitch, you ought to be ashamed of yourself; leaving your baby at home while you out here sucking dick!"

"I ain't got no baby," the whore said. "I just said that so y'all wouldn't rape me."

"Damn. That was pretty good," Kole said. "I believed yo ass. What about AIDS? Bet you ain't got that shit either."

"Oh, I *do* got AIDS," she said. "I wouldn't lie about that."

CHAPTER 57

KOLE AND MOON took their key back to the house in question to confirm it was what they thought it was. The whore pointed it out before they asked her.

"It's that one right there; the one with the blue trim."

"Why it ain't no traffic?" Kole asked.

"You gotta go through the back," she informed them. "They prolly won't open it for y'all, but if they see me, they'll open right up."

"Stop trying to make yourself seem useful," Moon said. "We can get in there just fine without you."

Kole grinned as he watched their back and forth. This was just like the old days. He was glad to be in an elevated position now, but damn if he didn't miss these nighttime missions – just a little.

They parked a few houses down and made their way to the alley that ran behind the crack house. Moon had a pump shotgun in hand and a pistol in the small of his back. Kole had an AK-47 with his 9mm holstered. He didn't like the assault rifle because it was not very accurate. But it was big and threatening, especially with the extended clip. It was the kind of weapon that made you think of nothing but self-preservation when he pointed it at your face.

When they got to the house, the men pulled on their ski masks and debated who should take point at the back door and who should enter through the front.

"It's my idea," Kole whispered. "I'm going in first."

"I ain't hit a lick like this in a long-ass time," Moon argued. "Let me do it. You can kick the front door."

"No! I'm going in the back," Kole hissed.

The three creepers were concealed by darkness and shrubbery, but at least one of them was anxious to get the party started.

"Come on, y'all," the prostitute whined. "Y'all being childish! It don't matter who go in the front or who go in the back. Both of y'all gon' get in there."

The men turn and sneered at her.

"*Shut up, bitch,*" they said in unison and laughed quietly.

Moon finally backed down and allowed Kole to take point. They agreed that Moon could be the first to enter their next house. Kole gave the prostitute $50 for her services and sneaked to the side of the house, while she emerged from the alley in plain sight. She walked to the back door and pulled the screen door open. Kole heard someone undo the locks before she had time to knock.

As soon as the last lock was disengaged, Kole sprang from the darkness like a black panther. He shoved the whore aside and pointed his weapon at what turned out to be a teenager. The boy was as freaked out as the dopefiend was when they first accosted her. Kole hated to go hard on the youngster, but he chose his own fate when he agreed to work in a dope house.

"*Get back!*" he shouted and charged inside the house. "*Get the fuck back!*"

The boy yelled and possibly pissed his pants. He didn't retreat quickly enough, so Kole kicked him hard in the stomach, sending him flying a good six feet. The teen collided with a wall and fell crumpled, gripping his stomach.

Kole looked quickly to the right and left. There was a goon at the kitchen table chopping up the product. There was another goon standing near the sink. There was a forth in the hallway on his left. There was a pistol on the table, so Kole aimed his death machine at him first.

"*Reach for it if you want. I got something for that ass!*"

The man's hands remained frozen.

"*Put your fucking hands up!*"

He did as he was told.

BOOMP!

"*You too, nigga!*" Kole yelled at the one in the kitchen. "Matter of fact, bring yo ass over here!"

"You fucking up," the dealer in the kitchen said. He was the oldest of the bunch. Kole could tell he was scared, but his demeanor said otherwise.

"No, *you* fucking up," he told him. "I'm 'bout to make an example outta yo bitch-ass!"

He raised the barrel of the AK towards the man's head and got the desired result. The man began to walk around the counter.

BOOMP!

"*Raise yo shirt up!*" Kole growled. "*Raise it up and keep it up!* Go sit next to that nigga."

The man reluctantly raised his shirt chest high and went to sit on the floor next to the boy Kole kicked.

"You, do the same thing," Kole told the one at the table.

As that one followed his instructions, Kole turned and saw that the fourth man was not standing in the hallway anymore. Rather than pursue him, Kole asked the oldest one, "The other guy, what's his name?"

The man played dumb. "What you talking about."

BOOMP!

"You ready to die?" Kole asked him. He pointed the AK at his face again. "The one that ducked in the hallway. Either call him in here, or take one for the team. After you dead, I'ma give these other two a chance to call him. After all three of y'all dead, I'll go get that nigga myself."

It was obvious the leader of the group had a hard time accepting the fact that one man was about to rob all four of them. He sneered at Kole, as if daring him to pull the trigger.

BOOMP!

That was the fourth time Kole heard the sound, but it was the first time it registered. *What the hell was that?* He knew it was coming from the front of the house, but–

"You know whose dope this is?" the leader of the group asked him.

"Yeah, I'm pretty sure I do," Kole said. "And I'm pretty sure Brass ain't here to save yo punk ass from this lead that's 'bout to be flying out the back of yo head. You better call that nigga back in here. *I ain't asking again.*"

The man took a deep breath, his eyes dark and furious. Before he had a chance to comply – or *not* comply and force Kole's hand – another dark figure appeared. This one came through the back door, behind Kole. For a moment he thought his goose was cooked. But he looked back and saw that it was Moon. The big man sucked air through the hole in his ski mask. He was winded from his sprint around the house.

"I couldn't, couldn't get that front door open," he explained.

"That was you trying to kick that shit?" Kole asked.

"I was kicking, using my shoulder," Moon replied. He took a deep breath and blew it out harshly. "That door didn't budge. I told you *you* should've went to the front. Yo muscle-man ass could've got it open."

Despite the level of tension in the house, Kole couldn't help but chuckle at that.

"Old, out of shape looking-ass," he told Moon. "Say, while you're here, it's another one hiding somewhere down that hallway." He nodded in the direction the missing dealer had gone. "Go find him and kill him."

"Bet," Moon said and headed that way.

Before he made it more than a few steps, they heard a voice coming from that direction.

"*Don't shoot!*" an unidentified person pleaded. "*I'm coming out! I got my hands up!*"

Neither Kole nor Moon let their guard down while they waited for him.

CHAPTER 58

THE ROBBERY DIDN'T go exactly as planned, but in the end, the desired result was achieved. All four dealers were bound and gagged. Kole and Moon collected a large amount of dope and a few weapons. They bundled their booty in a blanket they found in one of the bedrooms and returned to the kitchen like a ghetto Santa Claus.

"Don't forget," Kole told the apparent leader of the group, who still had a serious frown in place, "tell Brass to leave that mother and her son alone. Shank got hisself killed, and everybody know it. If Brass wanna take it to another level, he can. But he ain't gon' win. Make sure you deliver that message."

The friends left through the back door. They removed their ski masks before returning to the Altima. They deposited their reward in the trunk and laughed when they got back in the car.

"That was fun," Kole said as he turned the ignition.

"Yeah, it was," Moon agreed. "Think I'll leave it to the youngsters, though. I'm getting a little too old for this shit."

"Yeah, I see," Kole said. "Can't even kick a door in. What kind of goon are you?"

"A rich one," Moon stated. "You sure they didn't have it barricaded from the inside?"

"I'm sure," Kole said. "Just your average, every day deadbolt. I think you right about getting old."

"Yeah, well, at least I ain't retired. Yo ass will probably move to Florida soon..."

They repeated the same routine at the next dope house with better results. This time Moon followed a fiend through the front door, while Kole kicked-in the back. With attackers coming from both sides, the dealers dropped their weapons without too much barking. Moon thought they got more drugs from the first house, but that was okay. The robberies were never about profiting.

All of the crews returned to The Moonlight when they completed their missions. When the last group checked in, Moon was proud to say everyone had accomplished their goal. All in all, they shut down 26 MMG crack houses in less than two hours. No one from their side was injured during the raids. Kole was disheartened to hear that shots were fired at one of the locations.

"He said the dude tried him," Moon reported. He and Kole sat at the bar drinking aged bourbon. "The fool reached for his strap, and Lemon had to pop him."

Kole sighed and took a sip of his drink. He had a sinking feeling in his chest. It was silly of him to think they could do that much dirt in one night without hurting anyone, but he hoped they'd get lucky.

"He die?" he dared to ask his friend.

"He wasn't dead when they left," Moon informed him. "Lemon shot him in the stomach. They say he was bleeding like a motherfucker, but he was still alive. They tied him up with the rest. They didn't gag him, though. So I guess he got a chance."

Kole was quiet as he contemplated death's dark hold on his life. It seemed he'd never escape its cold clutches. He sensed it wouldn't be long before the Grim Reaper came knocking for him.

"It was his own fault," Moon said. "His dumb-ass shouldn't have reached. That ain't on you."

Kole disagreed with his friend about it not being his fault. "Fuck it," he said and brought his glass to his lips. The liquor was strong, but not strong enough. "I tried to talk to Brass man-to-man," he recounted. "He the one doing all that ho shit. Ducking and dodging."

Moon nodded.

Kole shook his head and asked, "How'd we make out?"

Moon grinned. "The boys did good. A shitload of guns and dope. I don't think it's no more crack in Overbrook Meadows. Look like we got it all!"

Kole wished he could find comfort in that.

"Yo, it was just one dude," Moon said, hoping to lift his spirits. "And they said he'll prolly make it. It's weird to be rooting for the other team, but don't count him out yet!"

Kole chuckled.

"That's what I'm talking about," Moon said. "We hit a hell of a lick tonight. We should be celebrating."

"The lick don't matter if it don't work," Kole reminded him.

"It's gon' work," Moon assured him. "They took a big hit. They not finna keep going after your friend. Far as I can tell, they only got two choices now: Either Brass is gon' meet with you to settle this shit, or he gon' try to retaliate. We'll be ready, if he try that retaliation shit."

Kole believed their soldiers would be ready, but that only meant more bodies would hit the floor. He downed the rest of his drink, savoring the burn of the alcohol as it heated his insides. He stood and gripped his friend's hand. He pulled him in for a brief hug.

"Alright, man. I'm outta here. You good? Need help with anything?"

Moon shook his head. "Nah. I got people taking care of it. I'm 'bout to leave in a minute my damn self."

"Call me if something pops off," Kole said. "Ain't no telling what Brass gon' do when he find out about them houses."

"He gon' call you and say, '*May I please have my drugs and guns back?*'" Moon predicted. "Watch what I tell you."

Kole wished he was as optimistic. "Alright, bro. Be safe."

"You too, man. I'll holler at you tomorrow."

PART SIX
INTENSITY

CHAPTER 59

IT WAS AFTER three a.m. when Kole returned to the hotel. He considered checking on Dana and the boys before he entered his room but decided against it. If Dana was sleeping on the sofa bed, he didn't want to wake her. There was nothing he needed to discuss that couldn't wait till morning.

When he stepped into his room, he was surprised to find her reclining on the couch. All of the lights were off, but Dana's face was illuminated in the glow of her cellphone. She looked up at him as he approached one of the smaller lamps.

"Mind if I turn this on?"

She shook her head. "No. Go ahead."

Dana sat up as she watched him. Kole was as brooding as he was before he left. He turned on the lamp and continued to the bedroom. Dana considered following him, but he returned a minute later. Her heart thumped when he came and sat next to her.

Kole stared straight ahead. His powerful chest rose and fell slowly. Dana thought she caught the scent of liquor on his exhalations. She waited, not sure if he wanted to talk about what happened. She reached and touched his arm. She ran her soft fingers towards his hand and held it comfortingly.

She finally asked, "Is everything okay?"

He turned slowly and met her gaze. Dana had never felt frightened of him, but for a moment his dark eyes looked menacing. Gradually his expression softened as he stared at her.

"Everything went as planned. I think we'll know if your problem is gonna go away by tomorrow."

Despite his comment, Dana's tension was steadily on the rise. "What, what did you do?" she asked.

He studied her features. Dana's eyes were anxious and hopeful.

He said, "You sure you wanna know?"

She thought she was, but the way he asked made her hesitate. "Yeah," she decided. "I – I wanna know. Why'd you ask me that?"

"Plausible deniability, for starters," he said.

"Was it something the police will question me about?"

He shrugged. "I doubt it, but ain't no telling."

"Why else wouldn't I want to know?"

"Because you have an image of me; what kind of man you think I am. It may be more comfortable for you to keep that image."

A shudder rattled her bones. "But you already told me about The Organization. You told me about the things you used to do."

"That's right." He nodded. His eye contact was unyielding. Almost unnerving. "I told you about things I *used* to do. That was the old me. Tonight the old me got resurrected."

Dana felt she might regret her decision, but if Kole had done things for her or in her name, she needed to know. She stared into his eyes, matching his intensity.

"Tell me."

A few heartbeats passed before he said, "Tonight we robbed people. *I* robbed people. They were members of MMG. We attacked their drug houses. Tied 'em up. Beat 'em up. Took their drugs and money. One of them tried to resist, and he got shot. They say he's still alive, but he might be dead by sunrise. I didn't pull the trigger, but I gave the orders, so that's on me."

Dana tried not to let on how stunned she was. Kole had told her he never wanted to kill again. She couldn't imagine how heavy his burden was. She realized the cross was also hers to bear, because he had done all of this for her.

"The goal," Kole went on, "is to force their hand. Brass said he didn't wanna meet with me. Now he's got to acknowledge me. We humiliated him. We interfered with his livelihood. If he's stupid, he'll continue to escalate things. But if he's smart, he'll call me, and we can talk about how to end this."

Dana didn't know much about gangs, but she understood that *escalation* would only lead to more bloodshed. Again, the blood would be spilled in her name. She didn't think she could live with herself if someone from The Organization was the victim.

"The worst thing about tonight," Kole said, "was how much I liked it."

Dana's heart skipped a beat. He continued to watch her reaction.

"I liked being out in the *witching hour* – that's what my granny used to call it. She said that's when witches and demons are at their most powerful. That's how I felt tonight; *powerful*. I felt like that was where I belonged; in a dope house full of crack and assault rifles. Now I'm sitting here wondering who I really am. Because when you turn away from sin, it's not supposed to feel good when you go back to it.

"So I can't tell you what kind of man you sitting next to right now. I'm not the retired house-flipper I told you I was. And I'm not the head of The Organization no more. But beyond that, I don't know."

He stood abruptly. Looking up at him, Dana saw the big, bad wolf again. Red eyes, fangs bared.

"You should go sleep in your son's room," he told her. "Think about everything I told you. In the morning, you can tell me if you want me to back off."

He walked away, leaving her seated on the sofa. After a few seconds, Dana stood and lifted her cellphone from the end table before leaving the room.

CHAPTER 60

KOLE WAS NOT yet asleep when he heard his door open and close again. By the time Dana appeared in the doorway of the bedroom, he had his pistol pointed at her. Kole's nostrils flared as he lowered the gun. He placed it carefully on the nightstand, his eyes glued on his visitor.

With no lights on, he couldn't make out her expression as she stepped slowly to the bed. He could barely tell that she had changed into a nightgown. She climbed into his bed without speaking. She brought a faint scent of perfume with her.

Kole's body tensed when she straddled him, like she had the previous night. She crawled over him slowly, until they were face to face. He stared into her eyes, unable to decipher her mood or her intent. Her sweet breath on his lips was titillating. He brought a hand up when she lowered her mouth to his. She kissed him softly, sucking his bottom lip between hers.

Kole's hand ran up her thigh, which he realized was bare. Her skin was warm and smooth. His hand continued its ascent as she peppered his lips with moist kisses. He did not encounter panties when he made it to her hip. His manhood sprang to attention when he reached further and palmed her bare ass. Dana moaned softly. Kole moved his left hand to cup the other cheek.

The rise and fall of his chest became more apparent as he caressed her, gradually applying more pressure.

Dana's tongue slipped into his mouth, coaxing him to kiss her back. He complied. He sucked her tongue and then her lips. A fierce shudder rolled down her frame, converging on her clitoris, where she felt his manhood growing steadily. Kole squeezed her ass as she grinded on him. She felt her essence leaking from her, onto him. Her clitoris pulsated when she sat up and looked him in the eyes.

She carefully placed something on his chest. As Kole reached for it, she reached back and unfastened her night gown. She pulled the garment over her head, revealing her nudity. Kole lifted the condom. He didn't ask where it came from. He barely looked at it. The wondrous vision on his lap held his full attention.

Dana's breasts were large, her nipples dark and perky. Kole's hands slid up her sides, but she backed away and out of reach. He watched as she scooted down the bed, and then he looked at the condom again.

"Stole it from Tariq's bag." Her voice was soft, barely audible.

Kole never thought he'd be so grateful to have a horny teenager around. He watched as Dana unfastened his pants. The feeling of déjà vu was strong, but with a condom in hand, Kole knew his appetite would be fully quenched tonight. He was rock hard when Dana peeled his underwear down. She caressed his manhood with soft hands that were truly magical. She looked up at him and took him into her mouth unexpectedly. Kole's eyes widened. He craned his neck and then sat up on his elbows to watch her.

She'd never pleased him in this manner, back when they were dating. Kole couldn't hide his surprise. Gradually his erogenous zones reacted to the sensations she was providing. Her mouth was delightfully hot and wet. She closed her eyes as her head bobbed slowly up and down. Her cheeks went concave as she increased pressure. Her tongue was delightful.

Kole muttered, "*Damn*," and she tasted his pre-cum.

She savored his manliness before swallowing it.

He did not have to reach for her head or pump his hips. Dana controlled the tempo perfectly. He couldn't stop watching her. Seeing his meat slide in and out of her mouth made him wish all of the lights were on. She pushed him past amazement towards sublime when the slurping sounds of her fellatio became audible.

Kole's head swam. "*Damn, baby.*"

She opened her eyes and looked up at him, as if responding to a question. The direct eye contact made another jolt of pre-cum shoot into her mouth. She pulled back and squeezed and stroked his shaft, bringing more of his juices to the tip. She licked him clean and then took him all the way in again. Kole reached for her. This time it was to stop her. The whirlwind of passion in his chest was rapidly descending. He was eager for a climax, but not before he penetrated her.

Dana was attuned to his desires, and she wanted the same thing. She backed away and stared hungrily at his piece as she slid off the bed. Each time it pulsated, she wanted it back in her mouth. She pulled his pants off completely and did the same with his boxers. Before she rejoined him on the bed, Kole yanked his tee-shirt off with enough force to rip the fabric. He used his fangs to tear the condom open before sliding the rubber down his shaft.

When he was ready, he beckoned with his eyes. Dana fought off a fit of nerves as she climbed onto the bed. His dick looked *huge*. She was soaking wet, but *damn*. Was she wet enough? She crawled on top of him. Once they were face to face, Kole could feel the heat radiating off her box. He grabbed hold of her hips and guided her down. Dana's eyes widened as he slid in deeper. Her mouth fell open, her breaths coming in shudders.

She placed both palms on his chest and lowered herself all the way down. The tightness was initially searing, but gradually her walls accommodated him. Kole looked up at her as she began to ride him slowly. Her expression was desperate, pleading even. After a minute she sucked her bottom lip into her mouth and bit down on it. She moaned and threw her head back, savoring every inch of him. When she got into her rhythm, Kole's hands moved from her hips to her bouncing breasts. He squeezed them and tweaked her nipples, much to Dana's delight. She looked down at him, a slight smile caressing her lips.

She moved her hands to the bed, planting one on either side of his head. From this position, she increased the speed and length of her strokes. Kole thrust his hips forward, matching her flow like two perfectly timed pistons. The clapping of their thighs was music to his ears. It was almost loud enough to drown out Dana's moans. He knew she was about to climax before her grip on his pillow tightened. She clenched her jaws, hoping to muffle her moans before they became screams.

Kole was normally a patient lover, but the drama he experienced that night had culminated in an adrenaline rush mixed with ecstasy. He reached for her hips and lifted her unexpectedly. His grunt was animalistic. Dana's head spun. She scarcely had time to decipher what was going on before he slipped from beneath her and reappeared behind her. Dana was still on her knees. She felt a rough hand on the back of her head a moment before he slammed in again.

Hard.

She couldn't stop a scream from escaping her.

"*Aaaah!*"

Kole gave her no time to recover before his hips started pumping. His strokes were long and fast. The sound of their bodies colliding was like an up-tempo rap beat.

SPLACK!

SPLACK!

SPLACK!

SPLACK!

His grip on her hair tightened. He yanked it back. Her head had no choice but to follow.

"*Ah! Shit! Kole!*"

Above the smacking sound of their skin and her own throaty screams, Dana heard him grunting behind her. She thought he sounded like a bull, but as his growls filled the room, she realized she was being taken by the wolf. Even if she had control of her head, she wouldn't have looked back, out of fear of what she might see.

But the thing she found most amazing was how much she loved it! He had dominated her, just as he dominated the streets. He wasn't a gentle or thoughtful or caring lover tonight. He was taking what he wanted. She had no choice but to give it up.

"*Fuuuck!*" she screamed. "*Fuck me!*"

She wasn't sure if she'd spoken those words aloud until Kole yanked her hair harder in response. He slammed in deeper, as if he'd been challenged. Dana's orgasm ripped through her body, from her head to her soul. Kole mercifully let go of her hair at that moment, and she had time to bury her face in the pillow before her clitoris exploded into a million sensual pieces.

The force of her climax made her lose sense of time, space and direction. She moaned loudly into the pillow. Kole grabbed her hips the moment her trembling legs gave out. Her walls gripped him even tighter. Her clitoris pulsated, milking every drop of pleasure from him.

When *he* came, Dana felt it in her whole body. He plunged in so deeply, she could taste him. She felt him in her chest, even in her toenails. He gripped her hips harder, yanking her towards him so that each thrust was deeper still. His grunts were so feral, Dana expected him to throw his head back and howl at the moon.

She didn't have an ounce of energy left when his movements finally slowed and came to a stop. He remained submerged in her oasis for a few moments more. She felt his dick, pulsating inside her. She heard him panting. She turned her head to the side and filled her burning lungs with oxygen. Kole blew out a pent up breath, and then he released her hips and allowed her to lie prostrate.

He stared down at her nude physique for several seconds before slipping off the bed. Dana tried to lift her head and watch him as he stepped into the bathroom, but she couldn't move at all.

CHAPTER 61

THE NEXT MORNING, Kole was fast asleep when his cellphone rang. It was rare that the sun made an appearance before he got out of bed. Considering everything that transpired last night, he didn't fault himself for sleeping till eight. By the time he found his pants and dug his cellular from the pocket, it had stopped ringing. He called his friend back.

Moon answered, "You sleep?"

"I was," Kole admitted. "What's going on?"

"Brass responded to our little outing," Moon informed him. "Sent some niggas to firebomb Moonlight this morning."

Kole was immediately wide awake. He stood completely nude at the foot of the bed. "He did *what*?"

"They torched my shit," Moon repeated. "Burnt up damn near half the club. Motherfucker still smoking. I got them niggas on camera."

The bright sunrays peeking through Kole's curtains were dark now. The darkness enveloped his whole body. Behind him, Dana sat up in bed, bringing the sheets to her chest.

"What about Hootie?" Kole asked, referring to his grizzly-size nighttime security guard.

"He was there," Moon said. "Couldn't do nothing to stop it. By the time he made it outside, they had took off. He lucky his ass didn't get burnt up."

Kole took a seat on the bed, his anger rising. "You alright?" he asked his friend. "I feel like this is all my fault."

"Man, don't even worry about it."

Kole shook his head. The Moonlight was Moon's baby. "I don't see how I'm supposed to do that. They wouldn't have never fucked with you, if it wasn't for me."

"Charge it to the game," Moon said casually. "Everybody knew the risks when we did what we did last night – me included. I got insurance on that bitch, so it ain't like *I'm* the one gotta pay to fix it."

"I feel you," Kole said, then, "Shit, man, I better go check on *my* shit. That nigga Ice know where I stay."

"Yeah, they got you, bro," Moon said somberly.

"What you mean *they got me*?"

"Yo shit burnt up too. I sent some guys to check on your place as soon as I found out about the club. They say the fire truck's still at your house. That shit damn near burnt to the ground. Sorry, man."

Kole's breathing grew heavier.

"They got Sherm too," Moon continued.

Kole's eyes widened. "*Sherm*? What they do to him?"

"Same as us," Moon said. "Set his house on fire – except he was home at the time with his wife and his little girl."

An icy chill washed over Kole. His heart stopped beating completely, he wasn't sure for how long. He was reminded of the time his crew set one of their enemy's house on fire. When the family fled the scene, they ran into a spray of automatic gunfire, courtesy of The Organization.

In a biblical sense, turnabout was fair play. But Kole didn't think he could handle it if something happened to Sherm's family.

"They made it out okay," Moon told him.

Kole was rocked again, this time by a tsunami of relief. He wondered if he was getting soft. Murder and mayhem was supposed to be an acceptable part of the job.

"Why they target Sherm?" he asked.

"Prolly 'cause he was the only one they could find," Moon replied. "You know my team keep a low profile. It ain't easy to get an address on one of us."

"Where is he?" Kole asked.

"Who, Sherm?"

"Yeah."

"They holed up in a hotel. But they alright. Nobody had to go to the hospital or nothing. Treated the little girl for smoke at the scene."

Kole could imagine Sherm's daughter in the back of an ambulance with an oxygen mask on her face. The vision made his eyes burn with fury.

"The MMG nigga that got shot last night, did he make it?" he asked.

"Yeah," Moon told him. "That lucky motherfucker pulled through."

Kole was quiet for a moment. After considering everything that had happened since Tariq ran over Shank, he came to the only rational conclusion: "Man, I'ma have to kill Brass."

"'Bout time," Moon said right away. "Time to take the kid gloves off. Niggas like that don't respect nothing but *murder*."

"We got the numbers for a full-scale war?"

"They got the numbers," Moon acknowledged. "But you know our team is smarter. Most of MMG is kids who ain't never seen nothing like what we finna lay on 'em."

Kole nodded, thinking about the boy he kicked in the stomach last night. If MMG bolstered their roster with punks like that, they wouldn't stand a chance. There would be bloodshed; funeral processions on both sides. But in the end The Organization would reign supreme.

"I'ma call you back," Kole told his friend.

"For sure," Moon said and disconnected.

Kole stood and crossed the room to grab a pair of boxers from his suitcase. Dana's eyes were apprehensive as she watched him. Kole's back was massive; fanning out like a cobra's hood. He turned and locked eyes with her as he pulled on his underwear.

She asked, "What happened?"

"They burned down my partner's club," he told her. "They burnt up my house, burned another homey's house. Fire trucks are outside my place now. I gotta go."

She had never seen him this angry. It was frightening, even though she wasn't the target of his rage.

"What are y'all gonna do?" Dana asked. "I heard you talking about killing that man, going to war."

"That's the only thing left for us to do." He turned and grabbed a pair of pants. "The only way to get through to Brass is with a bullet to the head."

"If you go to war, it won't just be him that gets killed," Dana said knowingly.

"There can be no war without casualties," Kole confirmed. "Hopefully all the bloodshed will be on their side. But I can't promise that. My crew, they know what's up. They know what to expect."

"I don't want that," Dana said. "I don't want anyone else to get hurt – not even Brass. Can't we – can't you just stop?"

"*Stop*?" Kole said the word as if it was a foreign language. He approached the bed and stood before her. "Ain't no stopping. Not now. Not till it's finished."

"*Please Kole!*" Dana's eyes were pleading, tearful now. "I don't want that. *I just want all of this to go away.*"

"That's what I'm doing. I'm gonna make it go away." Kole's voice was iceberg cold.

"*No*," she cried, shaking her head. "Not like that."

"He ain't giving me no other choice," Kole growled.

245

"That's because y'all keep escalating it. You do something to him, he does something to you. It'll never end this way! But if you stop right now, it might."

"If we stop right now, your life is still in danger. Tariq's too."

"We can go to the police."

"You already did that! Ain't nobody got arrested. The police ain't never did nothing to help me, and they can't help you either! In this world, you gotta help *yourself*. That's the only way!"

"*Please, Kole!*" She stood and grabbed hold of him. Without the sheet covering her nudity, her body and soul were laid bare. "*I don't want anyone to die! There's gotta be another way!*"

Despite Kole's anger, she somehow managed to touch his heart. She could see it in his eyes.

He sneered and told her, "I'll think about it." He returned to his suitcase to grab a shirt. "I'll be back."

"Where are you going?" she asked.

"To check on my house, talk to some people."

"I wanna go." Dana hurried to put on her nightgown.

He looked back at her. "I don't need you to go with me."

"I know you don't need me to go, but I want to. I wanna check on my house too."

"I can check on your house."

"Are you planning to kill someone *right now*?" she asked.

"No. I told you I wanna talk to some people."

"Then why can't I go? I'm sick of being left behind, when I'm the reason all of this is happening. I wanna check on my house, and I wanna make sure you don't kill nobody."

Kole couldn't say he was surprised by her stubbornness. She had always been strong-minded. It was one of the things that attracted him to her.

"Fine," he grumbled. "Get dressed."

"My clothes are across the hall. I'll be right back. *Don't leave without me.*"

In the boys' room, neither of the teens stirred while Dana dressed in jeans and a tank top. Before she left, she approached Tariq's bed and caressed the side of his face. His eyes fluttered open.

"Mama."

"Hey, I'll be back," she told him.

He sat up and blinked the sleep away. "Where you going?" he asked groggily.

"Me and Kole have to check on some things," she said.

"I wanna go."

"No, baby. You have to stay here."

"I'm sick of being in this room," he whined. "When are we gonna get out of here? I wanna go home."

"It's not safe, but I think we're close. I won't be gone long. Call me, if you need me for anything." She kissed him on the cheek. "Don't leave the room, baby."

"Mama, let me go with you."

It broke her heart to leave him like that, but she shook her head. "We won't be gone long. I promise."

Rather than lie back down, Tariq continued to watch her from an upright position as Dana exited the room.

CHAPTER 62

KOLE DROVE FIRST to their neighborhood. Sure enough his home had been destroyed. The walls were still standing, but the fire had reached the roof and spread quickly. The charred ruins broke Dana's heart. There was one fire truck and a patrol car on the scene. Some of their neighbors stood in the front yard gawking at the catastrophe.

"Oh my God," Dana breathed. She stared out of the window in a state of shock. "Kole, I am so sorry."

She looked over at him, wondering why he seemed so calm about everything.

"I got insurance," he said. "I can rebuild."

"*But this is my fault.*" Tears rolled down her cheeks. "None of this would've happened if it wasn't for me."

Kole didn't deny that, but he said, "These are material things. There was nothing in there that can't be replaced – not even a photo album."

Dana couldn't believe it was that easy to part with his possessions. She wondered if he was putting on a strong front for her sake.

Down the street, her home was still intact.

"Why didn't they do anything to my house?" she wondered.

"I don't think it's about you anymore," Kole said as he pulled to a stop behind the fire truck. "Their beef is with The Organization now."

Dana thought that was a horrible turn of events, but Kole said, "That's good news. It's better that they're picking on someone their own size, 'cause we got something for 'em."

Dana didn't ask him to clarify that remark. She didn't want to reignite the argument they had at the hotel.

"Is it okay if I go check on my house?" she asked him.

"We'll go together," Kole said. "Let me talk to these people first."

CHAPTER 63

KOLE SPOKE WITH the Deputy Fire Chief, who confirmed the fire was an act of arson. He asked Kole all of the pertinent questions, and Kole gave the expected answers: He had no idea who would've done this, and he was devastated that it happened. He reiterated this to the police. When they were done speaking, the officer gave Kole a report number he'd need to file a claim with his insurance.

Kole and Dana walked across the street and checked on her home. It didn't appear the thugs had returned since the driveby. It had only been a few days, but Dana felt as if she'd been away from her home for a month. She didn't have time to clean up after the shooting. Seeing the damage reminded her of the horror and despair she felt that night.

Kole noticed her change in demeanor as they stepped over the glass and sheetrock in the living room. He had never been the lovey-dovey type, but he cared for this woman. He stepped to her and pulled her into his arms. Dana was receptive. She held him tightly and buried her face in his chest as she cried.

Her life was in a freefall, and Kole was her anchor. He stood solid and firm, stroking her back until she was ready to leave.

When they got back to his Jeep, he called Moon. He didn't think there was anything salvageable inside the pile of charcoal that was once his home, but he told him, "Can you send some guys over to watch my place, until I have a chance to see if there's anything worth taking. I don't want the scavengers picking through it before me."

"No problem," Moon said. "You there now?"

"Yeah. About to take off." He glanced at Dana and said, "I need them to watch my neighbor's house too. We just came from there. It doesn't look like anyone's been inside. But I don't know if them niggas are done, or if they wanna set some more shit on fire."

"Say no more. You say you got your neighbor with you?"

"Yeah. I tried to leave her at the hotel, but she too damn stubborn."

Dana shot him a playful frown. Kole grinned at her.

"Where y'all headed?"

"I'm about to call Sherm and find out what hotel he's in. After I see him, I need to holler at you. You at home?"

"I'm at the club now," Moon said. "No telling where I'll be. Call me after you check on Sherm."

"Bet."

"The team I send to your place," Moon said, "what kind of reception you want them to give MMG, if they do come through again?"

Kole's smile went away. He looked straight ahead and told him, "Green light. Fire at will."

"That's what I'm talking about," Moon said. "Alright. I'll have someone there in thirty minutes."

Kole did not look Dana's way when he got his Jeep rolling.

CHAPTER 64

SHERM AND HIS family were in good spirits, despite their harrowing experience. Dana was surprised they all looked so *normal*. If she didn't know beforehand that Sherm was a gangster, she never would've pictured him as such. He seemed like a devoted husband and father. His wife was beautiful. His five year old daughter was adorable.

Another thing Dana noted was how loyal Sherm was to The Organization. Kole seemed more distressed about the fire than he did. Sherm consistently deflected his concern with comments like, "It's alright," "Ain't nothing," and "We good."

"What's next," Sherm asked. He and Kole had stepped away from the group, but the hotel room wasn't very big. Both Dana and Sherm's wife eavesdropped openly.

"Nothing for you," Kole replied. "You need to chill for a minute, spend time with your family."

"Yeah, but–"

"That's it," Kole said, cutting him off. "You need to chill for a minute, spend time with your family."

"Yes, sir," Sherm said, and that was the end of the discussion.

Dana looked at Sherm's wife, who was visibly relieved to hear that. Their daughter sat in the middle of the bed, totally consumed with an iPad. Dana found her youthful innocence a little heart-wrenching.

CHAPTER 65

THIRTY MINUTES LATER, Dana finally got to meet Kole's partner, who he had spoken very little about. Once again Dana was surprised by his lack of *gangster* characteristics. Moon was a large, bald man who appeared to be in his early forties. He didn't have any tattoos, gold teeth or facial scars. He was polite and well-spoken when Kole introduced him to Dana.

"Nice to meet you, young lady. I've heard a lot about you."

"Thank you," she said. "It's nice to meet you."

They met at a restaurant called *Carla's*. The specialty was home-cooking. They were open for all three meals of the day. Dana and Kole arrived before the lunch rush. There were only half a dozen patrons at the tables. Moon called a woman over and introduced her to Dana.

"This is my wife, Carla."

"Oh, wow," Dana said, her eyes brightening. "Is this *your* restaurant?"

"Sure is, hun," Carla said, beaming. She was a beautiful woman with rosy cheeks and wide hips.

"Could you show Dana around a little bit?" Moon asked her, "while me and Kole talk? Maybe she wants to get something to eat..."

"You hungry?" Carla asked her.

"I haven't eaten breakfast," Dana admitted. She looked at Kole, feeling guilty about eating without him.

"I'm fine," he told her. "What's your lunch special?" he asked Carla.

"Today it's meatloaf."

The thought of meatloaf made Dana's mouth water. Carla looked like she could throw down in the kitchen. "I'll have that, if it's not too early," she said.

"Me too," Kole said. "We can get some to-go for the boys," he told Dana.

"Come on, sugar." Carla took Dana's hand. "Let these men talk."

Kole and Moon took a seat at a table. Moon looked after the women before turning his attention to Kole.

"She's beautiful," he said. "Sounds sweet, too. I can see why you're willing to go through hell and high water to protect her."

Even with his best friend, Kole didn't feel comfortable discussing his feelings for Dana.

"What's our next move?" he asked. "We need to hurry up and end this, one way or another."

Moon didn't call him on the way he changed the subject. He said, "Depends on how you wanna end it. We can start laying them niggas down on sight. Or we can go after the lieutenants first and weaken their leadership."

"I want Brass," Kole said. "I ain't saying the rest of their squad should get a pass, but you know they're only doing what he tell 'em to. All he had to do was sit down with me and talk man-to-man when this first started. Now the whole situation's fucked up. I say we take out the head, and the body will fall."

"Maybe," Moon said. "You don't think his brother will pick up where he left off?"

Kole shook his head. "I think Ice is smarter than that."

"He got a cooler head," Moon agreed.

"So how do we get at Brass?" Kole pondered. "We ain't got no kind of address on him?"

Moon shook his head. "Closest we got is his mama. He don't stay there, but we can snatch her, use her to make him pop his head up."

It wouldn't be the first time The Organization had kidnapped someone, but Kole was against that idea. Technically he had retired because he no longer wanted to be a part of such tactics.

He told Moon, "Let's leave her out of it."

"Well, that boy's funeral is today."

That perked Kole up. "Who, Shank?"

"Yeah. You know Brass will be there."

"Do you know what time?"

"At two, I think."

Kole checked his watch. It was only ten-thirty. "Okay. That's promising. But I don't wanna shoot it up, or no dumb shit like that. I just wanna get at Brass."

"How you gon' isolate him?"

Kole gave it some thought. "You still got Timber and — what's that fool's name he be rolling with? Those Dallas cats?"

"Legend?"

"Yeah. You still got them on the payroll?"

"Naw, but they'll show up if we need them," Moon said.

"Here's what I'm thinking," Kole said. "We get them to infiltrate the funeral. MMG's so big, ain't no telling how many people gon' show up, with family and random well-wishers."

Moon nodded.

"Once Timber lays eyes on Brass, they can keep up with him for the rest of the day; follow him from the service to the graveyard and see where he goes after that. They'll probably have dinner at the church. After it's all over, Brass gotta go *somewhere* to lay his head. Once we figure out where that is, we can go get him."

Moon continued to nod. "That's when you wanna take him out?" He didn't bat an eye at the thought of killing a father on the day of his son's funeral.

"I'm gonna try to talk to him first," Kole said. "Give him one last chance to do the right thing and back down. We took from them last night, and they came back and took from us. It ain't gotta go no further. But if he don't wanna let it be, yeah, I'll murk that nigga myself. Then we'll get Ice and whoever else wanna stand up. Tonight we'll either call a truce, or it's gon' be the beginning of the end for MMG."

Moon considered the plan and couldn't find any holes in it. "That'll work. I'll give Timber a call."

Kole leaned back in his seat, confident he was doing the right thing.

"Y'all eating here or taking it with you?" Moon asked.

"Here, I guess. I ain't got nothing going on right now."

"Mind if Carla and I eat with y'all?"

"Course I don't mind," Kole said. "Just pull your wife aside and tell her not to be asking us a bunch of crazy stuff."

Moon chuckled. "Like what?"

"Like how long me and Dana been together and what our plans are." Kole grinned. "You know Carla been trying to get me married for ten years. She prolly tickled pink to see I brought a woman with me."

Moon laughed. "Alright. I'll tell her not to ask y'all a bunch of *crazy stuff*. But between you and me, what's going on? You just banging, or is this something serious?"

"Me and Dana are minding our business – like you should."

Moon frowned. "I don't see how you even got a woman like her interested in your *rude* ass. Not one romantic bone in your body."

Kole grinned and didn't respond to that.

CHAPTER 66

I sit and I pray at them graves
Dear, God don't let me die too
I really ain't got shit to lose
But I got a lot more to prove
There's too many guns
Them triggers, they cold
Keep laying brothers in the streets
My homies they die
My niggas they bleed
They got you G
Gangsta, rest in peace

ON THE WAY back to the hotel, Kole and Dana were stuffed and in good spirits.

She said, "Is that your partner, the guy you said is running The Organization?"

Kole frowned and didn't reply.

"Y'all been friends since you were kids, right? Is that him?"

Kole's frowned deepened. This time he told her, "I'm not about to snitch on nobody. It's bad enough I told you so much about me."

Dana's eyes widened. "*Snitch*?" She chuckled. "You think I'm the police?"

"Naw, I don't think that. But I'm not about to tell that man's business."

Seeing he was serious, Dana dropped that line of questioning. Instead she asked, "So did y'all come up with a plan – or *you*, I mean. Since you don't wanna talk about your friend."

Kole felt she was being sarcastic. But when he glanced at her, she looked serious.

"Yeah, I got a plan," he said, his eyes back on the road.

"Is it something you can tell me, or..."

"Today's Shank's funeral," he said.

"Really? So soon?"

"He's been dead for five days. How long they supposed to wait? It's not like they don't have the money to bury him."

"No, it's just... Jeez. It's been five days... I swear it feels like Tariq just had that accident yesterday. Everything's happening so fast."

"I haven't been able to get hold of Brass," Kole continued. "But I know he'll be at the funeral today. My plan is to follow him home, or wherever he's laying his head tonight."

"And then what?" Dana asked fretfully.

"And then we'll finally have our little talk," Kole said. "If he's agreeable, I'll let him live."

"Wha, what if he's not?"

"Then I'll kill him and everyone I think is in line to take his place." Kole's voice was calm, his expression deadpan.

"But I thought you weren't gonna kill anyone."

"I said I wasn't gonna kill anyone *this morning*."

Dana waited for the punch line. There wasn't one. "If you kill him, they'll go to war," she said knowingly.

"And they'll lose."

"You said you left The Organization because you wanted to stop killing. How can you go back on that so easily?"

"This is not an easy decision. You've seen me trying to avoid this."

"But–"

"*Enough!*"

Dana recoiled. Her mouth snapped shut. Kole had never addressed her with anger before. It was frightening as she'd imagined. But she knew he wouldn't hit her – at least she was pretty sure he wouldn't. So she quickly regained her composure.

"I'm going with you, when you talk to him."

He smacked his lips. "Get the fuck outta here."

"This is *my* problem," she argued. "*My* son is the one who killed Shank. I wanna speak to him, one parent to another."

"This ain't no Bonnie and Clyde thing we got going on here. You're a regular woman with a regular, lame-ass job. You don't know nothing about the type of people we're dealing with."

"Yeah, I think I do. They attacked my son. They knocked on my door. They shot up my house. I know a lot about them."

"Shut up. You just–"

"*Don't tell me to shut up!*" Dana didn't mean to raise her voice, but the way he was coddling her was annoying. And she got the desired response. Kole closed his mouth and gave her a look before his eyes returned to the road.

"*If this is my life you're trying to save,*" Dana said, "*then I deserve a say in it.*"

A deep sneer distorted his features. He cared about Dana, but there was only so much attitude he could take. "Stop yelling at me," he said through clenched teeth.

His expression made Dana rethink her belief that he wouldn't hit her. Nevertheless, she felt like she was fighting for his life as much as she was for Brass'. If Kole murdered the leader of a gang, it was only a matter of time before Brass' minions avenged him.

She lowered her voice and said, "If he won't listen to you, why not let me try to talk to him? You got nothing to lose."

"Yeah, nothing but your life."

Dana gave that some thought and didn't lose her resolve. "I know you're not gonna let anything happen to me."

Kole was at his wits' end with this woman. He doubted Dana could persuade Brass any better than he could. Then again, she convinced him to let her tag along this morning. Now she was on the verge of changing his mind about tonight. Maybe she could say something to make the MMG leader turn away from his path of destruction. If not, she was right that there was no harm in trying.

"Fine," he growled. "If you wanna meet Brass, I'll let you meet him. But if it don't work, you're gonna stand right there and watch me kill that man."

Dana thought that was a horrible condition to tack on, but she didn't back down.

Kole said, "That'll make you an *accomplice to murder*."

Dana continued to stare straight ahead, her lips pursed.

"You fucking crazy," he said and let the conversation die.

CHAPTER 67

BACK AT THE hotel, the boys were happy with the lunch Dana brought from Carla's. But what they wanted most was to know when they could leave the hotel and resume their normal lives. When they were finished eating, Kole came to the room to give them an update.

He told the boys to sit on the sofa, while he took the loveseat and Dana sat at the table behind them. Tariq and Brendon were always rowdy together, but they were quiet and attentive to Kole. They showed him more respect than their principal at school.

"We're leaving this hotel tomorrow," Kole stated. Before they could get excited, he said, "We're leaving if things go good, and we're leaving if things go bad. Either way, this will be your last day here."

The boys exchanged worried glances.

"Today they're burying Shank," Kole told them. "I've been trying to get in touch with his father, to see if we could work this out peacefully. But Brass doesn't want to talk. I tried a few things to force him to speak to me, but nothing's worked. Every move I make, he escalates it. No one's been killed yet, but people have been hurt. It seems like there's no end in sight, but I'm gonna try one more time. Today he's gotta show his face at his son's funeral. I'm gonna wait till it's over and confront him."

Tariq and Brendon remained silent. They hung on his every word.

"There's only two ways this could go," Kole stated. He clasped his bear paws together and rubbed them slowly. "Either Brass is gonna hear me out and stop this foolishness. Or he's gonna keep fighting. If he keeps fighting, more people are gonna get hurt. Some of them will probably get killed. If that happens, I'm afraid this city may never be safe for either of you. You'll have a price on your head."

Tariq looked to his mother, hoping she'd contradict what Kole just told them, but she nodded slightly.

"Don't give them too much credit," Kole said. "MMG's a bad-ass gang, but they're not the mafia. Their reach is pretty much limited to Overbrook Meadows. I'd say you could move to Dallas and be safe from them. If you moved further away, I'm almost positive you'll never hear from them again."

That comment provided Tariq a little relief. His mother had a skill that could get her a job at virtually any hospital. He'd miss his friends, but they didn't have any family in the city. Relocating wouldn't be the worst thing in the world.

Brendon, on the other hand, felt he was stuck in Overbrook Meadows. His mother was an absentee crackhead, and his aunt was barely making it. Victoria couldn't wait for Brendon to graduate and move out, or at least get a job and help with some of the bills. Much like the folks who got left behind during Hurricane Katrina, relocating is nearly impossible if you're poor.

"I'm sorry," Tariq said. "I didn't mean for none of this happen. It's all my fault."

"Naw it ain't," Kole said. "Shank was smoking wet when he ran out in the street. MMG knows it, but they'd rather find a scapegoat than accept that their OG's son was a dopefiend. There was nothing you could've done to prevent that accident, Tariq. It's okay to mourn the loss of life, but you gotta stop beating yourself up. At some point, you gotta let it go."

Tariq didn't think he'd ever feel better about his role in Shank's death. But he appreciated Kole for being straightforward with him.

"Thank you," he said, "for everything you've done to help us."

"Yeah, thank you, sir," Brendon chipped in.

Kole nodded and grunted as he rose to his feet. "I gotta make some calls," he told Dana before exiting the room.

CHAPTER 68

ACROSS THE HALL, Kole was able to monitor Shank's funeral with nothing but a cellphone. Timber and Legend, the operatives from Dallas, texted Moon with updates throughout the day. Moon passed the information to Kole.

The men were easily able to infiltrate the funeral. Shank's ceremony drew nearly 400 mourners. Most of them were members of MMG; sporting the gang's black and white colors or tee-shirts with the fallen soldier's picture on it. Timber said the mood was tense. Most of the conversation they overheard was the gangstas vowing to avenge Shank and retaliate against The Organization for an unspecified grievance.

The spies laid eyes on Brass for the first time as the church ceremony began. He sat in the first pew, with Ice and other family members flanking him. Timber indicated Brass wore a black suit with sunglasses, and he was easily distinguishable from the rest of the gang.

Timber said Brass' demeanor was subdued as his soldiers approached to pay their respects to him and the rest of the family. The gangstas left black and white handkerchiefs in Shank's casket as well as bullets, drugs and money.

Timber gave another update after the church service, during the procession to the cemetery. He momentarily lost track of Brass because he was in the first limo behind the hearse, and the line of cars following him was enormous. But at the gravesite, Timber was able to push his way to the front of the crowd and lay eyes on the target again.

He reported that the gangstas were more agitated and vocal at the cemetery. Without the confines of the church to keep them respectful, they openly cursed Kole, Moon and The Organization. Some vowed to murder the driver of the SUV that ran over Shank.

Later that day, at the repast, Timber said the crowd was still large, but it had dwindled to mostly family members, so he and Legend didn't attempt to go inside. They were able to keep an eye on the vehicle Brass was riding in.

Finally, as the sun began to set, tinting the skies above Overbrook Meadows a beautiful purple and orange, Timber called and said he and Legend were following Brass from the repast. Brass rode shotgun in a car with three other individuals.

Kole sat alone in his hotel room. He broke down his favorite murder weapon, a Smith & Wesson center fire revolver with a 6 ½ inch barrel. The gun was powerful enough to take down a rhino. Kole oiled the gun's components before putting it back together and loading it.

By then, Moon called to relay a final message from Timber: Brass, Ice and two other men had entered a hole-in-the-wall club on the south side. The club looked to be closed to the public. There were only two other cars in the parking lot. Timber couldn't say how many people were inside, but Moon was sure they could take control of the building with as few as ten gunmen.

"This is it," Moon said. "This is what we been waiting for."

"How long before you'll have the team in place?" Kole asked.

"About an hour."

"Alright. I'll meet you there."

Kole dressed in all black. He stopped by the boy's room on his way out of the hotel to tell them he was leaving. Not surprisingly, Dana shot to her feet.

She hurried to the door and said, "Okay. I'm ready."

Kole's eyebrows bunched together as he stared down at her. He looked past her and saw that Tariq was watching them.

Kole waited until they stepped outside the room before he asked her, "You really wanna do this? I told you I may kill this man tonight."

Dana understood that was a possibility, but she still believed no one would die if she was there. The men had testosterone-boosted egos pushing them towards a bloody disaster. She might be the only sober mind at the meeting.

"*I'm going*," she said.

Kole thought he had this woman figured out, but her tenacity continued to astonish him. He wasn't the marrying or even settling down type. But if he ever surrendered his heart, Dana might be the woman who'd change his life.

"Fuck it," he muttered. "Come on."

"Wait." She returned to the room and kissed her son on the cheek.

Tariq saw the foreboding in her eyes. "Mama..."

"I'll be back," she promised, her eyes glistening. "Everything will be alright."

She studied his features as she backed away, as if this might be the last time she laid eyes on him. She turned and exited the room before common sense could talk her out of it. She whispered a silent prayer before catching up with Kole in the hallway.

CHAPTER 69

My enemies wanna murder me
Shotgun blasts start to sound like bombs
Every slow car might bring defeat
Daily it feels like Vietnam
Last week they laid out our OG
The doctors amputated above the knee
Yesterday we lit up their whole street
We know today's their turn to creep
As we wait, I contemplate my fate
I've developed a theory two million strong
Even if we don't say
It's blacks that blacks hate
Two million blasting pistols can't be wrong

THE RIDE TO the south side was mostly quiet. Dana sat in the passenger seat of Kole's Jeep contemplating all of the things that could go wrong. Kole did the same, but if he was apprehensive, she couldn't tell by looking at him. It was as if he undertook these life or death missions on a regular basis. Dana didn't want to admit it, but she knew that probably was the case.

The further away they traveled from her son, the more Dana realized she'd made a mistake by accompanying Kole. Her vision of how she could save the day was not only romanticized, but it was foolish. When the men raised their weapons with murder in their eyes, would she rush into the fray, begging them to show restraint?

Don't do it, guys! This is what the white man wants us to do!

Even in her mind that sounded ridiculous. But if that wasn't her plan, what was? Ever since Tariq's accident, this tragedy was like a freight train storming downhill with no brakes. She'd get run over if she tried to stop it. But allowing Kole to murder Brass was just as reckless.

The sun was gone when they exited the freeway, but the moon was not yet on the rise. Dana had been gnawing on one of her nails throughout the ride. She chewed it down to the quick and winced when she went after the cuticle and drew blood. Kole looked over at her as she sucked the sore digit. It was the first time he had acknowledged she was in the car. Dana was eager for him to say something to her.

Anything.

"You never said why you were willing to help us," she told him.

He said, "They burnt up my house and my partner's club. This is personal."

"No, I mean in the beginning. You took us into your home after the driveby. You didn't have to stick your neck out for us."

He didn't respond.

"I don't know if you're the kind of man who expresses emotions," Dana said. "But I don't have a problem telling you how I feel: I love you, Kole. I appreciate everything you've done for us – good or bad."

Kole's stomach tightened, but she was right about the kind of man he was. Even if he was the romantic type, this wasn't the time for it. They were minutes away from murder and mayhem. A declaration of love might cloud his judgment in the heat of the moment.

When he didn't respond, Dana looked away and brought her hand to her mouth again. She nibbled on her ring finger this time. It had the longest nail on either of her hands. She reduced the nail to rubble within seconds.

CHAPTER 70

KOLE MET UP with Moon and his crew around the corner from the club Brass had retreated to. The men from The Organization were dressed in dark attire. They sat in four vehicles, waiting for Moon to give the word to commence the raid. Kole stopped at each car and greeted all of them. Some had participated in the dope house robberies the night before. They were all devoted to the cause; ready to take a life if Kole or Moon gave the word.

Kole left Dana in his truck, but nothing escaped his friend's watchful eye. Moon exited his vehicle as Kole approached him. After giving him dap, Moon eyed his Jeep warily.

"What the hell you bring her for?"

"Ain't have much choice in the matter," Kole replied, a bit sheepishly.

"What you mean you ain't have no choice? You a man, ain't you? You tell her to sit her silly-ass down, and then you leave. Works with Carla every time."

Kole agreed that would've been the best course of action, but he didn't think Carla had as much gumption as Dana did.

"She said if it comes down to me killing Brass, she wants to try to talk to him; give him one last chance to back down."

"What the hell she gon' say that a gun pointed in his face don't say?" Moon wondered.

Kole sighed. "Shit, man. I don't know. But I can't see how it'll hurt."

"It'll hurt if she get shot in the fucking head," Moon countered.

"She know the risks," Kole said, growing agitated. "She here now, so it is what it is."

Moon shook his head. "Nigga, you sprung."

Kole sneered at him. "I don't see what none of this got to do with running up in that club. So either talk about that, or shut the fuck up."

Moon grinned, unfazed by his outburst. "Yup. Yo ass sprung. Anyway, my man Timber just took off. He say Brass and his partners are still in the club. Ain't nobody came in or out since they got there. They prolly getting drunk, mourning that dopefiend, so they should be easy pickings. By the time they figure out what's going on, it'll be so many guns on 'em, they won't be able to do nothing but lay it down.

"Then you can go have your little talk with Brass," Moon continued. "If that don't work, I guess your little girlfriend can have a go at him." He chuckled.

Kole didn't respond.

"If she can't get through to him, you wanna be the one to do him?"

"Yeah, him and Ice," Kole said without a trace of compassion. "Prolly everybody else in there."

"You know that's coldblooded," Moon joked. "You gon' murk him right after he came from his son's funeral?"

"If he miss Shank so much, might as well be with him. You ready to roll?"

"Yeah. Let me give the M.O. to the boys, and we can hit it."

"Bet."

Kole returned to his Jeep. In the darkness, Dana's eyes looked larger than usual. He took a seat behind the wheel and turned to face her.

"Last chance to back out. You can bail and catch a cab to the hotel."

She shuddered involuntarily. "And then what?" she breathed.

"And then we do it my way."

"If your way means killing people, then no. I wanna try to work it out."

"Just because you try doesn't mean I won't have to kill anyone."

"Kole, we already talked about this. I wanna talk to Brass. You said I could."

He shook his head in frustration. "Okay. Here's the deal: Me and the crew are raiding the club. I'll be one of the first ones in, but I need you to hang back. I want you at the *back* of the line. You got it?"

Dana nodded, but she felt like her body was on autopilot. What the hell was she doing there? This was insane.

"It'll take a minute to secure the place," Kole said. "If everything goes well, I'll send one of the homies out to get you. But if you hear gunshots when we go in, that means something went wrong, and you need to hightail it out of here immediately. Here."

He took the keys out of the ignition and gave them to her. Dana squeezed them tightly in her fist.

"If you hear gunshots, don't wait on me," Kole instructed her. "Don't try to check on me. *Just run.* Go to the hotel, get Brendon and Tariq, and take 'em to another hotel. I would suggest somewhere in Dallas. If I make it out alive, I'll call you."

If?

But if you don't...?

The question hung in the air unasked and unanswered. Kole's stare was unsettling. Dana's eyes glistened in the darkness.

"You ready?" he asked her.

Hell no, she wasn't. But once again she nodded.

"Alright. Come on."

Kole exited the vehicle, and though every fiber of her being pleaded with her not to follow him, Dana did the same.

CHAPTER

71

THE INFILTRATION WAS loud and organized, flush with high stakes and adrenaline. Kole and his men had performed similar raids on everything from small homes to warehouses filled with armed men. They had honed their tactics down to a science. Counting Kole and 'oon, there were a dozen of them. Eight stormed the main entrance, while two stood guard at the back door and the others watched a side exit.

Like the police, they coupled noise with the element of surprise, barking orders at everyone they encountered.

"GET DOWN ON THE GROUND!"

"DROP IT!"

"HANDS UP!"

"HANDS UP, OR I'LL SHOOT!"

"GET ON THE FUCKING GROUND!"

Kole led the charge. His team fanned out like marines, making sure to stay out of each other's lines of sight. The club was small, about a third the size of Moonlight. Kole locked eyes with a man standing near the entrance, who didn't appear to be armed.

"GET YOUR HANDS UP! MOVE! MOVE!"

He ushered him towards the middle of the club as his posse did the same.

"GO! GO!"

They shoved men who weren't moving quickly enough. They gun-butted them, kicked them in the ass, all in a coordinated effort to herd them to a central location. Once there, they forced them to their knees. Five soldiers kept guns on them, while the others went to the side and rear exits to let their comrades in. Once everyone was inside, they swept the club to make sure they had gotten everyone.

All in all, the raid took less than two minutes – but it felt like *thirty*, especially for the folks on the wrong side of the guns. Kole measured their success by the fact that they didn't have to fire one shot. Most of the MMG thugs had been at the bar, totally unprepared for their impending doom. Only one had reached for a weapon. That poor sap got his head busted so badly, you could see the gash through his afro. Another had fallen down in the panic and skinned the side of his face.

When the dust settled, they held six people hostage. One was a female. She cried hysterically until one of Moon's men stepped to her and delivered a vicious backhand.

"Shut up, bitch, 'fore I give you something to cry about!"

Kole only recognized two of the hostages. One was Ice, and the other was the notorious Brass. *Finally* they were face to face. Kole strolled casually past the prisoners, while his men encircled them. The scene had the eerie feel of an Isis beheading video. By then the MMG crew knew they hadn't been raided by cops, and they were pissed.

The female was the only one who pleaded for her life. The men were older, seasoned thugs. It was hard to tell if they truly didn't give a damn, or if their bravado was a front. Either way, Kole wasn't bothered by their sneers and mean-mugging. It didn't matter if they looked as vicious as an escaped gorilla, because looks don't mean a damn thing when you're defenseless.

Kole lowered his weapon and told one of his men, "Pat 'em down."

He left the group and approached the bar. As he placed his pistol on the marble, he was alerted to a commotion. When he turned back to the crowd, one of the MMG thugs was face down with two men from The Organization on his back.

"Try it again!" one of them threatened. "Gimme a reason to wet you!"

Kole calmly leaned against the bar and spoke to Brass directly. "Tell your men to be easy. Ain't nobody gotta die tonight."

"Fuck you!" the leader of MMG spat. Fire blazed in his eyes. If looks could kill, Kole would've disintegrated into a pile of dust.

Kole shook his head and chuckled. He turned to Peabody, one of his good friends. "Go get her."

Peabody nodded and headed for the entrance.

The club was dimly lit and not much to brag about. Kole studied the MMG leader while his men completed their pat-downs. Brass was as tall as him, and his skin tone was dark, like Kole's. Brass outweighed him by about thirty pounds. Most of the extra bulk appeared to be muscle. Brass' brother, Ice, definitely got the looks in the family. Brass sported the outfit he wore to his son's funeral, minus the jacket and tie. His hair was styled low, in a crew cut. His face was clean-shaven.

Kole's men confiscated a handful of weapons from the MMG crew. Only the first one had resisted the shakedown. When they were done, they ordered him to, "Get back on your knees," and he complied. His nose was busted now, which made two MMG goons who had shed blood. Kole was almost certain they wouldn't be the last.

He noticed Dana when she entered the club, but he didn't acknowledge her. He could imagine the thoughts running through her mind when she surveyed the scene and saw what his team had done. To her credit, Dana didn't gasp or make any other sounds as she stepped closer to the bar. She didn't tuck tail and run, which said a lot about her. Kole was curious about her upbringing in Chicago. What exactly had she seen in those foster homes? How extensive was her knowledge of gangs?

Those questions would have to wait for another day. Kole pushed off the bar, just as Dana approached him. He returned to the MMG crew, until he stood before their leader.

He told him, "I guess you know what this is about."

Brass snorted, sneering at him. "You got some nerve, pulling this shit on the day I buried my son. You niggas ain't got no respect. Got me on my motherfucking knees. Don't think you getting away with this."

"Don't talk to me about respect," Kole retorted. "I asked to speak to you when this first started. You the one ain't have enough respect to get at me."

"Fuck you!"

"Yeah, fuck me," Kole said. "You sound like a dead man right about now."

"*Kill me then*! What the fuck you waiting for?"

Despite their differences, Kole decided he had a little respect for Brass. He was a fool, but at least he wasn't going out like a coward.

"I'm waiting on you to tell me if we can resolve this without killing all of y'all," Kole stated.

That brought more whimpers from the female. Brass' men continued to snarl and breathe heavily.

"You owe me a new house," Kole told him. "And you owe my man a new club."

"You robbed my dope houses!"

"That don't make it even," Kole stated. "But I'm willing to call it square, if you drop whatever problem you got with that lady and her son."

"Nigga, you still on that shit?"

"I'm still on it till she can go home safe. All you gotta do is tell your people to leave her alone. That lady ain't did nothing to you."

"Her son killed Shank!"

"That nigga got hisself killed!" Kole said, matching his volume. "And you know it! He ran out in the middle of the street, full of that dope. What the hell you wanna avenge that for?"

Kole was pleased to finally deliver that message face-to-face. He wasn't surprised when Brass jumped to Shank's defense.

"How the fuck you gon' be talking shit about my son after I just buried him?"

"*He was a fool!*" Kole bellowed. "Fucking with that wet. You know he was fucked up."

"*Shank wasn't no goddamned dopefiend!*" Brass was so upset, his body trembled. "Fuck you for saying that! You a coward, nigga! You wouldn't be talking shit, if you didn't have all these guns on me! *Shank was my only son!*"

Brass' eyes were red with rage. Kole was surprised to see them fill with tears. He could tell Brass hated showing such emotions to an enemy.

"Are you really this goddamn stupid?" Kole asked him. "This what y'all dealing with?" he said, addressing Brass' soldiers. "I know y'all been telling him Shank was skitzing when he got killed. Or are y'all part of the problem? Y'all been keeping the truth from him, so he can live in his little bubble, thinking it wasn't nothing wrong with his son? Y'all ready to die over a lie?"

Brass' men didn't look like they were ready to take their last breath. But out of loyalty, none of them spoke up. Kole shook his head in disappointment. He returned to the bar and hefted his pistol. He'd almost forgotten Dana was there until she rushed forward, screaming.

"*No! Please, no!*"

She stood between Kole and his enemies, tears streaming down her face. She turned to Brass and implored him, "*Please stop this! This is crazy!*"

Brass stared at her like she was the crazy one.

"I don't know you," Dana told him. "I don't know anything about what you do, and I don't wanna know. What I do know is you had one son, just like me, and you love him – regardless of his

279

faults, just like I love my son. But you gotta step back and see when your son did wrong!"

Dana sniffled. She wiped her tears and runny nose with the back of her hand.

"*Nobody has to die!*" she wailed. "There's nothing anybody can do to take back what happened to Shank, but we can change what happens next. All you have to do is back down. *Please,*" she begged. "*Please, just stop!*"

Her impassioned plea tugged at Kole's heart. He suspected every man in the room felt *something*. Even Brass' expression changed. When the MMG leader spoke, Kole knew he'd make the right decision.

"Is this her?" he asked, looking past Dana and locking eyes with Kole. "This the mama?"

Kole's nostrils flared. He didn't respond.

"Tell you what," Brass said. "Why don't you leave her here, with me and my partners, and we'll call it even. We'll even drop her off at home tomorrow, when we get through with her."

Dana's mouth fell open. Kole's jaws clenched. He momentarily blacked out in a fit of rage. He barely felt like he was in control of his actions as he rushed forward and shoved Dana aside. He threw a mean hook that caught Brass squarely on the jaw. The blow sounded off like cymbals in the small club.

The MMG leader fell to the floor, but he didn't stay down for long. He pushed up on strong arms that looked as sturdy as tree branches. From all fours, he looked up at Kole. Kole could tell the blow had hurt him, but Brass had a big head and thick neck. It would take a lot more than that to knock him out.

Brass rose to his knees and continued rising, until he reached his full height. Expecting him to rush forward, Kole raised his weapon. But Brass didn't take a step in his direction. He spat blood and wiped his mouth.

"I knew you was a coward," he snarled. "You gon' hit me while all these guns on us... You want this to be over? Step to the square!" Brass said, inviting him to a fight. "After I whoop your ass, we can call it even. Yo niggas can drag yo bitch-ass up outta here, and I won't fuck with this bitch or her son no more." He snorted and spat more blood. "If you ain't no punk, show me what them hands do!"

Kole was not eager to tussle with the man. Not only was Brass bigger, but Kole had just put all he had into that punch, and the OG made it to his feet within seconds. But the curse of gangsta bravado wasn't only on MMG's side. Kole would lose major respect if he declined the offer. Even if he murdered Brass and all of his associates at that moment, the men in The Organization would know that he'd done it with his tail tucked between his legs. The streets would know.

Kole nodded and stepped to his closest soldier. He handed him his pistol and instructed his men to, "Clear the floor. Move them motherfuckers out the way."

Dana's eyes were wide with fright. Her heart thundered, even as it was ripped in two. Part of her thought a fist fight was the best they could've hoped for. If Brass was a man of his words, no one would die that night. On the other hand, Brass was such a formidable figure, she thought he could kill Kole with his bare hands.

"Get up!" one of Moon's men ordered. "Move!" he shouted, as he ushered Brass' crew to the side of the room.

Moon made his way to his best friend and asked, "You sure about this? We can kill all these motherfuckers right now, get this shit over with."

Brass heard him and shouted, "*Coward*! I'ma die a *legend*! You niggas gon' die *cowards*!"

"Fuck that," Kole said to Moon. "I got this." He kept his eyes locked on his adversary, as if he and Brass were staring at each other across a boxing ring.

Moon tried not to look doubtful, but he failed. He looked at Brass, thinking he should off him anyway.

Kole read his mind and said, "Don't do it. Don't nobody jump in!" he shouted across the room. *"No matter what happens, don't nobody jump in!"*

He looked at Dana before pulling his shirt up and over his head. Twenty feet away, Brass stared him down and removed his shirt as well. With both of them topless, it was clear this would be a fight for the ages. Kole's muscles were more defined, but Brass' chest and arms were clearly bigger.

Dana took a step towards Kole, but he yelled for her to, *"Get back!"* before she reached him. "Take her over there," he instructed Moon.

Moon took hold of her arm and pulled her away. "Come on."

Tears streamed down Dana's face as he led her away.

With just the two monsters on the dance floor, there was nothing between them but space and opportunity. Neither of them asked if the other was ready before they collided like pitbulls in a dogfight.

For the next five minutes everyone in the building held their breath as the men traded blows. The sounds of their grunts and heavy fists impacting skin was cringe-worthy. Kole started off strong; delivering quicker, more precise blows that left cuts and bruises on Brass' face.

But the MMG leader's strikes were heavier, like George Foreman in his prime. Kole was able to duck and dodge most but not all of them. Each time he got caught, Dana's heart jumped up her throat. One of Brass' punches to the head staggered Kole. Brass lunged forward and delivered a straight jab that bloodied his opponent's nose. Despite the pain and the stars twinkling before his eyes, Kole dodged him like a bullfighter when Brass tried to go in for the kill.

After shaking the fog from his brain, Kole reevaluated his opponent when they squared up again. He had delivered enough head strikes to topple a normal man, but Brass had an iron chin. When they traded blows again, Kole did his best to dodge haymakers as he delivered uppercuts to the sides and gut. When Brass wasn't able to stop a surprised "*Oof!*" from escaping him after a particularly brutal liver shot, Kole knew he had him.

Brass reached to grab him and possibly wrestle him to the ground, but Kole maintained his balance and kept peppering his gut with hooks and uppercuts. For the first time in the fight, Dana felt like he'd be victorious, but then someone in the crowd yelled, "*He reaching! He reaching for something!*"

Three soldiers from The Organization broke from the crowd, but they didn't make it in time. Kole never saw the blade, but he felt the sudden, searing burn when Brass submerged the knife in his midsection, all the way to the hilt.

Everyone's gun came up.

Someone shouted, "*That nigga stabbed him!*"

Someone else wanted to, "*Kill his ass!*" and all hell broke loose.

Half of the men from The Organization hurried to the dance floor and trained guns on the fighters. The other half made sure the MMG crew stayed put. Both of the women in the club screamed bloody murder, and Moon yelled for his men to, "*Back up! Move, so I can get a shot at him!*"

In the midst of it all, the OG's kept fighting, and Moon couldn't get the clear shot he wanted.

Blood spilled on the dance floor. Kole knew it was his. He was infuriated but not surprised that Brass had stooped so low. Everyone knows there are no rules in a street fight. There was always a rock or brick or stick nearby. Kole thought Brass had showed himself as the *true* coward, but that wouldn't matter if he succumbed to the stab wound. Brass would surely die tonight, but he'd take Kole with him.

The fighters slipped in the blood as they continued to wrestle. Kole heard Moon imploring him to, "*Let go, so I can shoot him!*" but Kole felt Brass reaching for the knife, which was still embedded in his side. Kole knew that if he let go of the big man's arms, Brass would yank the blade out. Who could say if

Moon would get his shot before Brass plunged the knife in again, possibly in his chest this time?

So Kole held on for dear life and tried to overpower his foe. He thought he'd sufficiently weakened Brass with the body shots, but the MMG leader seemed as strong as ever. If not for the blood, Brass might have gotten the upper hand. But the adversaries lost their footing and fell together. Kole landed on his back, with his enemy on top. The pain in his side exploded, as if he'd fallen directly on the knife. Kole couldn't help but cry out.

With Brass on top, Moon *almost* took his shot, but Kole quickly scrambled from beneath the pile. He grabbed Brass by the shoulder and twisted to the side, throwing all of his weight into it. When they stopped rolling, Kole was on his back again. The pain in his side was thunderous, but he was grateful that he'd secured the position he wanted.

Brass' back was pressed against his chest. Kole quickly wrapped his legs around his opponent and snaked one arm under Brass' chin. Before he could react, Kole brought his other arm behind Brass' head and locked in a rear-naked choke. Brass began to gasp and claw at Kole's arms and face, but it was no use. Kole held on for dear life as his blood spilled freely.

Realizing Kole had somehow taken a superior position, Moon lowered his weapon and ordered everyone to, "*Back off! Get back!*"

His men reluctantly retreated. They watched with wide eyes as Brass struggled for breath. The MMG leader's eyes bulged. His mouth opened and closed, like a fish out of water, but his windpipe was completely cut off. Behind him, Kole's grimace was terrifying. The muscles in his arms bulged as he tightened his grip. The women continued to scream, and now it was the MMG crew who wanted to stop the fight. But they couldn't take a step towards the dance floor without getting their wig split.

Dana didn't realize she was witnessing a murder until Brass' eyes rolled to the back of his head, and all of his movements gradually came to a stop. His mouth hung open, in what was clearly a death mask, and his arms fell limply to his sides. Dana wasn't an MMA fan, but she'd seen enough fights to know this was when the referee rushed in to stop the bout. The problem was there was no referee, and no one from The Organization was inclined to play that role.

Kole sucked air through his mouth and maintained his anaconda hold. His busted nose spilled blood, as did the wound on his side. An agonizingly slow ten seconds passed, but he wouldn't release his foe. The clamor from the MMG crew grew steadily.

"Tell him to let go! He killing him!"

"That nigga stabbed him!" their captors replied.

"That sneaky motherfucker deserve to die!"

"Get him off! Kole, let him go!" Brass brother pleaded. *"You got him! You won! Let him go!"*

It didn't appear Kole heard any of them. Even when Dana joined the chorus begging for mercy, he didn't look her way.

Another scuffle ensued when Ice threw caution to the wind to save his brother. He ran towards the dance floor but didn't make it far before someone from The Organization stuck out a foot and tripped him. Before Ice made it to his feet, four men converged on him, kicking and pistol-whipping him.

Dana screamed as she watched this prolonged tragedy. She ran to the dance floor and grabbed Kole's arm, trying to pry it from beneath Brass' chin.

"Let him go, Kole! Please!"

But his arm didn't budge. He still wouldn't look her way. He didn't let go of his enemy until he was good and ready. By then thirty seconds had passed since he initiated the hold. When he shoved Brass' limp body off of him, there was no doubt the man was dead. A ghastly silence enveloped the club.

Moon stepped forward and helped his friend to his feet. Kole grimaced and clutched his side, but he knew better than to remove the knife. Dana didn't know what to think of him when his deranged eyes finally swam in her direction.

"*Brian!*" From his defeated position between the legs of Moon's men, Ice called out to his brother, using his government name. "*Brian!*"

Tears streamed down his face as he crawled towards him. Moon's men made no attempt to stop him this time. When Ice reached his brother, he lifted his head and cradled it on his lap. Moon's crew had left Ice bloody and bruised. Tears ran from his swollen eyes.

"**Why you didn't let him go?!**" he screamed at Kole. "**Why you didn't let him go**?!"

Kole looked down at him but said nothing.

Dana stood between them, once again torn, this time between her allegiance to Kole and her disapproval of what he had done. Brass had stabbed him, true enough. It was his goal to take Kole's life. But it appeared he had failed. Whether out of anger or revenge, Kole had made a conscious decision to kill a man. Once Brass passed out, it was no longer self defense. Now The Organization had no choice but to kill every witness in the club. But even that might not be enough to stop a war between the two factions.

"*Let me, let me...*"

Dana couldn't formulate a sentence as she knelt next to Ice and reached for his brother. Ice turned his cold eyes on her but didn't intervene when she checked his pulse. Sure enough, there was none. She instructed him to, "*Lay him, lay him down flat.*"

Ice was reluctant to listen to someone who had arrived with his enemies, but Dana had already proven herself the most capable medical professional in the building by checking Brass' pulse. Ice lifted his brother's head from his lap and carefully lowered it to the floor.

Everyone in the room watched with confused expressions as Dana commenced CPR. She wasn't a nurse or even a PCT, but her job at the hospital required her to renew a CPR certificate annually. She knew the basics. She knew when to blow a breath into Brass' lungs and when to do the chest compressions. Her tears flowed uncontrollably. Everyone was stunned by her efforts. No one offered to assist.

After a full minute, Dana's arms were tired, and Brass had not responded at all. His eyes were half open, his eyelids turning blue. Dana would've given up if everything she held dear didn't rest on the outcome.

It took another thirty seconds of compressions before Brass coughed and sucked in a breath of air on his own. Although this was the outcome she prayed for, Dana was startled. She slowly backed away. Ice stared at his brother as if he was Lazarus. Brass didn't regain consciousness, but he began to breathe on his own. If someone got him to a hospital, Dana was confident he would survive.

The men from The Organization looked around in confusion, not sure what should happen next. It seemed wrong to kill everyone anyway, after Dana had gone through so much trouble to bring Brass back to life. But leaving an enemy behind was not a smart option either. Moon knew what he wanted to do, but he let Kole make the call.

After surveying the scene and taking in all of the eyes looking to him for guidance, Kole made a decision.

"Let's go." He was winded, his voice raspy. The blood from his nose had bloodied his bare chest. The blood from his stab wound soaked his pants and leaked to the floor.

Moon nodded and pulled his friend's arm over his shoulder. Kole grunted and leaned heavily on him as they made their way to the exit. Dana was right behind them. The rest of the crew kept their guns trained on the MMG squad, lest they try something stupid at the last moment. But no one did.

EPILOGUE

CHAPTER 72

KOLE'S STAY IN the hospital was uneventful. The blade in his side was deep enough to pierce his large intestine, but he was fortunate to avoid injury to his lungs, liver or kidneys. After surgery, he remained at the hospital for two days with trigger-happy men from The Organization by his side at all times. Thankfully their presence was not needed. Moon visited him on day two with news from the streets.

"It's over," he announced. Moon leaned forward in a chair next to Kole's bed. A smile lit his eyes as he delivered the good news. "Brass says we're square. He don't want no more trouble."

Kole grunted as he tried to sit up straighter.

His friend told him, "Whoa. What you trying to do?"

"Just adjust this pillow," Kole explained. His wound didn't give him any trouble when he was lying still. But due to the location, the pain slapped him in the face whenever he tried to sit up, bend over or get out of bed.

Moon stood and readjusted the pillow for him. "Is that good?"

Kole scowled at him. He appreciated the help, but he couldn't stand feeling helpless. "Yeah. Thanks. Brass came and talked to you?"

Moon shook his head and returned to his seat. "Naw, he called me. Brass ain't showing his face. I don't blame him. You whooped up on him pretty good."

"I'm sure I look worse than him," Kole stated. There was a huge mirror on the wall next to his bed. He had taken multiple blows to the head during the fight, and the contusions hadn't gone down yet. "That nigga hits hard," he told Moon.

"We should've killed that dirty motherfucker," Moon replied. "Maybe we'll get a chance later. But for now, he's calling it quits. He's ready to stop retaliating, if we are."

"What about the shit we got from his dope houses?" Kole asked.

"That's all mine," Moon replied. "I told him we *was* gon' give it back, but he went and burned down my club, so I'm keeping it now."

Kole grinned. "What he say?"

"What could he say? It was either accept that or go to war."

"What about Dana?" Kole asked him. "They gonna leave her alone?"

"That's the word," Moon confirmed. "They're squashing the beef on all fronts. We're ready to get back to business as usual."

"That's what's up," Kole said.

"What about you?" his friend asked.

"What you mean? What about me?"

"You ready to resume your retirement or..."

Kole waited, but his friend just stared at him. "Or what?"

"You can't tell me these last few days didn't make you rethink things, just a little," Moon said.

Of course he was right about that. Since he'd been laid-up in the hospital, Kole had time to consider a lot of things. He had retired from The Organization because it was his time to go and also because he'd lost the taste for murder. His efforts to save Dana pulled him back into the gritty underworld so easily, Kole felt like he'd never left. He couldn't deny that he missed the raw excitement of gunshots and screaming, the possibility of death around every corner.

But he told Moon, "Naw, I'm good. I think it's best if I leave that shoot-'em-up-bang-bang shit to the youngsters."

"*Youngsters*? I'm older than you," Moon replied.

"Yeah, and you should probably retire too."

"Man, I'm 43. Don't know what I'd do with myself if I didn't have this shit going on."

"You could work fulltime at your club," Kole suggested. "I know the legit life ain't all that exciting, but it's a helluva lot safer."

"Nah, I'm good," Moon told him. "To each his own, I guess."

Kole nodded. "I feel you. Are you rebuilding the Moonlight at the same spot, or you looking at other locations?"

"It's gotta be at the same spot," Moon said. "The south side needs that joint. Still ain't never had no shootings there, even with all that MMG shit going on. What about you? You gonna rebuild your house in the same neighborhood?"

"Haven't decided," Kole said. "I was thinking about moving on."

"Not too far, I hope."

"I'll only be a phone call away," Kole assured him.

"You going with Dana when you get discharged?"

Kole nodded. "For a little bit. Till I get back on my feet."

Moon already knew the answer, but he asked anyway. "You gon' marry that girl?"

Kole frowned. "You tripping."

Moon laughed and told him, "You can deny your feelings all you want, but *I know you, Kole*. Don't forget, I been knowing you for twenty-five years."

"And? What that mean?"

"You acting like you ain't in love what that woman, but I know better."

Kole shook his head, in addition to frowning. "Nigga, you tripping."

CHAPTER 73

DANA WAS GRATEFUL to take Kole home with her when he left the hospital. And although Tariq never said so, she could tell he liked having him around as well.

She had already cleaned up the mess from the driveby when Kole arrived, but she hadn't completed the repairs to her walls and windows. Even though Kole's story about being a house-flipper had been fabricated, it turned out he had a lot of connections in the remodeling business. Within a day of his arrival, he had a crew of workers strolling in and out of Dana's home. They completed the work in just three days.

When Dana got home from work on their last day, she had tears in her eyes as she walked through her home. Kole had replaced all of the windows; even the ones that weren't damaged. He bought her a new big screen television to replace the one that was destroyed. The new TV was bigger and professionally mounted on the wall, rather than sitting atop the TV stand, like the old one. Dana knew there were bullet holes in her walls, but for the life of her, she couldn't remember where they were. The workers left no evidence of the repairs.

Kole managed to get out of bed and limp into the hallway as she rounded the corner. The sight of him filled Dana's heart with love and compassion. She hurried to support him with an arm around his waist.

"Baby, what are you doing out of bed?"

"Can't stay on my back all day," Kole complained. "Doctor said I need to do some walking."

"Want me to get your walker?" Dana asked, her voice drenched with concern.

Kole sneered at that. The hospital made him take the clunky contraption home when he got discharged, but he'd be damned if he'd ever use it. What kind of invalid did they take him for?

Dana laughed at his expression. "Well, what about your cane?"

"Yeah, I'll take that," Kole conceded.

"I don't know why you keep getting out of bed without it," Dana chided. "Are you gonna be okay for a second, while I go get it?"

"I'm pretty sure I can stand up by myself."

She rolled her eyes playfully and backed away from him. Kole maintained his balance without her support.

He did not like being doted on, in general, but Dana was an exception, as she was an exception to a lot of things he normally wouldn't tolerate. When she turned and disappeared into the bedroom, he admired the sexy sway of her hips and the way her ass poked out in her scrub pants. He still had a dreamy look in his eyes when she returned with the cane.

"What's that look for?" she asked. She kissed him softly. Her lips were warm and sweet. His were the same.

Kole took the cane and leaned on it as they walked to the front room.

"I can't tell where any of those holes were," Dana gushed. "Your men did an excellent job. They matched the paint perfectly. And, *oh my God, this TV!*" She admired it, as if it was a painting. "This is amazing, Kole! But you didn't have to do this. I was gonna get another one."

"It's okay."

"I feel like you've done too much," Dana said. "This TV, the windows... You gotta let me pay you back."

"You're giving me a place to stay," Kole reminded her. "Taking care of me, till I'm back on my feet. I'm the one who owes you."

She shook her head. "No. I'm doing that because I love you. You don't owe me anything."

"Then you don't owe me anything either."

Dana knew he wouldn't take money for the things he'd done for her. She also noted how he didn't say he loved her when she expressed those sentiments to him. This had been a pattern, for as long as she'd known him. She wasn't sure if she should ever expect more from him or if she even needed to hear him say something sentimental. Kole showed her how much he cared for her at every turn. It was okay if he wasn't the type of guy who vocalized his feelings, wasn't it?

As much as she tried to convince herself that it was, in the back of her mind, Dana knew that she did need to hear those things. Because if he never said it, she'd be a fool to take it for granted. What if Kole decided to disappear from her life in a few days? She couldn't tell him, "I thought we were in a relationship" or "I thought you loved me," because he could look her in the eyes and honestly say, "I never said that."

But he hadn't disappeared, and Dana tried to find solace in that. She found peace in his gentle caresses at night and the way his eyes sparkled for her during the day.

She stepped across the room and kissed him again. "Thank you," she said, her voice soft and breathy. "But I'm still waiting for you to tell me why you stuck your neck out for us..."

Kole smiled. He snaked his free arm around her waist and pulled her closer for another kiss. Dana decided that was a type of response, and it meant something. She closed her eyes and appreciated the affection he provided, as she always did.

CHAPTER 74

DURING HIS RECOVERY, Kole decided to rebuild a new home from the ground up, to replace the one that was destroyed by the fire. Dana was not pleased to hear his new house would be in a new neighborhood. She was even less pleased when she returned from work one night to find all of his things packed and sitting by the front door. In the bedroom, Kole was stuffing the last of his belongings in a duffle bag.

Dana paused in the doorway, her arms crossed over her stomach. "What's going on?"

He looked up at her, his expression unreadable. Kole was fully dressed in black jeans with a blue tee. He didn't have his cane with him. Dana saw that he had managed to tie his own shoes. Not being able to do so for the past few weeks was one of the things he hated the most about his injury.

"I'm leaving," he said simply. He grabbed the remaining items on the bed and placed them in his duffle bag. "I'm gonna stay at one of Moon's rentals until my house is finished."

Dana didn't mean to let on how much that news hurt her, but Kole saw it in her eyes. His eyes narrowed as he watched her.

"I thought you were gonna stay here until your house was done," she told him. It was hard to speak while her heart was breaking, but she managed.

Kole left his bag on the bed and approached her. "I never said that."

Dana's eyes filled with tears. She'd warned herself that it was foolish to expect anything from him if he didn't tell her directly. But somehow she'd allowed it to happen anyway. She wondered how many of the other things she expected and hoped for were figments of her imagination.

Kole stood quietly, staring into her eyes. Dana hated how he made her feel small and immature. They were around the same age, but Kole's mindset seemed leagues ahead of hers. He was too smart to let silly things like *emotions* and *love* muddle his thinking or interfere with his future. Every move he made was calculated, which was why he'd been successful with everything he laid his hands on.

He told her, "I can't live up under no woman. I'm sorry if that bothers you."

"I, I just..." She sighed and sniffled. "You didn't tell me you were leaving. I just, it feels like, I don't know. Out of the blue. Were you even waiting for me to get home, or did I happen to catch you before you took off? If I got off ten minutes later today, would you have been gone already?"

A tear rolled down her cheek. Before she could wipe it, Kole reached and touched the side of her face. He wiped the tear with his thumb. His hand was large and battle-scarred, but his caress was gentle.

He said, "I was waiting for you. I didn't plan to leave today, but Moon got the place ready sooner than we thought."

Dana took a deep breath. Her chest shuddered when she blew it out. She knew she shouldn't ask her next question, but the lack of communication in their relationship – if it even was a relationship – had led to the heartache she was experiencing. If Kole wanted to remain a man of mystery, that was his choice. But she could no longer accept a life with so many uncertainties.

"What about us?" she said. "If you're leaving like this, does that mean you're gone for good?"

Both of her eyes were leaking now. To his credit, Kole did not shy away from the pain he had caused her. He shook his head.

"That's not what I want. But there are things you want from me, things a man should give his woman, that I'm not comfortable with. I haven't had a real girlfriend since high school. Now I'm in my forties, and it's hard to give a woman that label. It's even harder to tell a woman I love her. I've never planned a future with a woman. I'm not saying I don't want that for us. It's just – to be honest, I don't know how."

Dana wanted to find comfort in his words. This was the most heartfelt conversation they ever had. But he still hadn't made any declarations that she could grasp onto and ride out the storm.

She wiped her eyes, so she could see his expression clearly when she asked, "Do you love me? Do you want to be with me?"

Kole opened his mouth to respond and then closed it. Dana's heart thumped sickly as she waited. He took a deep breath and nodded.

"I do wanna be with you."

That statement made Dana's heart want to soar, but she grabbed hold of it and held it down. There was too much at stake to go another day or even another minute with doubts.

"Do you love me?" she asked again.

She watched the conflict wash over Kole's face as he struggled to come up with a suitable answer. He shook his head slightly.

"I – I've never told a woman I loved her. That's, it's not something that fits my lifestyle. Love has always been a hindrance. It's a weakness my enemies could exploit."

"But you're not in that lifestyle anymore. You said you retired because you wanted something different for yourself; something better. A new life where you wouldn't have to look over your shoulder all the time."

"I know. That is what I want. But old habits die hard."

She nodded. Her tears flowed even harder. She wiped them angrily. "Okay. That's fine."

She turned, to leave him to his packing. Kole reached for her arm and pulled her back to him.

"So, you don't want to be with me," he asked, "if I can't tell you I love you?"

"No, you don't have to tell me you love me, Kole. But you do have to tell me *something*. I don't wanna be with someone who can't say if we have a future together. I don't wanna be with someone who packs all of their things and tells me they're moving at the last minute."

"I been on my own for a long time," he argued. "I'm not used to explaining myself."

"That's fine, Kole. But I'm not gonna be in a relationship with someone who can't even tell me *we're in a relationship*. If you're moving to another place, that's something we should talk about. I'm not saying you have to ask my permission, but you do have to let me in, Kole. You can't be with me and still act like you're by yourself."

"Okay, I..." He reached and rubbed his forehead. "You're right. I'm sorry."

Dana knew she was in the right, but she was surprised that he agreed with her.

"I wanna be in a relationship with you," he stated.

His eyes never left hers. His gaze was a bit unsettling, but it also gave her life. Dana took deep, slow breaths while she watched him.

"I do wanna communicate with you more," he revealed. "I don't know if I can open up like you want me to. But I wanna try. I care for you, Dana. You already know I'd move a mountain or kill a man for you. I don't know if that's *love*, or if I'll ever know what love really is. But I know it's *something*. I know I don't wanna see you cry. I know my whole day goes better when I see you smile."

Dana brought a hand to her mouth as her expression deteriorated even more. Kole thought he'd said something wrong, but she closed the distance between them and threw her arms around him. She hugged him tightly, momentarily forgetting about the wound on his side.

"I love you," she breathed against his chest. "Thank you, Kole. I know this is all new to you. We can take it as slow as you want."

"I'm cool with slow," Kole said. He wrapped his arms around her, pulling her deeper into his embrace. "Just as long as we don't stop."

Dana's heart fluttered and attempted to soar again. This time she allowed it. The tornado of fear and uncertainty that had been barreling through her chest dissipated as she gave in to her feelings for him and looked forward to their future. The sweet emotions stretched her smile from ear to ear.

Her heart thumped even harder when Kole's hands sank down her back and settled on her ass.

He asked, "When's Tariq coming back?"

She backed away, just far enough to look up at him. She thought she looked a mess after working all day and crying for the past five minutes. But Kole looked down at her as if she was the most beautiful woman in the world.

"I'm not sure," she said. "He's at Brendon's. I don't know what they're up to."

"You think he'd mind spending the night?" Kole asked.

Dana eyed him suspiciously. "Probably not, but I thought you were leaving?"

"I don't have to go tonight," he replied. "Probably better to take off in the morning anyway – or the day after that." He shrugged. "No rush."

Dana's eyes brightened. Her smile was delightful.

"But what about your side?" she asked him.

"Feels a lot better," he said. "I got it wrapped up good. But if I'm not up for it, I'll lay back, and you can get on top."

A minute ago, sex was the furthest thing from Dana's mind. Now it was a primal desire. She reached down to see if Kole felt the same way. His soldier was standing, almost at full attention. An erotic heat blossomed between her legs.

"Okay," she said. "I'll call him. And I gotta bathe." She broke away from him, heading to the living room where she left her purse.

"Are you hungry?" Kole called after her. "I can whip something up while you're in the shower."

Dana knew her man's culinary skills were noteworthy. She looked back at him, curious to see what he'd produce in such little time. "Okay. That would be nice."

"Alright. Go ahead and call Tariq."

He watched her until she rounded the corner, a satisfied smile parting his lips. The notion of love was a conundrum, but Kole accepted that it wasn't completely out of the realm of possibilities. If Dana's happiness meant the world to him, and the thought of not having her around hurt him to the core, that meant something, right?

For the first time in recent memory, Kole accepted that he was wading into uncharted waters without a game plan. He knew he wouldn't drown, because Dana wouldn't let him. All he had to do was reach for her, and she'd be there.

He shook the last vestiges of doubt from his mind and headed to the kitchen to make a late dinner for his woman. He had been marinating several chicken breasts for the better part of the day, so maybe this was his plan all along.

KEITH THOMAS WALKER

ABOUT THE AUTHOR

Keith Thomas Walker, known as the Master of Romantic Suspense and Urban Fiction, is the author of more than two dozen novels, including *Fixin' Tyrone, Life After, The Realest Ever,* the *Backslide* series, the *Brick House* series, the *Finley High* series, the *Asha and Boom* series, and the *Blurred Lines* series. Keith's books transcend all genres. He has published romance, urban fiction, mystery/thriller, teen/young adult, Christian, poetry and erotica. Originally from Fort Worth, he is a graduate of Texas Wesleyan University. Keith has won numerous awards in the categories of "Best Male Author," "Best Romance," "Best Urban Fiction," "Best Young Adult Romance," "Best Duo," "Book of the Year," and "Author of the Year," from several book clubs and organizations. Visit him at www.keiththomaswalker.com.

www.ingramcontent.com/pod-product-compliance
Lightning Source LLC
Chambersburg PA
CBHW031221120726
47905CB00002B/425